HARSH HERITAGE

HARSH HERITAGE

NIGEL TRANTER

EDINBURGH
B&W PUBLISHING
1996

Copyright © Nigel Tranter
First published 1940
This edition published 1996
by B&W Publishing Ltd
Edinburgh
ISBN 1 873631 65 0

British Library Cataloguing in Publication Data:
A catalogue record for this book is available from
the British Library

Cover illustration: detail from *Hills of Ross*
by Sir David Young Cameron (1865-1945)
Photograph by kind permission of
The Flemings Collection

Printed by Werner Söderström

CONTENTS

THE SOWING

1817

THE work went merrily, for it was merry work, with the anticipation of still merrier work to come. At present only the livestock was being cleared, a mere preliminary to the more exciting business of the afternoon, when bonfires would be the order of the day and some sensation assured. Still, the immediate work was far from dull, and opportunities for recreation not infrequent.

It was quite an animated scene in that small green glen amongst the crowding hills. On either side of the amber waters of the burn men were busy rounding-up and herding the small black cattle, the stumpy sturdy ponies, the nimble-footed goats, and the scraggy assorted poultry, that, with the meagre crops in the tiny unfenced fields of the glen-sides, appeared to sustain the life of this God-forsaken community. There was much hallooing and shouting, much whacking and cursing, as the shaggy cattle charged hither and thither, the shelts clattered and wheeled, the goats leapt and skipped, and the screeching fowls flapped in and out of the tumbledown croft-houses. The men, big-boned burly keepers and the like from the laird's fine southern estate, forgot their dignity and station and much else in the scramble, pursuing the bewildered animals with sticks and stones and peats and heartsome swearing; and if frequently they followed the ridiculous hens into the black interiors of the hovels and did not always emerge therefrom immediately, who was to blame them? Not Mr. Simmonds, certainly; he was a liberal-minded man, and wisely tolerant of his men in small matters. And it was very dark in those black-houses.

Despite all the commotion it was a common enough scene

3

for the Scottish Highlands in the year of Our Lord and of grace, eighteen hundred and seventeen; and of all the sixty-odd inhabitants of that small glen, one old woman alone continued to protest against the inevitable, and that despite her reputation for wisdom. The others, men, women and children, apparently recognising and accepting the hand of Fate, stood by and consented. What else indeed was there to do? The laird wanted the land for sheep, and the land was the laird's—of this they were left in no doubt, though when it had ceased to be the clan's and become the laird's it would be hard to say. Tales had been reaching them from the South for long enough, of war and threats of invasion, indeed most of the younger men had already been recruited to fight for the English king. The French were like ravening wolves devouring all before them. Homegrown supplies, it appeared, were in demand, and were likely to remain so. The Highlands, it was discovered, could support sheep, and mutton and wool prices were soaring. The laird, then, in common with so many other lairds, had turned patriot. It was unfortunate that with the arrival of the sheep the people must go, but there it was. The little crofting townships took up much of the best and most sheltered land in the glens, hirsels necessary for sheep in a Highland winter; their lean half-wild cattle fouled the ground and wasted the pasture, it was said, also, the sheep-farmers considered the crofters a disturbing influence in their new sheep-runs, and doubtless they knew their business. Then again, it was discovered that these glens-people's standard of living was deplorably low; they were poor, indolent, dirty, and backward, their houses were hovels, and their stock and crops wretched. In fact, they were found to be a sore on the face of the land, and the laird, adding social reform to his patriotism, found it expedient to remove them. It had all been explained to them. A written notice even had been nailed-up—in English, unfortunately, and therefore indecipherable—setting it all forth, and

4

quoting the expert opinion of many important people "that these mountainous districts were as much calculated for the maintenance of stock as they were unfit for the habitation of men, and that it was as if it had been pointed out by Nature that the system for this remote district, in order that it might bear its suitable importance in contributing its share to the general stock of the country, was to convert the mountainous areas into sheep-walks, and to remove the inhabitants to the coast or to the valleys near the sea." So they looked on, passive if not disinterested, with only an occasional entreaty, fruitless as it was unfitting. All but the old woman.

They were an unkempt company, these crofters, not at all romantic, and slight in comparison with the factor's men. Mr. Simmonds agreed with the laird that the place would be well rid of them. Idle, lazy, thieving, good-for-nothings, that's what they were, and Catholics to a man—though little good even that graceless religion seemed to do them! And the airs they could assume on occasion; wrapping themselves up in a dignity ill-befitting their filthy rags, looking down their dirty noses at him—him, John Simmonds, lately steward to the Marquis of Welby—and referring familiarly to the laird as Neill More or some such disrespectful term, as though they were his equals if not his betters. Thank God he wouldn't have to put up with them much longer!

Mr. Simmonds smiled grimly as a woman's scream pierced the general hubbub. Let them screech! It would do them not a bit of harm to shed a little of their damned exclusiveness. It was little enough any of his men had got out of them hitherto, barring a mouthful of their heathenish gibberish. They were good fellows, his men, and deserving of a little fun. Mr. Simmonds, as has been remarked, was tolerant in small matters.

The appearance of a strolling elegantly clad figure from the direction of the strath-road, roused the factor out of his musing. Hurriedly he sprang up from his overturned meal-chest, to hasten in the direction of the newcomer. Mr. Edward was a rather difficult young man and apt to be autocratic, but he was the laird's son and therefore entitled to his whims. Mr. Simmonds was as admirable a servant as he was a master.

"I have wandered along to see the fun, Simmonds," the elegant young man remarked, "if there is any fun to see! Are they going quietly, d'you think?"

"They'll go quietly, sir, I'll see to that," Mr. Simmonds assured him.

"A pity!" Edward Macarthy Neill yawned. "I had hoped for a little amusement. Things are devilish dull." He glanced about him languidly, groping in his coat-tails for his snuff-box. "You haven't even got the cattle away yet, I see. I might have spared myself the walk. You're damnably slow about it, man."

"That's the last of them now, sir," the factor said. "After this, we'll be able to get on with the burning. That ought to be worth seeing."

"Ah, yes, the burning!" the other murmured. "I had forgotten the burning. I'll wait a little, then. As you say, that might be worth seeing—if the filthy stuff will burn!"

Mr. Simmonds nodded confidently. "It will burn, sir," he said.

It was the old woman alone, not forgetting the white calf, that was the cause of all the trouble. Why couldn't the old hag take it philosophically, like the other occupants of the glen, quiet, mute even, in their ejection? After all, her house was little more than a hovel of mud and turf and stones from the burn, ill-roofed with a crazy thatch of reeds and bracken—little enough to make such a fuss about. And Mr. Simmonds was providing a fine cart, gratis, to take her and her belongings anywhere that she might want to go.

It was all so useless, this clamour. Obviously it was so

6

much wiser, so much more fitting, to go quietly, unprotesting, as did the other evicted tenants. What if their parents and forefathers had dwelt there for generations, centuries perhaps, safe and secure as members of the sept of which Macarthy Neill, their landlord, was chief? Times changed, and there was no putting back of the clock. It was the chief's land now—though it had been the sept's land once—and if Macarthy Neill wanted the glen to breed sheep on, who were they, as loyal clansmen, to stand in the way? A sad state of affairs if a man could not do as he liked with his own land!

Yes, it was foolish, useless, to resist; everybody, everything even, seemed to realise that—all but the old hag, Elspeth Macarthy. The brown hills looked down through the thin autumn sunshine, unmoved and withdrawn in their silent dignity, rank upon rank of them, lifting their stony brows up and up to the vague outline of Beinn Buidhe itself, austere and aloof in its sterile majesty. The burn winding its accustomed way down the glen to the Feith River, murmured and chuckled to itself just as it had done for countless ages, and would do for countless more, little caring whether men or sheep tenanted the glen. Certainly the wind, that already had the cold breath of coming snows in it, sighed fitfully amongst the scattered birches of the braeside, but it was a sigh infinitely remote, concerned only with its own vacant affairs. Even the sun had little warmth about it, its slight solicitude soon obscured by the billowing acrid smoke of the already burning thatches and tiny stacks of bog-hay.

No, nothing seemed to be very deeply affected. One or two scrawny hens still pecked about as nervously as was their wont, casting only an occasional wary glance at the intruders, while even the white deer-calf looked on with timid interest but no anxiety. Nevertheless, Mr. Simmonds was annoyed, and with reason. There were few things Mr. Simmonds enjoyed less than a scene, the more particularly

7

when the maker of the scene insisted on making it in the outlandish Gaelic. It wasn't as though the old runt had no English—he had talked with her before this. Probably she felt that she owed it to her reputation as a seer of sorts to make a demonstration. Well then, she had made it. She must not impede the work of clearance further.

"That'll do now, mother," he gestured, patiently firm. Mr. Simmonds prided himself on his patience as on his firmness, two qualities invaluable in a factor. "You will bring out your personal belongings and place them on the cart there. You should have had them all out before this." He swung on his interested henchmen. "You, Thomson, give her a hand. You, Smith, catch those damned hens and truss them up. We'll be here all night at this rate!" He turned again to the crone. "And the less fuss you make, the better it will be for you!" he added significantly.

The old woman, bent in the squat doorway of her poor cottage, spared him not so much as a glance of acknowledgment. The gaze of her beady eyes went on and past him to the slim, fashionably clad figure that lounged behind him, and the spate of her Gaelic flowed on unchecked.

Mr. Simmonds spoke again, sharply. "Elspeth Macarthy, come out of that house, I tell you! What way is this to behave . . . and in front of the young Chief, too!" he added, sententiously reproachful.

For an instant the black eyes flashed on him. "Chief!" The word was spat out, and the cackle which followed it only rivalled it in scorn and eloquence.

Mr. Simmonds, with a half-glance at his companion, hesitated. Edward Macarthy Neill appeared to be as oblivious of his factor's presence as was the old hag.

Then, with a shrug, he resumed. "Come on then, woman! I have my duty to do—we've wasted too much time as it is."

The old woman forsook her Gaelic. "Duty, is it?" she screamed. "Your duty is it to be turning me out from the

8

house I was born in, me Elspeth Sean with the gift and the sight, turning me from the glen, and it that my people have held since Fergus Dubh mac Niall! *Dia!* Ye lick-spittle!"

Mr. Simmonds' patience had its limits. "Hold your foul tongue, you old bitch, and get your wretched things out of that place, or by God I'll burn the roof over ye!" he shouted. Nor was his wrath appeased by the light mocking laughter from at his back.

" 'Pon my soul, Simmonds, I do believe it was worth my while staying, after all. You become considerably more impressive when you are . . . shall we say, heated?"

Mr. Simmonds could have gladly seen the speaker in hell, but he most assuredly could not tell him so. Instead, "I'm glad indeed that you've found something to amuse you, Mr. Edward," he said. By a considerable effort his tones were level. "So far it has not been very exciting, I'm afraid."

"Deuced slow!" the other agreed casually.

"Well, it won't be now," the older man grunted, and his voice was grim. "Thomson," he ordered, "fire the thatch!"

The man Thomson grinned, and did as he was bid.

With a crackle and a roar the dry thatching caught, and, shrilly screaming within the doorway the old woman stood, lips drawn back from toothless gums.

Cursing, Mr. Simmonds took a couple of steps forward and grasped her roughly. "Out you come, you old she-devil!" he bawled, and half of her poor clothes came off with the wrench he gave.

And with cold ferocity the old woman spat, full in his great red face. "Lick-spittle," she cackled, "lick ye that!"

With a great oath he struck her, a furious blow that sent her staggering back and back, coughing convulsively, while from behind, mocking laughter pierced the hiss and crackle of the burning thatch. The crash of her fall was drowned by a greater, the crash of the blazing roof. For a moment the roar of the flames was paramount, then through and above

9

it shrilled a thin screaming that rose and rose to an intensity of agony inexpressible, to cease suddenly, entirely.

Into the throbbing silence that succeeded, the lazy, modulated voice of Mr. Edward Macarthy Neill sighed, "You're a rough fellow, Simmonds. Quite a man of action when you get roused, begad! A dramatic ending, too. Devilish appropriate . . . for a witch!" and he laughed lightly as he turned on his heel.

When, presently, the flames died down, two men lifted out the pitifully charred remains of Elspeth Macarthy, and laid her on the scorched grass at her own doorway. Mr. Simmonds, hands clenched tightly, looked down and hastily glanced away, muttering something. Mr. Edward did not look at all—it was not a pretty sight. Only the white deer-calf, approaching diffidently, looked for long, a close searching stare, its great eyes like peat-pools in a still river. Long it looked, immovable, then gently, deliberately, it stooped its head and nuzzled and licked that blackened face. Mr. Simmonds, turning to drive the brute away, stopped in mid-stride, his breath catching in his throat, his protuberant eyes held by the steady glare of a pair of others, beady black. "My God!" he gasped, his hand at his throat. "My God, she's alive!"

Mr. Macarthy Neill strolled over. "Damme, you're right!" he murmured. "A *bona fide* witch after all," and he laughed, as ever, but his laughter was strangely harsh.

For a full minute they stood hesitant, florid factor and pallid elegant, uneasy beneath the blaze of those unwinking eyes, yet unable to transfer their gaze elsewhere. Gradually, painfully, the scorched and cracked lips began to move. Little by little they worked, blood welling thinly from the cracks at every movement, and still the eyes glared unswervingly, malevolent. Then remotely, like the sigh of a dry wind in a dead wood, came the whisper. "Curse you, curse you, Niall Og. Curse you and your false house that would be selling

10

your own people for the yellow gold. Curse this fair glen that you have ravished. Curse you and your house and your glen, all the days of yonder *Laoigh Feigh Ban*!"

Still the jet-black eyes stared, fixed immovably on the face of the young chief, but presently the metallic glimmer of them waned, faded, and died. The black eyes were like the naked windows of an empty house—no life moved behind them. Elspeth the seer, the wise woman, had gone to her fathers in the glen that would never be cleared.

It was some little time before the watchers appreciated that it was a corpse that they were watching. Mr. Simmonds shook himself and coughed uncomfortably. "Well, she's dead this time, devil take her!" he said. He glanced doubtfully at his companion. "Mad, she must have been," he suggested.

With a seeming effort the other roused himself from a grey meditation. "Mad!" he repeated absently. "Mad . . . oh, yes, mad probably . . . mad undoubtedly!" He forced himself to laugh again, a laugh with an edge to it. "Anyway, we will settle her curse right here and now," he said, and from his coat-tails he drew out a small silver-mounted pistol, richly wrought. Carefully he adjusted the charge and the lock. Deliberately he turned to where the white deer-calf, the *Laoigh Feigh Ban*, nibbled uncertainly, and as deliberately fired.

The crash of the report echoed and re-echoed amongst all the slumbering hills. A puff of blue smoke drifted to join the darker clouds from the burning crofts. The white calf looked up, startled, his velvet-brown eyes showing a rim of white round their edges. And the strangely-hunched, red-spattered figure of Edward Macarthy Neill fell limply across the blackened corpse of Elspeth Sean, the burst pistol still gripped by some of the fingers of a bloody hand.

And the white deer-calf, great ears back, haunches down, leapt past the smoking ruins of the cottage that had sheltered it, over the clearing where the bog-hay struggled with

11

the ever-encroaching bracken, and up through the scattered birches of the braeside, with never a pause nor a backward glance, while the gathered hills looked down unmoved, the small wind sighed resignedly, and the burn murmured and chuckled on its way to the Feith River.

THE FRUIT

1847

A DISCREET tapping at the door interrupted the Major's contemplation of his brandy and the gentle current of his thoughts: Fully fifteen hundred acres of fat land, two villages and three livings, a good house—old-fashioned, but quite imposing—another place in Wales which he hadn't seen, but was told that the shooting was good, also a tidy house in Portland Square, which could be sold—his own was well enough. Say two thousand a year in all, or to be conservative, make it eighteen hundred . . . and a pretty piece of goods thrown in as make-weight . . . pretty, though a shade fickle, perhaps. But that could be attended to. Of course he couldn't take possession straight away, as it were—he'd have to let the dust sink down a bit; stay out of England a few months, a year perhaps, and then a quiet wedding and the reward of patience. He might need the year, anyway, to square off certain affairs. . . . Confound the fellow, what was he wanting at this time of night? "Well, dammit, Nixon, what is it?" he called.

Nixon opened the door apologetically, to close it carefully behind him. "Beg pardon, sir, but there's a lady to see you, sir," he informed.

"A lady, eh?" The Major's reflective tone held no hint of surprise. He looked at his man keenly. "Well, out with it, then!"

Nixon, his eyes on the stained carpet, gave the smallest shrug of the shoulders. "She spoke English and she gave no name, sir, but"—he coughed circumspectly behind a plump hand— "she said it was—er—a matter of life and death, sir."

A faint frown came and went on his master's fine forehead,

15

and for a second or two his long, carefully-tended fingers drummed a tattoo on the arm of his chair. Then he rose to his feet and tightened the cord of his be-furred velvet dressing-gown, and ran a sure hand over dark hair and silky moustache. "Show her up, then," he directed curtly. He turned on an afterthought. "Where is she now—in the lobby, or in that room of yours at the back?"

"In my own room, sir. I assumed that you would not want the inn people to. . . ."

The Major smiled a little, to himself necessarily, and his hand went up to his moustache again. "Perhaps it would do no harm for the inn people to . . . observe, a little," he considered. "But don't overdo it—these Frenchies are pretty sharp. And, Nixon, stay near at hand . . . but not too near. You understand?"

And Nixon, meeting the fixed stare of cold eyes, repressed a shiver—as he was constrained to do quite frequently—bowed and withdrew.

When, a minute or two later, he ushered the lady in, the Major had a silk scarf to his neck, two more candles lit, and a welcome on his lips. He stepped forward to greet her gallantly, hands outstretched. "My dear, this is indeed a happy surprise. Come over here by the fire, it's a cold night." With his eye on the closing door, he slipped an arm round her. "Though perhaps you are not cold, Millicent?" he whispered, smiling.

The woman, wrapped in a dark travelling-cloak and hood, drew away. "Ranald!" she gasped, and not even her generous covering could hide the tumult of her breathing. She put out a hand to him, upturned, suppliant, and he grasped it and pulled her to him. "Milly, you little devil," he grinned, "I knew you were keen, but. . . ." He wagged an admonitory finger at her, and stooped to push back her hood, his eyes on her lips. "For a married woman you're distinctly. . . ."

"Stop!" she entreated, and even he could not pretend to

16

misinterpret the sincerity with which she thrust him away. She stood, in the mellow radiance of the candlelight, a young woman, fair, fresh-complexioned, her hair, released from the hood, gleaming subduedly. Round-cheeked, wide-browed, full-lipped, hers was a comeliness that did not aspire to beauty, but tonight in that pale luminosity, with the lines and shadows drawn by anxiety and tears, her features held a quiet loveliness that was not lost on her companion. The Major was something of a connoisseur of beauty, feminine and equine.

"B'gad, Milly, y'know you're damnably good-looking tonight," he told her.

The girl gave a half-shake of her head. "Ranald, I did not come here to listen to compliments, or . . . what you suggested." She laughed, shortly, harshly. "Our time for that is past, I'm afraid. I heard this afternoon that you and George are to fight. Ranald, you won't, you can't do it. Say you won't do it!"

The man inspected his fingernails appraisingly. "Afraid it's all arranged, m'dear," he said.

"Then cancel the arrangement," she cried. "You can do it easily. You must—you shall! Surely, if you love me as you say, you will spare me this!"

"Spare you what, my child? I can conceive of not the slightest danger in it . . . for me, so your concern is quite uncalled for." He smiled at her sardonically. "Unless, of course, your alarm is on George's account? Though it's rather late to be thinking about George, eh?"

She drew herself up as though she had been struck. "Late, as you say," she admitted quietly, "but not too late, perhaps. I am still his wife." Her shoulders drooped again, and she took a step toward him. "But you can't do this thing, Ranald, if I ask, pray, that you won't, after what we've meant to each other. It would be so easy for you with your reputation. . . ."

17

"Easy!" The man's lean jaw thrust forward on the word, and something of his reputation was apparent in that handsome face. "By God, your husband insulted me, actually struck me in public!"

"And what have you—what have we done to him?" she demanded wearily. "I have let you borrow from him, fleece him at cards, debauch him. In his own house we have betrayed him, made him a laughing-stock, dragged a good name in the dirt—and, God, you say that he has insulted you!" She looked him straight in the eye now. "I may have cheated him, lied to him, and wounded him, but I will not stand by and see him . . . murdered!"

While the inexorable clock on the mantelpiece tick-ticked, they stared at each other, hot blue eyes meeting cold grey eyes, each seeing in the other something that they had not noticed hitherto. At length the man shrugged and turned to the table and the decanters. "This is ridiculous. I had thought better of you, my girl. Here, have a glass of something—brandy, port?" he suggested, not entirely equably. "And for the Lord's sake, sit down. There's no call to stand there like a heroine in a melodrama. You take the whole affair too seriously, Millicent. Why talk about killing? A mere matter of two shots exchanged at so many paces, a slight wound, a little bleeding—vastly beneficial, I am told—and honour is satisfied."

"Honour!" the girl repeated scornfully. "I think that we can leave honour out of it. And was your fame built on a few slight wounds and a little bleeding?"

"Accidents will happen!" he protested piously. There were two boxes on the table. One contained cigars. The Major selected one, and glanced towards his visitor. "D'you mind if I smoke?" He lit his cigar from a candle, and made two puffs at it, blowing out the smoke appreciatively between pursed lips. With a curious semi-abstraction the woman noticed how red and moist his lips seemed in that pose beneath the sleek luxuriance of his moustache. "This is all too theatrical," he went on. "Come on, Milly, let's stop this bickering. You're much too charming to quarrel with. George isn't worth it. You know that this affair has to go through, but I'll let George down lightly . . . if he lets me, though I'm damned if he deserves it. Come along and sit down—I'm going to, if you're not. You know how I detest scenes." Seeing she still made no move, he took his seat and glanced at her curiously. "And why, may I ask, if you're so put out about this business, why don't you go to George and get him to back out of it or do a bolt or something? As you so aptly put it, we've made his name so—er—soiled, that it could hardly do him much harm. If he was to apologise— publicly—and—h'm—accommodate me otherwise, I suppose I'd be almost bound to let him off."

The other's hands tugged agitatedly at her cloak. "Do you think that I haven't tried, hateful though that would be? I'd rather see him degraded than dead! But George won't hear me, won't even see me."

"Foolish fellow!"

"Not that he would do it, anyway. You know that. George is still the remains of a gentleman."

"So you come to me! And I, pray, what am I, my dear Mrs. Pomeroy?"

"I begin to think that you are nothing more than a cold-blooded, soulless adventurer, despite your romantic name, Major the Macarthy Neill!"

He got to his feet, frowning. "I thank you for your frank-ness, at any rate," he snapped, "though I think it scarcely comes well from you. And Ranald Neill will suit me better for any further compliments you may have to present, if you please!"

The girl bowed mockingly. "Forgive me, I forgot that you are so . . . modest about your Scottish title." She stopped, and bit her lip. "Oh, I'm sorry, Ranald."

The man said nothing, but, his hands busy with his moustache, he resumed his seat. For half a long minute Millicent Pomeroy eyed his shapely back, shapely even in a dressing-gown, before she moved over to his chair, swiftly, urgently, to lean over him and take his hand. "Ranald," she said, "I'll agree to anything, anything, if only you'll cancel the duel. I'll do whatever you like. I'll give up George and all that George means. I'll run away with you, if you want, anywhere, just you and I, for good!"

If the woman had expected an emotional reaction to her offer, she was disappointed. Her companion, far from exulting, gazed up rather coldly. "Run away with you—and leave George?" he repeated, frowning. "What good would that do? Please use your intelligence, Millicent, for my sake if not for your own. A man in my position can't afford to run off with the wife of a diplomatic colleague who'd been his host up to the previous day. B'gad, I'd be recalled from the Embassy. I'd be struck off my clubs. I'd probably lose my commission. I'd be ruined socially!"

"I see! You may kill your erstwhile host with a pistol, but you may not elope with his wife and remain respectable."

"I don't like your choice of terms. And as you know very well, a duel is a perfectly honourable arrangement between gentlemen, no favour, seconds and witnesses, doctors and so on."

She smiled acidly. "I am learning things tonight. Can you inform me where lies the difference in respectability between seducing a man's wife in his own house, and running away with her?"

The Major looked his handsome bleakest. "Once again, I resent your way of putting things, Millicent. You don't require me to tell you that a small—er—affair is winked at in all circles, always has been, but an elopement is a vastly different matter."

"A small affair!" she reiterated, and laughed jarringly.

"Lord, what fools we women can be! And I actually thought that you loved me!"

He jumped up at that. "Of course I do, Millicent," he affirmed, "but let us look at the thing like reasonable beings. You must appreciate my position. . . ."

She stopped him with a gesture, dignified in its finality. "I think that you can spare me that, Ranald," she said, frigidly. "I may take it, then, that nothing that I can say or do will alter your decision about tomorrow?"

He shook his dark head. "I'm afraid not! After what he has done, I owe George altogether too much for me to do as you ask."

"I believe you. Somewhere in the region of eighteen hundred pounds, I understand," the woman amplified, bitingly.

She had touched him this time. "My God, woman, I've stood enough of this!" he shouted, and strode towards her. Clumsy in his violence, he overbalanced the light pedestal table beside his chair. Almost automatically the man and woman grabbed at the table's plenishings, Neill at the decanters, Mrs. Pomeroy at the two boxes. The cigars she failed to catch, but the weightier box she gripped and held. With a muttered apology, he righted the table, and she set down the box again, a flat, handsome mahogany box, inlaid with satin-wood, with the initials R. M. N. inscribed in mother-of-pearl. With the jerk the lid had become unfastened and would not shut tightly again. Unthinkingly the girl opened it to re-arrange the box's contents.

"Oh!" she gasped at what she saw there, and stepped back, her hand to her throat.

The Macarthy Neill smiled slowly. "Thank you for catching them, my dear," he said. "It's as well they didn't fall—I had them all prepared for tomorrow. I always try to be very careful with these toys—my father was killed by a bursting pistol, you know. They are rather a handsome pair, are they

21

not? A presentation from some friends after the de Noilly affair—he was a fearful bore and very unpopular."

She made no acknowledgement of his humour, but continued to stare, as if fascinated, at the two small chased and inlaid duelling-pistols in their case. At length she withdrew her eyes from them. "These things, then, are all ready for use—for the . . . business tomorrow?" she inquired, quickly, tonelessly.

"I naturally keep them in working order," he agreed, shortly.

"Of course!" She stooped to pick up a stray cigar from under the table. "Nevertheless, I trust that despite your refusal to do as I ask, they will not be required tomorrow."

"Indeed?" he wondered complacently, eyebrows raised.

She nodded. "I shall inform the authorities, scandal or no. I shall go tonight to the Prefect of Police, and get him to stop the whole affair."

The man laughed easily. "The Prefect will do nothing of the sort. You forget that you are not in England, m'dear. The French authorities are much more sensible than our own about this sort of thing. They appreciate that a gentleman's honour is a matter of some consequence, and must be preserved in a suitable manner. I'm afraid you'd have no success with the Prefect."

"But the Prefect must enforce the law!"

"The law is, shall we say, elastic, but not to be hurried, never to be hurried. With your well-known persistence you might get something done within the week perhaps, but. . . !"

Something of the girl's distress and despair must have shown in her eyes, for Neill moved towards her, striving hard to be affable. "But how absurd this is, Milly. Have I not told you that I will let George off lightly—barring accidents, of course—one can never be certain in a meeting of this sort. I might even get shot myself, you know!"

"You might!" she agreed evenly. As he had been speaking her expression had changed. Her chin lifted, her eyes narrowed, there was despair in them still, but something else also. Like a flash she moved back to the table, and snatched one of the pistols, pulling back the hammer and pointing it at her companion in the one movement. "Stay where you are, Ranald Neill," she directed, "and promise me not to fight this duel, or I swear I will shoot you where you stand!"

The Major eyed her amazedly. "B'gad," he jerked, glancing from her hand to her face. "I believe that you mean it, too, you little devil!" Then he nodded to the pistol with a half-smile. "So you would shoot me, would you! You were kinder two nights ago."

"Promise!" was all she said, but her finger was steady on the trigger.

He still stood, lounging easily. "You certainly have spirit, but then I never denied you that. Yes, two nights ago you were adorably spirited!" He paused, then went on again. "Might I ask, by the way, what you intend to do with the corpse when you are finished with me?"

"That does not concern me," she answered, her voice tense as her trigger-finger. "There are two pistols, fortunately. The second one will be used also. Now give me your promise, or . . ."

He sighed, and shook his head. "Murder and suicide—melodrama still. You must have become devilish fond of George all of a sudden!" At that he laughed again, a laugh with an edge to it, and straightening up, stepped over to her.

Her eyes shut, her lips moving, she pressed the trigger. As the hammer clicked, her hand was grasped roughly and the pistol was wrenched away and flung carelessly on to the chair. "You little fool," he cried hoarsely, "I thought even a woman would have known that pistols are not kept loaded in a box!"

23

For a moment the girl stood motionless, her face devoid of all expression. Then silently, without warning, she slid to the floor, unconscious.

Neill swore feelingly, with the resentful anxiety common to men with a fainting woman on their hands. He stooped and lifted her, having some difficulty with the cloak, and, gasping just a little, set her down on his chair. She was a well-made young woman. He was reaching for brandy to revive her, when he paused, thoughtful, and nodded grimly. "Nixon!" he called loudly. Ranald Neill was something of an opportunist.

With commendable celerity the door opened and Nixon stood framed therein, deferential, impassive.

"The lady's fainted," the Major said, briefly. "Has she a conveyance waiting?"

"Yes, sir, there is a carriage outside."

"Good! Well, give me a hand with her down the stairs. You take that side, and put her arm round your shoulder. Quick, man, she'll come round any moment, and I want her out of here before she does."

Dutifully expressionless, Nixon did as he was told, and, after the other had pulled her hood well forward over her face, they supported the drooping girl between them, somewhat hastily, out of the room.

On the stair her eyelids flickered and opened, and a violent shudder ran through her. Then she looked rather wildly from one man to the other. "What is this . . . ?" she began, uncertain.

Neill patted her shoulder. "It's all right, my dear," he said soothingly, "you are a little over-wrought, that's all. We'll have you in your carriage in a moment. Just keep quiet, will you?"

Her eyes searched his face for a moment. "I understand!" she said, and then, disengaging both arms, she moved forwards and downwards, her face set and white. Straight

24

through the public room of the inn she passed, glancing neither to left nor to right, the Major half a pace behind her and Nixon rather dubiously bringing up the rear.

The *aubergiste* stepped forward hopefully, but was waved away in curt dismissal, and the trio passed out into the night, leaving behind them an interested company that nodded and winked and expressed itself with considerable freedom and much ingenuity.

"Captain O'Hara and the Marquis de Nerville are below, sir," Nixon announced, almost apologetically.

The Major yawned. "What, already? They're deuced early." He peered at the clock. "Dammit, I can't even see the time. All right, help me on with these things and take away that tray, then show them up." He stretched his arms and yawned again. How he detested early rising!

O'Hara and the Marquis were shown in. They greeted him effusively and characteristically. "Well, me boy, the top of a fine morning to ye! All ready for the fray, eh?" and "Good morning, *mon cher* Ranald! Do we find our champion flourishing and full of resolve, steady of hand and clear of eye?"

"You find me damned sleepy," Neill retorted. "You are confoundedly punctual, gentlemen!"

The visitors laughed in unison, a guffaw and a snicker. "He's a cool card, b'dad!" the Captain chuckled. "Sure, he'd be more excited to be going wenching." De Nerville agreed. "The so admirable *sang froid*! *Le flègme brittanique*! To our good friend, a duel is a mere nothing, just *pouf*—so!" The Marquis was as elegant in gesture as in person.

Major Neill shrugged. "This duel is, anyway. Fellow can't shoot. Never handled a pistol in his life, so I'm told."

"Rumour can be a liar," O'Hara warned him genially. He was a large untidy man with a cast in one eye and an atmosphere of extreme joviality.

The other shook his head. "Not this time. I have it on the

25

highest authority." He stepped over to a wall-mirror, and adjusted his stock carefully. "On the authority of no less a person than Mrs. Pomeroy. She is much—er—exercised over George's uncertain future." And he smiled with a certain satisfaction at his reflection.

His two companions exchanged glances. "The lady, then, she knows about this meeting? You have seen her since the—hum—since the affair?"

The Major yawned elaborately. "I had the honour of entertaining the lady here last night." One eyelid drooped suggestively. "Perhaps that is why I am so deuced sleepy . . . though you must admit, gentlemen, that this is a devilish uncivilised hour to be out of bed!"

Captain O'Hara slapped his massive thigh a resounding whack. "That's rich, b'dad!" he roared. "The fellow arranges to shoot a fellow in the morning, and then spends the night with the fellow's wife."

"Not the whole night," the other protested mildly. "Let us be accurate at all costs."

The Marquis almost choked himself with his mirth. "*Mon Dieu*, Ranald, you are . . . gigantic! You surpass yourself! *Mon frère*, I salute you!"

Neill waved a casual hand. "You exaggerate, gentlemen, I assure you." He glanced about him. "Well, I think that I am at your service. Will you have a drink before we go?"

"Thank you, no!" De Nerville shook his head. "At this hour—impossible! I have not the courage."

"Courage be damned!" O'Hara snorted. "Is that brandy you've got there, Neill, me boy? I'd drink any man's brandy any hour in the twenty-four!" He filled a generous glass, and held it up. "Well, here's to our friend's shooting, and our mutual prosperity!"

"And a pleasant journey to our Monsieur George!" the Marquis added, imaginary glass raised.

"Amen!"

The Macarthy Neill put on his beaver, a single tap on its tall crown settling it at precisely the right angle. Then he picked up his gloves, and the mahogany box from the table, tucking it under his arm. "Nixon!" he called. "The coach—is it ready?"

Nixon was always there when he was wanted. "Yes, sir. Everything in order, sir."

His master consulted the clock. "It is seven-thirty now . . . ugh! How far will it be to the venue de Nerville? About ten kilometres—say, six miles? Then two hours ought to be ample time for the whole business. I'll be back by nine-thirty, then, Nixon. Have everything here packed up—it may be advisable for us to leave almost at once for Paris. Now, gentlemen, if I cannot offer you anything further!"

Captain O'Hara had said it was a fine morning. A sharp touch of frost overnight, after a day of rain had made a glassy cover for the puddles through which the coach-wheels crunched exhilaratingly. The wan light of morning held that peculiar quality, sharp and clear within a short radius, hazy and indistinct beyond, fading into a vague smokiness that rose only a little way over the tree-tops, and would diminish and disappear with the rising of the cold November sun. Above was nothing of vagueness, but rather a stark emptiness, a chill, toneless vacancy, out of which one or two pale stars still gleamed, frigid and remote. It was as fine a morning as that.

Inside the jolting, swaying coach, Captain O'Hara waxed reminiscent. "This will be the fourth meeting where I've acted as your second, me lad . . . and you with never a scratch to show for any of them, too! Ye have the devil's own luck, for sure. D'ye remember de Noilly . . . and Crossley . . . and Crossley's sister? A handsome piece, that Crossley girl, as ripe a plum as any I've seen. Bye the bye, what happened to that lass, Neill? It's long enough since I set eyes on her."

"I'm afraid I have no information," the Major answered coldly.

"Yes, oh yes, indeed! Why should ye, b'dad?" He winked heavily. "Then there was Paterson—still is, to be sure. Ye never met Paterson, did ye, de Nerville? Well, ye'd be knowing him now by the unusual face that he has on him, no bridge to his nose, and one eye short. That was a damned peculiar thing, the way that ball took him. A glancing shot—ballistics or something would explain it, I suppose," he mused, loudly of necessity, owing to the clip-clop of the horses, the rumble and bump of the wheels, the groaning of the springs, and the creaking of the leather upholstery. French roads were no better than English in the eighteen-forties. "Anyway, it was the kind of thing that happens only once in a lifetime. Paterson was lucky."

"From your so admirable account, most lucky, most fortunate!" the Marquis smiled. "It is not to be expected that our young friend George should be so fortunate, is it, Ranald?"

The Major withdrew his regard from a protracted study of the carriage-roof, to turn it, with almost a trace of wonderment, on the Frenchman. "Of course not!" he said briefly.

"Of course! *Naturellement!*" de Nerville nodded, still smiling. He had most excellent teeth. "It is only fitting—and necessary! The unfortunate young man, besides possessing a most charming wife, and certain other . . . provocations, is it? . . . is, of all follies, meddlesome. To meddle in the affairs of others is unforgivable, is it not? And the young man is a fool, and confirmed in his foolishness—he accepts the challenge of the so celebrated Major Neill of the Blues. *Nom de Dieu!* What would you!"

O'Hara grinned. "The young man had small choice," he grunted. "Our friend saw to that, eh, me boy?"

Ranald Neill, beyond a shrug of the shoulders, did not reply. He transferred his gaze from the roof to the window, already steaming over. He was hardly a sociable man, and paid little court to popularity—masculine, at any rate.

The coach was rattling its way through a level, glistening country of small hedgeless fields, patches of heath, and scattered cottages, from the chimneys of which blue smoke-columns coiled lazily. Here and there, isolated trees raised naked arms in mute appeal to the indifferent void, sweating in the grip of the cold, and over all the rime glittered and sparkled. Already, as the Major noticed with a certain distaste, men and women were at work in the fields, patiently, doggedly, toiling; at the sight of women forking and spreading manure that smoked obscenely, he turned away in disgust. The country and its drudgery was brutish, barbarous, he decided, and distressing to a sensitive man. Also, in some way that he could not quite apprehend, it reminded him of Scotland, a place he preferred to forget. Ranald Macarthy Neill closed his eyes, and resigned his mind to mental arithmetic: five hundred, three-fifty, four-fifty, four hundred . . . seventeen hundred, and a few odds and ends, small obligements . . . b'gad, she'd been near enough to it! Money was the devil! Then he smiled to himself. The widow, fortunately, would hardly be likely to press for payment!

The others, accustomed to their associate's comparative aloofness, conversed animatedly, if not entirely freely. In fact, it might be that they were too loquacious altogether, O'Hara almost too jovial, the Marquis over-witty. Unlike their principal, it seemed they could not remain entirely unaffected by the contemplation of their journey's end and object. Major Neill's detachment was, of course, proverbial. Twice amid their chatter he yawned and settled himself more comfortably in his corner. It almost appeared as if the Macarthy Neill was going to sleep. His companions shook their heads and shrugged and lowered their voices. A queer, cold-blooded devil! And the coach lurched onward.

It was out of a pleasant doze that Ranald Neill was

aroused, perturbed, suddenly alert. The other two were still talking. Something that had been said had penetrated his somnolence sufficiently to leave an impression, a distinctly unpleasant impression. Eyes still closed, but very much awake, he listened. O'Hara was speaking. ". . . the Lord knows why it should be such a popular name for an inn. 'Tisn't as though it was an everyday sort of a beast like a black bull or a grey mare. There's one of the same name in my own village of Ballyrane, back in County Cork, but here in France. . . ."

Neill interrupted. "What did you say the name of this place is—the place we're making for?" He spoke sharply.

The others glanced at him in surprise. "Sure, I thought ye were asleep, Major!" the Captain exclaimed. "Dreaming of blue eyes and golden hair, eh!" He turned to de Nerville. "The sly dog's been sitting there listening to us. . . ."

"The name, please!"

The peremptory demand raised the Irishman's eyebrows. But he laughed, as ever. "Gervaix, isn't it, de Nerville?"

"I know that!" the Major snapped. "I mean the name of the place where the meeting is to be held—the actual venue."

"Oh, the inn, y'mean? *Le Cerf Blanc*, it's called. Quite homely, isn't it—the White Hart!"

"And a most convenient appointment," the Marquis confirmed. "In the Forêt de Gervaix, quiet, secluded—entirely suitable. We are nearly there."

Ranald Neill said nothing, made no comment, only his mouth tightened strangely at the corners and his fine nostrils flared and quivered. For a matter of minutes he remained silent, not reclining now, but upright in his seat. Then, without warning, he jumped to his feet, opened the window, and thrust out his head. "Stop, driver! *Arrêtez!*" he shouted. "At once!" As the coach lumbered to a stop, he opened the door and jumped out. Turning to his astonished companions, he spoke, jerkily, harshly. "Come out, gentlemen! You say that we are nearly there. You may finish the

30

journey on foot, then. You will convey my regrets to Mr. Pomeroy and his supporters. I cannot meet him today . . . at this place. You understand!"

"I do not, b'dad!" O'Hara spluttered. "Have ye gone crazy, Neill? What in the name of Beelzebub's come over ye?"

The Major continued to hold the door open. "You will please descend, gentlemen!" he said quietly, but his voice quivered a little.

The Marquis gazed down at him, bewildered. "But this is astounding, impossible! *Mon Dieu*, but you cannot mean that you do not wish to fight?"

"I will not fight!"

"But you must fight, *mon cher* Ranald. You cannot now withdraw. It is out of the question. *Sacré*, what can we say?"

Neill said nothing.

O'Hara jumped down from the coach, his joviality for once forgotten. "Look ye here, Neill," he growled, "I don't know what the devil's the matter with ye, but ye can't back out of an affair like this—ye know that better than I do. Get back into the coach, man, and enough of this. Ye've been dreaming, to be sure!"

The Major gripped his arm in a hand that trembled. "O'Hara," he said, almost beseechingly, "I must get away from here. I can't go on. I can't—I won't go to that place. I know what it means. I'll be killed—killed, I tell you!" His voice rose shrilly. This was a very different man from the cold, imperturbable, celebrated Major of the Blues, manner changed, voice changed, eyes changed, eyes that now held what looked uncommonly like stark terror. With an obvious effort he took a grip of himself. "You must go on. Tell them I took ill—tell them I had an urgent call, tell them anything you like. Another time, perhaps. . . . But I will not fight. My God, I dare not do it!"

De Nerville wrung his hands. "But this is terrible! This is unbelievable!" he wailed.

31

The Captain looked his erstwhile principal up and down, and wagged his head. "I would not have believed it," he agreed. "Saints of Glory, I would not! Ranald Neill, of all men!" He took hold of the other's coat lapel, a liberty he would not have dared an hour before. "Now, see here, m'lad," he growled, chin out-thrust, "whether ye like it or no, ye'll go through with this. It is absolutely necessary—ye know that. Necessary for us all. Pomeroy knows too much. Have ye forgotten the von Hochstein business? The man must be silenced."

"Then shoot him yourself!" Neill flashed. "I tell you it's no use. I've made up my mind."

O'Hara tried again. "Made up your mind, have ye? Have ye made up your mind for the result of this folly? Ye'll be ruined—we'll all be ruined! Ye'll be ruined socially and financially and every other way besides, b'dad! Ye'll never live it down, ye'll never dare show your face anywhere that ye're known. Ye owe the man a cool two thousand, I'll wager, and the Lord knows who else as well. Man, ye've debts all over the face of Europe! Even if Pomeroy holds his tongue, ye'll be bankrupt and disgraced, and if he speaks and gives evidence, it's finished ye are, entirely!"

The other shook his head. "I will be alive, at any rate. You don't understand, O'Hara. I am of Highland blood—maybe I have the sight, the vision—but I know, I know, I tell you, that if I go to that place and fight, I am a dead man. It is no use fighting with Fate." He turned from them quickly, and climbed into the carriage, while de Nerville and the Captain looked at each other hopelessly. From the open window he spoke again, with a trace of hesitation. "O'Hara, would you . . . could you lend me something, a small advance? I'm short, damnably short . . . a hundred francs would do!"

The Irishman snorted. "A hundred francs! Where the devil d'ye think I'd get a hundred francs? M'lad, any few francs I may be able to raise will have to get me out of

32

the country, *tout de suite*, thanks to ye. A hundred francs, indeed!"

"De Nerville, would you. . . ?"

The Marquis sighed. "Mon ami, I am desolated! But I never carry money with me, not a franc, not a sou. So risky in unsettled times, you will understand. Is it not unfortunate! Perhaps. . . ."

"Back to Saint-Martel!" the Major shouted, and almost on the word the window slammed shut. The driver flicked his whip, the steaming horses stamped, pawed, and swung round, and the ungainly vehicle rattled away whence it had come. And the two men remained alone on the road among the skeleton trees of the Forêt de Gervaix, their breath forming little clouds about their heads. It was a fine morning, but cold, cold.

*   *   *

Excerpt from 'The Times', London
5th September, 1849

DEATH OF HIGHLAND CHIEFTAIN

An inquest yesterday revealed the death, in distressing circumstances, of the Macarthy Neill, twenty-fourth of his line, formerly Major in Her Majesty's Life Guards (the Blues) and sometime attached to the British Embassy in Paris. Previously well known in London and Paris society, and celebrated as a duellist, Major Neill disappeared in a mysterious manner from the public eye during the winter of two years ago, rumour connecting him with the von Hochstein scandal. His name, however, was not mentioned at the inquiry. Since then, it appears, he has been living in straitened circumstances and under an assumed name in the Wapping district and elsewhere.

33

Major Neill, whose identity was established by certain papers found on his person, apparently died by his own hand, a discharged duelling-pistol being discovered lying beside the body. Mrs. Green, his landlady, testified to his frequent attacks of delirium and light-headedness, when he appeared to be under the delusion that he was struggling with some large animal. A verdict of suicide while of unsound mind was returned.

1878

SIR NEILL MACARTHY NEILL had his feet firmly planted on the ground. And he could say—and did say— with complete justification, that he had planted them there by himself and for himself. In nothing had his parentage and upbringing assisted in the stabilising process. His father, a man of singular levity, having already drunk himself into a premature grave, young Neill, while still in his teens, had inherited as heir of entail his deplorable Uncle Ranald's embarrassed estate of Inverfeith and the dubious honour of the Macarthy chieftainship. A legacy well calculated to confound any man, it did not confound Neill Macarthy Neill. Far from it. Two factors contributed to his achievement, the one proceeding from the other. Firstly, it had been his inestimable good fortune to perceive, from a very early age, that money was the essential element in successful living; without it, a man was nothing, could do nothing: with it, he could do and be anything. Secondly, he had the discernment to marry a suitable wife, plain, obedient, and well-dowered. On these sure foundations he built ably; on this firm ground he planted his feet, and stood.

Characteristically, as soon as young Neill apprehended the impossibility of divesting himself of either his encumbered, entailed estate or his family reputation, he endeavoured to turn the tables on destiny, and capitalise his inheritance in the only way left to him. He turned romanticism to a current account and made notoriety pay a dividend. He wore Highland dress on all possible occasions, and cultivated an air of colourful but aristocratic poverty. He, as it were, penetrated

London Society with eagle's feathers as an introduction and a proud melancholy as a passport. His sad smile was a lament for passed glories and forgotten splendours, his lofty pensiveness a memorial of a dying culture and an age-old tradition. He put on the coat of dignity and the cloak of indigence, and prospered. He was one of the early pioneers of the uses of publicity. He also was one of the first to perceive the possibilities of the Queen's autumnal infatuation for the Scottish Highlands. With every penny that he could scrape together he made shift to modernise the old house of Inverfeith, and to advertise the scenic glories and sporting facilities of his leagues of rock and heather. Scotland had been discovered. Scotland was Romantic, romantically poor but romantically barbarous. Neill ordered bales of Macarthy tartan for the Inverfeith gillies to wear as plaids during the months of August and September, and he let it be known that the name of Macarthy would go well with the tartan, during the season at least. He acquired several old sets of bagpipes from an Army contractor, and sent them North with definite instructions. He even went the length of organising a local Highland Games festival amongst his reluctant tenantry and neighbours. He attended to details and did nothing by half. And when the demand for "Scotch" grouse-moors and shootings and fishings followed intrepid Royalty, he reaped the reward of his perspicuity.

With successful matrimony came a widening of scope and opportunity, but no change of direction. Servants were imported from the North, and dressed accordingly. His personal piper was conspicuous, especially at meal-times. A large wolfhound was ever at his heels—Irish, but most effective. He even learned a few words of the Gaelic for use at public functions and the like. The Macarthy Neill, from being a Character, became a Personality.

But a social position, a degree of fame, and financial independence were not his goal, nor, most certainly, did he seek any sort of Gaelic revival. He required wealth, required it rather than desired it, as the ultimate requisite of success. With the directness of purpose that was the man himself, he sought out wealth. Essentially practical, he had little difficulty in deciding where lay his best chances of achieving his end—whisky. *Uisge beatha*, water of life, the national beverage of Scotland, what more suitable medium of effort and profit for a man in his position! To assist in the introduction of the amber dew of the mountains to the great English public, was his privilege, almost his obligation. He also made it his business.

Contacts already made, he had little trouble in accomplishing his purpose. As he had not failed to appreciate, he was a walking advertisement in himself. Messrs. Grant & Ogilvie of Glasgow and London recognised this also, and after a certain amount of mutual adjustment, he was duly elected to the board of that enterprising house. There, in due course, his colleagues were surprised to discover that in the Macarthy Neill they were dealing with a business man, as distinct from a piece of expensive publicity. The day came when, instead of occupying a chair at the foot of the boardroom table, he sat at the right hand of John Grant himself, facing a handsome full-length portrait of Neill, twenty-fifth chief of the Neill Macarthys. That picture was the seal and token of his success, a noble canvas in all the pride of tartan and lace and feathers, from the cunning brush of the great de Lessels. It was an outstanding portrait of an outstanding man, and it was famous too, for reproduced, it adorned and identified every bottle of Grant & Ogilvie's special "Chieftain" whisky.

Thus far, and farther. From the boardroom table to Westminster is but a step, and Buckingham Palace but two paces beyond. Parliament received him as the elected representative of South Hammersley, and the accolade was but a fitting acknowledgement of the nation's appreciation. As has been said, Sir Neill Macarthy Neill had his feet firmly planted.

As always, people looked at him, eyed him frankly or covertly, turned when he was past and stared after him. Some thereupon hastily became interested in shop windows, in their feet or in the scudding grey clouds of January, others smiled at each other sheepishly, some of the baser sort even winking and jerking their heads, one going so far as to raise his elbow suggestively. Few were indifferent. Sir Neill Macarthy Neill saw to that. He strode down Vere Street on his way to the new offices of Messrs. Grant & Ogilvie in Oxford Street, a striking figure of a man, tall and wide-shouldered, in an alder-sprigged Balmoral bonnet and an enormous Inverness cape that flapped open to reveal shepherd-check trousers of vigorous pattern. In his hand he carried, or rather wielded, a roughly-trimmed ash-plant, half as long again as an ordinary walking-stick, and at his heels loped the inevitable wolfhound. Fellow-citizens were entitled to look, indeed they were encouraged to do so. He did not walk all the way from his house in Wilton Square to his business for the sake of exercise, or because he had no carriage. He was a conscientious man, and exceedingly thorough.

No expense had been grudged in the erection of the new offices in Oxford Street—in the portion that mattered, at any rate. Impressive without, the interior was almost awe-inspiring—the public parts that is, of course. No embellishment had been spared, in stone, or wood, or paint. The vast entrance hall was a temple of white marble and dark mahogany crowned by a dome of plaster that left no inch unelaborated, and from which, among many lesser pendants, hung an enormous cut-glass chandelier. The grand staircase was grand indeed, marble again, turkey-carpeted and brass-railed, branching halfway to the first floor and finishing in duplicate. The landing was adorned with numerous busts on black marble pedestals, conspicuous amongst them a handsome effigy of the late John Grant donated by his successor in the chairmanship. Above, more marble, more mahogany, more statuary, more plaster scrollery and flowers and fronds.

Higher still need not be described, this being merely office space and unnecessary of adornment. The whole was a monument to the taste of the management, and an example of what could be achieved by the progressive and enlightened conduct of commerce in the year of grace eighteen hundred and seventy-eight.

Sir Neill, to whom the credit for all this largely went, paced across the hall with measured step and justifiable pride. He crossed over behind the staircase, deposited his bonnet, cape, and stick in a cupboard there, peered briefly into a dark room under the stair where a number of clerks scraped pens industriously, their noses close against their pages, re-crossed to one of the hall's two noble fires, where he rubbed his hands briskly, and the hound Luath crouched and appeared immediately to doze. For a minute or two the Macarthy Neill, back to the fire, surveyed his handiwork complacently, frowned momentarily when an undersized clerk appeared for an instant from under the stair, to scurry back hastily whence he had come, glanced at the cupid-supported clock, and then with habitual dignity ascended the grand staircase toward the business and burden of the day.

In the magnificent boardroom, Sir Neill's fellow-directors awaited him. There were six men grouped about the fire, an impressive phalanx, with something of the substance and dignity of the building itself about them. Their chairman favoured them with one of his melancholy smiles, improbable on such dominant, rather dour, features. "Good morning, gentlemen! I have not kept you waiting, I hope." Unnecessarily, he drew out his massive gunmetal watch from the pocket of his well-worn sealskin waistcoat. "No, it is just on eleven now. We are all here, I see." A short greeting or two, and, very much the master of the situation, he turned to the only youthful member of the company. "Lancelot, you might ring the bell for Stevens, and we'll get on with the business." Lancelot Grant was a plump, pink-faced young man, with a dashing taste in neckwear and hose. Sir Neill eyed him with a certain distaste; one spectacular member of the board was sufficient, but as son of the late chairman, and principal shareholder in the company, he was something of a necessary evil.

They took their seats at the somewhat apologetic entry of Stevens, the secretary, and under the lofty regard of de Lessels' masterpiece, reflected admirably by the subject thereof, the meeting commenced. The secretary's report was read amid studious disregard, which altered to a respectful concentration when the chairman rose to his impressive height. He was fully six feet four inches tall, and broad in proportion, and in his check suit, loosely worn, he was a figure to fill the eye. Like all his race he was a dark man, and his square black head and strong black beard betrayed no hint of grey. He made a point of standing at the commencement of these meetings; it seemed to induce the right atmosphere. "Well, gentlemen," he began, "you have heard the report, and, no doubt, have studied the statements which each of you will have received by post. I think that you will agree with me that we have had a prosperous year, quite a prosperous year, and with the general trade outlook and our own projected expansion, the prospect for next year looks reasonably encouraging."—"Hear, hear!"—"You will have noted the figures for the gross and net profits, and the sum that it is suggested should be set aside to augment the reserve, allowing for a final dividend of twenty-five per cent, making a total of forty per cent for the year. I think, from our previous conversations, that we all agree to these figures?"

A restrained nodding of beards seemed to indicate that these figures could be accepted as reasonable, but one dissentient voice was raised. Lancelot Grant spoke languidly from the foot of the table, addressing his fellow-directors, rather than the chairman. "I say," he drawled, "don't you think that eighty thousand is a devilish large sum for reserves? They stand at over two hundred thousand already! D'you know, I don't think it's quite the thing to—er—defraud the shareholders of their due share of the profits for the sake of piling up these enormous reserves. I mean, fine buildings and all that are well enough, but—well, there y'are." He smiled on them all engagingly. "Personally, I could do with a spot more myself. 'Magpie' dropping out like that cost me a reg'lar pot o' money, believe me!"

His five colleagues all became interested in their finger-nails or their watch-chains. The Macarthy Neill, eyeing them keenly and noting the noncommittal murmur, smiled patiently. "My dear Lancelot," he said, "we all deplore your misfortunes on the racecourse and sympathise in your . . . hardship. Nevertheless we must consider our duty to the business, especially in view of the large new programme we are now launching. I am afraid that we cannot consider a reduction in the figure specified. You agree, gentlemen? You, Lord Sedley, you agree?"

"Eh—me? Yes, oh yes! Ah—of course! Quite right, Sir Neill. Naturally! Ah!" Lord Sedley's imposing bulk sank back again into its chair, while its owner mopped his brow.

Sir Neill spoke swiftly. "That's settled then, I take it, gentlemen?" The low murmur was repeated. Young Mr. Grant seemed inclined to continue the discussion, but his chairman gave him no time. "Mr. Secretary, have you any further matters to bring up before we go on to consider the new whisky?" It was not by mere melancholy smiling that he occupied the position he did.

The secretary coughed nervously. "Well, sir, if you don't

41

mind, I have a petition here from the distillery hands, a combined petition I'm afraid, requesting a—er—slight increment in their wages. They think, sir, that twenty-five shillings is . . ."

"More than sufficient!" the chairman cut him short. "This is a business, not a philanthropic institution, Mr. Secretary. You will instruct them to that effect." This time the murmur was in no way noncommittal. "Anything further?"

Mr. Stevens looked quite distressed. "I am sorry, sir, very sorry indeed, but I have two—er—problems relating to the office staff. It seems that there are complaints about the heating in the upper rooms, sir, and the lighting downstairs." He glanced anxiously round the seven directors, and swallowed. "But as it is not an urgent—an important matter, and you are so busy, I think perhaps we might . . . that is, you might—er . . ."

"As you say, I think we might." Sir Neill agreed, rather grimly. "Unless any of you gentlemen have anything to say on the subject?" He rightly interpreted the silence. "In my opinion the eminent architect who has so ably designed this noble building must be credited with knowing more about the requisite heating and lighting than do a few clerks."— "Hear, hear!"— "Anything else?"

"Only the matter of bottles, sir."

"Ah, yes, the bottles! That will be more suitably brought in later, I think." He leaned forward. "Now, gentlemen, we come to the new venture. Though no doubt you are all perfectly conversant with the facts, perhaps a brief résumé of the position may not be out of place. As you know, we took over some time ago, at an economic price, the very large stocks of matured spirit held by the late Messrs. Maclellan & Sons of Edinburgh. Since then we have been considering the most satisfactory and profitable way of using this excellent liquor, and it has been decided that by judicious blending with our own No. 1 and No. 3 grades, a very superior—I might almost say exceptional—liqueur whisky results. It is intended that we issue this blend at eighteen under proof, as against our 'Chieftain' brand at twenty-five, the price being three shillings per bottle as against two-and-sixpence. While admittedly this is a dear whisky, I think that with suitable advertising, the superfine quality will ensure it a warm reception, and from a better class of customer than we now normally supply. It is even possible that through this we may yet be able to supplant brandy as the favourite of the upper classes."

Amid the general satisfaction aroused by this able exposition, one doubt was expressed. "But how much of this Maclellan's stuff have we?" a venerable, white-haired gentleman demanded. "The supply can't be inexhaustible. What is to happen when we have finished it?"

Sir Neill coughed. "I thought that had all been made quite clear, Mr. Darbyshire. Actually, we have a very large stock, but as time goes on we shall use more and more of our own grades in the mixture, keeping it always at the same strength of eighteen u.p., of course. I am assured that the change will be quite imperceptible."

"Maybe, sir, maybe! But is it a wise policy to allow the quality to deteriorate like that? It strikes me as just a little like cheating the public, sir. Yes, it does, sir!"

"Hear, hear!" said Lancelot Grant, as a matter of principle.

The chairman smiled long-sufferingly, but the glance he swept on—or rather over—young Grant was frigid indeed. Mr. Darbyshire was the veteran of the board and apt to be a trifle cautious and old-fashioned. "My dear sir, there is no question of cheating anybody," he protested. "This issue can be envisaged as something in the nature of an advertising campaign, preparing the ground, blazing the trail, as it were. We wish to educate another strata of the community to an appreciation of our whisky, and we are going to use this blend to do it, that is all. "He paused impressively. "And as to deterioration of quality, my friend, surely you do not suggest that Grant and Ogilvie cannot make as good whisky as Maclellan's?"

"Hear, hear! Hear, hear!"

"Might I ask how much this experiment is going to cost us in extra labour?" another gentleman wanted to know. "Important item, labour!"

"I quite agree, Mr. Campbell. I am glad to say that the additional cost is relatively insignificant. It is on the bottling department, of course, that the bulk of the extra work will fall, and there, fortunately, juvenile labour can be largely used, at suitably low rates. On the blending side, a certain amount of overtime work and a general tightening-up should be all that is necessary, I think. Now, there is this matter of the bottles. You remember, we chose an entirely new and very distinctive bottle for this whisky, and the first delivery of these is now on hand. Spence, the manager, however, doesn't seem to be altogether pleased with them. Just what is it that he objects to, Mr. Secretary? Are they not up to specification, or what?"

"No, sir, it is hardly that, I think. You will recollect, sir, that he was never very—er—enthusiastic over the sample that you approved. Well, sir, having now seen the new delivery and while recognising that it is a very handsome and unusual bottle, he feels that it is not entirely satisfactory. He thinks that it's just a little bit on the light side—flimsy was the word he used, sir—and the shape not very suitable for packing. Also he says that the necks are just on the narrow side for our standard corks, of which we have such large quantities in stock . . ." Mr. Stevens' voice trailed away in his humility, and he was very much aware that certain of the directors were actually looking at him. He felt, rather than saw, their expressions. How he hated board meetings! Desperately he made a suggestion. "Perhaps, sir—gentlemen—you would like to see Mr. Spence himself?"

"I don't think that will be necessary," Sir Neill said crisply. "Spence is a very excellent man, but something lacking in imagination. He has been used to dealing with clumsy massive bottles all his days, and doesn't appear to realise that we are trying to start a new tradition in whisky-marketing. As for the packing difficulty, I myself have evolved a method of getting round that, a very simple device, of which I can draw a diagram if anyone wishes, involving only a honeycomb packing instead of the usual chessboard pattern. But this is the first that I have heard about the corks. Are we to understand, Stevens, that our corks won't fit these bottles?"

"Oh, no, sir, they do fit—I mean, they go in all right, but they are rather tight, I believe, that's all." Abjectly he broke his promise to the manager. "It's a small matter, sir. We can always get smaller corks, if that should be found to be necessary."

"I like a well-corked bottle, myself," a hitherto quiescent gentleman observed. "Keeps the liquor in good condition." He wiped his iron-grey moustaches, as though already savouring a tightly-corked, well-conditioned whisky. "By the way, Neill, what about the name for the stuff, that you've got up your sleeve?"

The Macarthy Neill sat back in his chair, and considered the striking picture on the opposite wall. His hands were busy with a paper-knife in the shape of a *sgian dhu* ornamented with cairngorms. He spoke slowly and distinctly. "Gentlemen, I propose that we call this whisky 'White Stag'!" For a moment he continued to stare at the picture, then he swung on his fellows, a certain tenseness, almost fierceness, in his attitude. "Well?" he demanded. Then, noting their unchanged expressions, he laughed curiously. "Does it not appeal to you?"

"Quite good!" said the iron-grey gentleman.

"Not a bad name, ah!" gasped Lord Sedley.

"We could do worse," Mr. Campbell considered.

45

"Rather meaningless, isn't it?" young Mr. Grant objected. "Wouldn't 'Dew of the Glen' or something of that sort sound better?"

Sir Neill rose to his feet; his companions knew what that signified. "It is not entirely meaningless," he said evenly. "Actually, gentlemen, I am rather anxious that we should use the name I suggested. It is more than just a whim. For a long time my family has been oppressed by a foolish superstition, a kind of bogy, common enough in the Highlands of Scotland. It is time that bogy was laid, and that superstition shown to be what it is, a mere shadow to frighten children. I intend to make our White Stag a symbol of progress and prosperity and good cheer, instead of a bugbear. I am afraid that perhaps I have anticipated your approval in this matter, gentlemen, and have commissioned Mr. de Lessels—personally, of course—to paint me a representation of this animal, which will hang in my dining-room. It is unfortunate that Sir Edwin Landseer is dead, as he would undoubtedly have been the man to do it, but I am sure that de Lessels will do a thoroughly satisfactory and spirited piece of work. This will, of course, be available for reproduction on our labels, should you agree to my choice of name. You do, do you? Thank you! That is very gratifying, gentlemen. 'White Stag' it is, then! It but remains for me to invite you all, with your ladies, to a little unveiling ceremony at my house in about one month's time, when we shall admire the masterpiece and celebrate the launching of our new venture at the same time. I will let you have details later. Not at all, not at all, my friends, the pleasure is entirely mine." He sat down, smiling. "Well, gentlemen, is there anything further before we close the meeting?"

Lord Sedley heaved himself forward. "Fees!" he puffed. "Matter of fees, ah! Very necessary matter!"

"Of course!" Sir Neill nodded. "How foolish of me to forget! An increase of twenty-five per cent in the directors' fees, owing to increased responsibility, will be passed at the general meeting in February. You have a note to that effect, Stevens? Then, gentlemen, I think that will be all. Thank you!"

The party at Wilton Square was a subject for discussion for long afterwards. Here, at any rate, was no suggestion of poverty. It was quite an ambitious affair, nearly thirty guests receiving invitations. Nor was one of the male guests unnecessary; that is, each one of them had, or was hoped to have, some part to play in his host's scheme of things. Sir Neill was careful in his choice of friends. In addition to the six directors and their accompanying ladies, there were four fellow-members of the House, including a junior Minister, one of Her Majesty's equerries, two financial nabobs, one a deputy-governor of the Bank of England, and, of course, Mr. de Lessels.

The unveiling ceremony was performed as soon as all the guests were assembled and in their places at the great table in the brightly-lit dining-room. First the piper did his necessary part, amid giggles from the ladies and assumed passivity from the men, then the host, resplendent in black velvet, white lace, and the rich red and green Macarthy dress tartan, delivered from the head of the table a brief and admirable speech outlining the object and significance of the occasion, at the same time paying graceful tribute to the artist.

"This gathering here tonight gives me great pleasure," he concluded. "In opening, as it were, a bright new chapter, we close a dark old one at the same time." He gestured first to the be-ribboned whisky-bottle enthroned in the centre of the table, and then towards the still-shrouded work of art. "May we not hope that, as today, the firm of Grant and Ogilvie enters on a new phase of progress, so may my distressed people, led most graciously by our beloved sovereign, be commencing a happier and more noble period of their long history." He was most affecting. "I now call upon my son, Edward Macarthy Neill, to unveil this symbolic picture."

Amidst much clapping, a small boy appeared from behind a group of tartan-clad servants. Slight, dark-haired and dark-eyed, and wearing an exact replica of his father's splendid costume, he stumbled, acutely miserable, past the ranks of applauding adults, towards his appointed place beneath the draped gilt frame. There he stood, eyes downcast, his hand gripping the cord he was to pull, while the piper produced another resounding selection from his repertoire, mercifully short. Then, at a sign from Sir Neill, he called out, *"Ard mo cheann, airde mo dhream!"* The high-pitched voice almost screamed into the quivering silence that succeeded the piping. "High my head, higher my race!" he translated, and tugged at the cord. The sound of tearing fabric, and a titter of amusement, resulted. Fear in his dark eyes, Edward looked guiltily at his father, but Sir Neill only smiled. "Try again, my son," he said. For a moment the boy continued to stare strangely, then he turned. *"Ard mo cheann, airde mo dhream!"* he mumbled, and pulled. This time the cloth at his feet and the general applause assured him that all was well. With all eyes turned up to the picture, the boy slipped out of the room almost unnoticed, but his own gaze never left his father's face, even when he passed his mother at the foot of the table. Edward's relations with his father appeared to be unusual.

Mr. de Lessels had made a stirring picture indeed, out of his semi-mythical subject. While admittedly the anatomy and posture of the beast was more than a little reminiscent of Landseer's "Monarch of the Glen", that was no doubt inevitable, stags being what they are. It was no slavish imitation, however; the background was as majestic as sheer cliffs and rolling mist-wraiths could make it, and the animal itself was of a pure and snowy white, striking in the extreme, while the antlers could only be termed luxuriant. Mr. de Lessels was obviously a man of initiative.

The acclamation was loud and prolonged. The picture was all—and more—than could have been expected; undoubtedly it would look highly effective on a whisky-bottle.

The host turned to the artist with a courtly bow. "Need I elaborate?" he asked. "The applause speaks for itself!"

De Lessels, an impressive small man most impressively attired, rose to his feet. "It was nothing—a mere *tchik, tchik!*" He made one or two lightning and obviously inspired strokes and passes with an imaginary brush, head back and to one side, eyebrows active. "Thus—and thus!" he demonstrated. "A small thing—a mere gesture in paint, ladies and gentlemen, though not perhaps unworthy of this noble apartment." He beamed on them all. "I thank you all for this appreciation. Appreciation—ah, appreciation is the coin in which we artists must be paid." The Macarthy smiled, a trifle grimly. "Without it we are nothing, we die; with it—*tchik, tchik!*" his expressive hand delineated the stag, the hills, and the mist, in one comprehensive, intricate gesture, indicating what could be done when appreciation was assured. His audience did not fail to recognise, that despite his modesty, "The White Stag" was to be considered one of de Lessels' most successful canvases. He went on, "I thank my friend the chief of the House of Neill"—he bowed to his host, who frowned again before he smiled. How often must he tell these fools that it was the Macarthys that he was chief of, that the final Neill was but a title?—"and I thank his engaging small son and heir!" He had nearly sat down when he recollected, "and, of course, our charming hostess, Lady Neill."

Lady Macarthy Neill, a disappointing lady, quietly dressed and in evident discomfort with her rather generous tartan plaid, nodded her head. "Thank you!" she said. "Shall we start dinner?" She was an excellent foil for her husband.

*   *   *

49

The guests leaned back in a state of repletion and satisfaction, as Sir Neill rose once again. The dinner had been worthy of the occasion, and the piper had been banished to the basement whence the background that he continued to provide acquired a compassionate remoteness. "Before the ladies leave us," he began, "it is my pleasant duty to ask you to drink to the success of our new product, 'White Stag' whisky. I am sure that when you have tasted it you will agree with me—the gentlemen, at any rate—that for quality, body and flavour, it is superior to anything at present on the market. Seumas—the bottle!"

A servitor stepped forward and removed the decorated bottle from its pedestal, handing it to his master, who unwound the tartan ribbon, revealing the "White Stag" label. Three-sided and slightly barrel-shaped, it was indeed a notable and handsome departure from the ordinary run of liquor containers. Sir Neill picked up a corkscrew, gestured towards the picture, and with quick decisive twistings of the wrist, prepared to draw the cork. He pulled. He pulled again. He changed his position, and pulled once more, but without effect. A little red about the cheekbones and brow, he straightened up. Seumas held out a tentative hand. "Let me be trying, sir," he suggested.

"Not at all!" Sir Neill snorted. The guests watched, interested. He stood back from the table, stooped, placed the bottle between his thighs, gave the corkscrew another turn, drew his breath, and pulled. The cork remained immovable. With a muttered curse he bent, put all his great strength into a supreme effort, and wrenched. There was a crack, a splintering, and the crash and tinkle of broken glass, and Sir Neill staggered back, clutching the bottleneck in a hand that spouted blood over his lace and finery. As the guests watched, horrified, they saw the strong dour face soften, the full lips draw back to reveal teeth tight-clenched, and a trickle of saliva run down the black beard, the whole proud figure crumple and slacken, as the twenty-fifth Macarthy Neill sank back into his chair. A severed artery and an inhibition, a flimsy bottle and an oversized cork, or the White Stag of Glen Raineach, Neill Macarthy Neill was dead within a week.

THE HARVEST

I

THE last lift of those lifting purple moors behind him, and Jonathan Maitland paused, to face the rolling immensity of An Moine Liath, and his breathing, if deep, had no catch or hurry to it. Two miles or maybe three backward and downward over the shelving heather, and the white of the Lodge gleaming out of its sheltering belt of pines marked his starting place; and his climbing had been steady, unhurried and uninterrupted. A day or two more of this, with maybe a go at the grouse over dogs, and he would face the forest with devil a care!

Jonathan sat himself down upon a flat granite outcrop and consulted his map. Cross An Moine Liath he must, and since the map displayed never a track, he must follow such paths as his own eye showed him . . . and good luck to him! His objective was the three-miles-distant summit of Beinn Buidhe, undisputed lord in a land of giants, today thrusting its pale head in somnolent majesty into the arch of the sky. There, from a buttress on its massive south flank, they told him, he could survey practically the length and breadth of his temporary domain . . . and the mist letting him.

Buidhe was no deer-forest in the accepted sense of the word. Certainly it was a forest, or what passes as a forest north of Tay, and equally certainly there were deer on it, but it was no preserve rigorously be-keepered and be-fenced, equipped with sanctuaries and artificial feeding-grounds and so on. It was, in fact, nothing more nor less than a representative stretch of Highland scenery comprising some twenty thousand acres of floating moor and bog, of high tops and sheltered corries, of green glens and scattered woodland, where a reasonable man might shoot a sufficiency of grouse and hares, as well as an odd ptarmigan when he felt energetic, and a clever man might kill a nice stag, or maybe two . . . with the luck with him.

Just as such had Jonathan Maitland leased it, since neither his inclination nor his purse would run to a first-class forest, where the sport was apt to be a business, and the large and expert staff must be paid as well as lived-up to. Rather would he find and stalk and grass his own stag, even gralloch him thereafter, the fates being kind to him, and if he failed in any or each of these tasks—well, hadn't he doubled his sport and nary a one to apologise to afterwards?

It was pleasant sitting on that outcrop, warm beneath him, and watching the far-flung panorama of the hills pale in the faint haze of midday, watching . . . and watching. No life moved, no breath of wind stirred the heather, no sound broke the stillness, not even a cloud drifted in the vague infinity of the sky. A man might sit there in that gentle quiet, sit and watch and let the brooding impersonal spirit of the hills flow over him and enter into him; sit and watch and think not at all, and in time perhaps, the calm inscrutable peace of the high places might enfold him and possess him, and he would be a god and no man. . . .

Damnation! Jonathan Maitland twisted sideways off his outcrop and lifted to his feet in one complex movement. That sort of thinking was not good for a man. Neurosis, was it, or merely a touch of the sun? Either, or both, it had got to be stopped, with him aiming to reach Beinn Buidhe!

On his two feet Jonathan Maitland displayed exactly five feet and ten inches of lean manhood, his carriage exhibiting a strange union of tensity and looseness, clad in comfortable, faded tweeds that at, say, a quarter of a mile, could be guaranteed to fade completely into any moorland background . . . if the wearer was reasonably still. He had a peculiar face on him, the young man, by no stretch of the imagination to be termed handsome; bright, deep-set eyes, grey beneath a dark bar of eyebrow, a high, white forehead, a great beak of a nose, and a tight-shut mouth over a square jut of chin. Forcible, yes; stubborn, yes; but handsome—no! Anyway, a strong face—at first glance perhaps, a hard face.

With just half a shrug he grinned to himself, and the hardness went out of his hatchet-face like snow off a dyke. "You haven't got me yet!" he jeered, and his grey eyes challenged the serried ranks of the enclosing hills, to lift and check and narrow as they focused into the glare of the midday sun.

And the whisper of a sigh quivered over the heather and was gone; a vague tremor of wind perhaps, on a windless day, as the young man picked up his stock and faced the watershed.

An Moine Liath—the Grey Moss—a vast amphitheatre of the mountains, heaved before him cordial under the sun, like a rolling sea, its brown waves rising and falling in unvaried succession, to break themselves upon the barren flanks of the enclosing braes . . . and never a hint of the tortuous ravines, the quaking bogs and the awesome peat-pools that scored and pitted its deceptive expanse.

The man was perhaps halfway across that measureless desolation when he saw the deer. They were feeding uncertainly along the sun-soaked face of a rounded knoll that lifted like an island out of that tumbled sea. It was an unlikely place for them on this day of heat when the high-tops should have beckoned them with their coolth, and the young man squatted himself into the knee-high heather and got to work with his deer-stalker's glass.

There would be over a dozen of them, and all hinds, barring the one old "switch", a nasty brute Jonathan took mental note, and ripe for the larder. The watcher knew his deer, and as he watched, his interest quickened. These deer were acting strangely. Instead of grazing peaceably or chewing the contented cud in all the warmth of the mid-day sun, they were moving and nibbling tentatively and moving again, not aimlessly, casually, as deer will, their hunger satisfied, but steadily and of a set purpose, and that over unlikely country. An aged hind, all nose and ears, led the way, but unwillingly, and strung-out behind, the others drifted after her, the old switch bringing up the rear, again unwillingly. To the man with the glass, the unwillingness was obvious in every line of them.

For all of ten minutes he watched, while the beasts moved stiffly, doubtfully, yet ever in the same direction, half-towards him. They left their knoll reluctantly and finnicked down a spine of basalt and heather that reached out into the emerald unpleasantness of a stretch of bog. At the very lip of the bog they hesitated, and made to turn along the edge. But no, they wheeled again, to waver just for a moment, till, led by the old hind, they took that quaking morass in Indian-file, fastidiously dainty.

Almost forgetting to breathe, the man watched fascinated, and as he watched, the conviction grew upon him. Those deer were being moved; not driven as sheep or cattle are driven, but subtly, insidiously, disturbed but not dismayed, irritated but not affrighted, always agitated but never alarmed . . . and them asking nothing more than to bask in the smile of the sun. The man, no fool at this sort of thing himself, appreciated what he was watching. Whoever or whatever was moving those deer knew his job down to the very last degree; one gliff of the wind here, just a suggestion of the unusual there, perhaps a mere hint of a doubtful sound now and again, working on those suspicious beasts as a sculptor works on his clay . . . and one false move, one degree over-close into the wind, and those deer would be off like the wind itself.

Jonathan Maitland lifted his glass from the herd to rake the ground three hundred, four hundred yards behind. With

58

the wind—and little enough of it—in the airt it was, blowing towards his half-right, and the beasts moving half-across the wind, the "mover" must be working somewhere within an arc over to his half-left. Back and forward, up and down, he raked with his glass that arc of peat-hags and heather-clumps; further back he lifted, closer in he drew, and never a trace of movement, not so much as a shudder among the heather. He shut his telescope carefully. The deer were now within half a mile, and, continuing their present line of advance, they must presently get his own wind . . . which might be a pity.

A hasty but comprehensive survey of the terrain and his mind was made up. To reach the position that he wanted, he would require to fetch two-thirds of a circle to his right— the shorter curve to the left would give those deer his wind in no time.

It was a long stalk though a quick one, and the best of practice with the season opening in earnest in a day or so. In the main, there was plenty of cover for a man who knew how to utilise it, though one stretch of dwarf-heather, flat as a billiard-table, had to be crossed in full view of the oncoming herd. However, your deer's eyes are not a patch on his nose, moreover the beasts were to a certain extent preoccupied by the mysterious influence to the rear, and Jonathan was soon breathing freely again. A sunken burn-channel proved a useful friend, more especially when it provided a tributary curving away in the direction he wanted to go; and even if the tributary grew shallower as it progressed necessitating a certain amount of belly-scraping in its peat-stained waters, the young man was not resentful . . . he was no churl, and wasn't it all part of the game?

He had chosen his landmarks with care, and the reaching of a certain jagged outcrop advised him that he was level with the rounded knoll whereon he had first spied the deer. Well behind them now, he was right out of their wind. A few minutes more, and he was round the back of the knoll and climbing up, to worm himself with infinite caution on to the summit.

Long he lay behind a convenient clump of heather, the tang of it strong in his nostrils, watching, not the deer still moving slowly, but rather the land between them and himself. It was some time before he was rewarded by just a hint of movement amongst a welter of peat-hags, maybe three-hundred yards off. He had his glass on the spot like a flash, but look as he would he could make nothing out of it. Apart from the drifting deer, An Moine Liath might be as empty as the abyss of the sky.

Jonathan Maitland scratched his head. It was queer, devilish queer! That those deer were being moved he was morally certain, but the why and the wherefore of that moving he couldn't for the life of him understand. One thing he did know, that whoever was doing it was a mighty fine stalker—he might say the hell of a fine stalker—and he took off his hat to him. For all that, it was poaching, and ought to be looked into. He was the tenant wasn't he? Well then!

Cautiously he slipped back down the side of that knoll, and worked round the flank of it to face the bright green threat of the bog. That was an unpleasant crossing, and him bent double, the reeds tickling his chin, but it was expedient and expeditious . . . moreover he was wet already. Thereafter the peat-hags received him into their black melancholy, and warily he twisted through their sodden maze, and always his eyes were busy. Anywhere, anytime now, should see the end of his search. And what would he do then? Heaven alone knew! Better just wait and see—no good making too much fuss. All the same, this sort of thing wasn't to be encouraged, or the stalking would be all gone to glory. Must assert himself for the good of the sport, and all that! He'd just—Suffering Saints!

It was a pair of legs that he saw, long, shapely and unclad

60

legs, legs such as never grew on any man born of woman, and occupying a tiny hollow among the hummocks. They commenced their delectable course out of a pair of small but serviceable brogues, and terminated, in course of time, in what, at second glance, Jonathan Maitland realised must be a kilt. These charming peat-stained limbs, not forgetting the suggestion of kilt, had the hollow all to themselves, the presumably attached torso being visible to the eye of faith alone, swallowed-up in the heather at the top of the little bank.

Silent as the grave the young man looked . . . and looking, scratched his black head. A woman, by all that was wonderful! This was the devil and all . . . what in the name of glory was he to do now? A remark about the weather or the state of the crops would be scarcely apt; maybe an observation on the fairness of the landscape would meet the case? Maybe the best plan would be for him to go even as he had come . . . why did he have to come poking his long beak of a nose in, anyway? Why couldn't he have minded his own business? But then, it was his own business! Wasn't he the tenant of the place, and wasn't this woman trespassing —which was a small matter enough—and disturbing the deer—which wasn't—and potentially poaching? All the same, he was no woman-fighter, and an unseemly squabble with a lady over his rights and her wrongs was not to be considered. Ye gods, anything but that! Yes, he'd stand not upon the order of his going but go.

A last glance at those legs, quite involuntary, and he prepared to retire . . . quietly. And retire he did, but not quietly. Back he wriggled silently enough, but it was unfortunate that his stick failed to wriggle with him. A small bit of a jerk and it came, but in the coming it had to strike what was in all probability the one and only piece of stone in that sodden bed of peat, and stone and stick-ferrule tinkled musically.

A gasp, a flash of white quickly overwhelmed by hunting-tartan, the convulsive twisting of a lissome body,

61

and the distant patter of many sharp hooves, all registered simultaneously on the young man's horrified consciousness.

"Oh!" A gasp, scarcely lady-like, and again "Oh!"

Jonathan gulped. Snakes! He was for it now. What was it that he was going to say? The weather—no, the landscape! that was the cue. "A wonderful view one gets from here, don't you think?" he blurted. The words were no sooner out than he was cursing himself for a blundering fool. View was the last word that he should have used here and now!

The girl all but choked. "Oh, you beast!" she whispered, the apprehension of that display of leg flaming in her face. "You beast!"

Jonathan plunged desperately "Oh, I didn't mean . . . you must realise that I didn't . . . you misunderstand me entirely." He paused. This would never do . . . only making matters worse. A change of subject perhaps. "We've alarmed your deer, I'm afraid. A mighty fine piece of work you put in there, positive work of art . . . though reprehensible all the same. Trespassing and all that, you know." Jonathan's attempt at playful reproof was hardly a notable success. Queer what an abject fool he always made of himself, with a woman to face! Of course he was handicapped with the face he had to take about with him . . . enough to frighten an Amazon, and didn't he know it! Trespass was a foolish word to use, and the girl seized on it quick as greased lightning. "Trespassing, is it?" she flashed on him. "Me trespassing, and the Neills holding this country since before history?"

"Maybe trespassing wasn't just the most suitable word," he allowed hastily, "but nevertheless . . ."

"But nothing," she snapped. "I am Barbara Macarthy Neill!"

"Well!" said Jonathan Maitland inadequately.

So this was Edward Neill's daughter—and a chip off the old block too. An evil-tempered race, apparently, for a harder man to get along with than Captain Edward Neill would take some finding. She had something of her father's appearance about her too, now that he came to look at her, the same raven hair . . . black as his own . . . and eyes that were grey or green or a mixture of both, set in a face of vital pallor. Yes, the strong nose, the high forehead, and the sweep of the chin were the same, but the mouth now—the mouth was different, which was just as well for her looks. The Macarthy Neill's small thin-lipped scimitar of a mouth was not the mouth for any woman. This mouth was larger, fuller, less fractious, a woman's mouth . . . but an angry woman's mouth! Oh, yes, she had her looks but for himself, he didn't greatly admire your dark, sulky beauty. He preferred something a bit more human and kindly. For the rest, she was well-made, tall and slim and supple, and her plain close-fitting jumper and skirt were entirely suitable. Definitely, he decided, she looked what she was, daughter of a hundred chiefs . . . and most of them no better than they ought to have been, by all accounts!

Of a sudden Jonathan realised that he was still grovelling on his belly, a position hardly advantageous to himself in what, seemingly, was likely to develop into a verbal duel. He scrambled to his feet and bowed stiffly. Astonishing how much more of a man he felt on his two feet. He'd let her see that he wasn't to be "but nothing-ed" to, like a bit of a school boy. "Madam," he said, "I am Jonathan Maitland, and I have leased Buidhe Forest for the season. Would you be so good as to tell me why you were moving those deer?"

That was plain enough and to the point, but he was scarcely prepared for the spasm of fury which clouded that peculiarly beautiful face. "The new shooting-tenant, is it?" she cried. "And do you think that by signing a paltry cheque you can buy . . . this?" and her arm swept in an expressive curve to include all that land and all that was on it.

The scorn and contempt in that voice lit the spark of his anger. "The law thinks so," he gave back, frowning.

"The law!" Barbara Macarthy Neill dismissed the law with another sweep of the hand.

"Captain Neill leased me this land." The young man spoke quietly. "I did not anticipate having to settle with his daughter also."

Haughtily she considered him. "Even The Macarthy Neill may not barter away the Macarthy's land to the first comer."

Jonathan noted the way she said that, and wondered. There was a world of bitterness behind her enunciation of The Macarthy Neill, bitterness and more than bitterness. He tried to speak reasonably. "Miss Neill, your attitude can serve no useful end. If you challenge my right to be here, you make your father a robber."

"I don't challenge your right to be here—I don't challenge anyone's right to be here! There are no fences on Buidhe, are there? What I deny is your—any man's—right of sole possession. These hills are too big, too fine, to be made one man's playground!"

"Jove! A socialist!"

"No, I am no socialist," she said levelly. "And . . . I hate deer-stalkers!" That last was not level at all.

Jonathan swallowed his astonishment and near choked on it. "You . . . ?" he gasped. "And after your late performance?"

Impatient she rounded on him. "I didn't say stalking, I said stalkers . . . killers!"

He winced at the hard word. By heaven! If it was naked steel that she wanted, she should have it. His voice then, was as steely as her own when he answered. "Miss Neill, I don't feel myself obliged to defend the sport of deer-stalking, nor to account for my actions to you or any woman. . . . Or man either, and though I can't and won't ask you to keep off the ground, I must demand that you refrain from interfering with my sport on the hill."

"Demand?" queried Barbara Neill.

"Demand," agreed Jonathan Maitland, and their voices were as crossed rapiers.

For perhaps a minute there was silence between them while dark man glowered at dark woman, and the bar of his eyebrows answered the arch of hers.

At length she spoke, and her tone had changed strangely. Quietly, almost gently, she murmured, "You are a bold man, Mr. Maitland. I wonder if you are a wise one?"

"Maybe not, Madam, but I know my own mind."

She let that pass and swung on a new tack. "The deer have never done you any harm," she said, and her voice held the subtle sweetness of the south wind over bog-myrtle. "Why must you kill them?"

But Jonathan was not to be drawn into the morass of an argument on principles. "Shall we say because I like killing them?" he short-circuited her brutally. "Why were you moving those deer today?"

She was not defiant at all. "Shall we say because I like moving them? They are beautiful beasts to watch, don't you think?" The barbed gentleness of her!

The man was not impressed. He shrugged. "They may be, but I came here to shoot stags, and shoot them I will . . . if I can!" he said.

"If you can," she repeated and once again her anger was naked and undisguised. "If you can, Mr. Maitland . . . but I will make it my task to see that you don't!"

"You wouldn't dare!"

"You will see!" Barbara Macarthy Neill said simply, and with the word she turned and left him standing, and An Moine Liath swallowed her up.

And Jonathan Maitland, going his own way, frowned on the fair face of the land.

II

THE tired sun had sunk behind the western hills and the wan solitude of the gloaming lay on the earth as Jonathan Maitland reached the head of Gleann na Mallachd. He had climbed Beinn Buidhe and done his surveying, no mist hindering, and what he had seen had been worth seeing. There was good deer ground in plenty and one or two fair corries set at varying levels, suitable for a variety of weather. But there was no enthusiasm in him. Yon slip of a girl had spoiled his day for him, confound her for a besom!

Gleann na Mallachd was born of twin corries out of the great side of Carn Garbh, and ran its pleasant course for something over two miles between ever-widening walls, to open on to the broad strath of the Feith River. Always a quiet place, sheltered alike from all the boisterous winds that might play on An Moine above, or sweep down the wide strath below, it was never quieter than in the hush of a still evening . . . such an evening as this present. To Jonathan Maitland, as he slanted down through the silver and shadows of the birch-woods, it seemed to hold a peace scarcely of this earth.

The murmurous burn, but lately sprung from the green heart of Coire nan Daimh Ban, welcomed him with its subdued chuckle, and he followed its reed-lined bank companionably. So cheering was the chatter of the leaping waters that presently an accompanying whistle was forced out of tight-shut lips, despite themselves. His was a good whistle, a tuneful honest-to-goodness whistle, no thin mournful piping such as has to serve so many, and thus in harmony they moved together through the gathering shadows. And the birches of the braesides stooped to listen, and the gossiping reeds nodded in tune though no wind stirred them, and even the bog-myrtle contributed its sweet incense to the praise of the evening.

When it was that the whistling ceased, Jonathan was not aware; he did not of intention stop whistling. When the grey mood came upon him he was not aware either, nor of what caused it. Perhaps it was the closing shadows that started it, though of all the long day Jonathan loved the creeping dusk. Perhaps it was the chill of advancing night, though the young man's vigorous blood felt it not. Perhaps it was the lonesome cry of a whaup from the moor above that started it, or of a white owl from the darkening woods, or of a sleepy oyster-catcher from the reeds? Perhaps, perhaps. . . . More likely it was an empty stomach that had had nothing more solid in it since breakfast than sandwiches and chocolate!

Be that as it may, a grey mood was upon him, and growing. The glen-sides seemed to be closing in on him, their bald brows frowning in the nebulous light; the drooping birches appeared to be weeping now, not listening; the whispering reeds were sighing, gossiping no more. Only the brown burn sang on unchanged, and its very changelessness spoke of indifference, insincerity.

Not that there was anything gloomy about the place, physically gloomy. It was none of your dismal glens, scree-lined and bare, bedded in dark bog and crested in sweating cliffs. Many such, this man had known. But this place was quite the reverse; a bonnier pleasanter glen he could not remember. And far from narrowing-in on him, it was widening with his every step.

Silent he strode on down the silent valley, and imperceptibly but as steadily, the sense of sadness, of melancholy, grew upon him, and became an oppression, a consciousness.

Frowning, he brought himself to heel. This was not good enough; he was becoming moody, an old maid. This morning hadn't he been mooning about the peace that passeth understanding, and here and now he was wallowing in some sort of melancholia. Presently he would be seeing things! It might be that it was his stomach? He had heard things about stomachs.

Once again his tuneful whistling rose up through the still of the evening, a cheerful air—The Road to the Isles—an air with the lilt of the pipes in it, and the twisting deer-path along the burn-side echoed his quickened step. Gallant the tune and gallant the cock of his head over squared shoulders, and gallant the speed he made down the glen. How was it then that bye-and-bye he discovered that his pace had slackened, that his shoulders had sunk, that his chin was on his chest, and that he was whistling Seumas Og Macallum's Lament? Queer. . . .

Lengthening his stride he cursed himself for a fool, a very dam' fool, and felt no better for it. And even as he cursed, a sigh, a breath, a shudder out of nowhere ran down the glen, to send an answering quiver down his spine.

"Go you to hell!" he said, fiercely, and his face was set. He was not such a hard man as he looked, you will see.

He was nearing the mouth of the glen and walking fast when the desolate hunched figure on the broken-down moss-grown wall stopped him in midstride. He had never a moment's doubt as to the identity of the sitter, and strangely, he had no surprise. At that time and in the mood that was on him, it seemed perfectly natural and to be expected that she should be sitting there in the half-light in the jaws of the glen, and in just that attitude, despondent, despairing almost.

Though he had come upon her suddenly round a bend of the path she made no start nor movement, she gave no sign that she had seen him; but she spoke, and her voice was impersonal, remote, and in the pallid light of that place she seemed infinitely lonely. "You hurry, Mr. Maitland?" was all she said.

The man, still as herself, nodded and said nothing.

She went on, quietly, levelly: "Why do you hurry?"

Simply, he answered her: "To get out of this glen, Miss Neill." An honest answer.

She looked at him sharply at that. "You do not like this glen then?" she questioned, and there was an odd eagerness in her voice.

Jonathan shrugged his shoulders ever so slightly. "There is a sadness about it," he said. That was all.

She was interested, manifestly. "It is strange that you should say so," she murmured. "I wouldn't have thought it . . . not of you. . . ." She seemed to be speaking to herself rather than to him. "You, of all men!"

"And what makes you think that?"

Her glance left him for the birch-clad slopes, dark and mysterious in the failing light. "It is a beautiful glen, don't you think . . . despite the name it has?" was all the reply she gave him. "Goodnight, Mr. Maitland!"

Jonathan accepted his dismissal, so abrupt, so final, but he felt no resentment; only an obscure pity, a vague regret for something or somebody. He nodded silently and passed on, leaving the girl to the glen and the glen to the girl. A queerly beautiful glen . . . a queerly beautiful girl, and both lonely, waiting it might be, waiting for something . . . something that he did not know, nor ever could supply. A sad girl and a sad glen, beautiful both of them, but he loved neither the one nor the other.

And presently he was out of Gleann na Mallachd, out in the wide strath of the Feith River, his feet on the rutted road to the Lodge—and dinner—and the skirl of his whistling rose up clear and tuneful toward the wakening stars.

III

PETER CHISHOLM'S arrival at Buidhe was opportune. Another day or two of his contemplative solitude, and the hills and all the spirits of the hills might have had their strange way with Jonathan Maitland. For despite his rat-trap of a face Jonathan was an imaginative man, and it is not a good thing for an imaginative man to be alone in hills like those for over-long. And alone he had been at Buidhe, since the half-deaf housekeeper and the slim fawn of a girl from the croft down-bye scarcely constituted company.

Buidhe was a small lodge with not over-much in the way of comfort about it. It had the resentful air of a house long unoccupied and suddenly disturbed, which was natural enough, this section of the Inverfeith estate never having been let previously, the mansion-house being but three heather miles away.

Peter Chisholm was a cheerful individual, and the most unlikely lawyer you ever saw. He was large and sprawling and untidy, in person as in attire, with a correspondingly large and good-humoured face, the mouth of which, at its norm of smiling geniality, threatened to engulf an otherwise rather featureless expanse. Incidentally, he was something of a celebrity as an amateur boxer—and he was not quite such a fool as he looked.

He was speaking now, and his rolling voice had something of the thunder of clamorous waters in a deep gorge, hollow and remote. One felt that if it were possible to reach the deep-seated source of that voice, the din would be overwhelming.

"Man, Jonathan," he rumbled, "where women are concerned, you're nothing better than a ruddy fool! The creature was bluffing you, and you played into her hands."

Jonathan Maitland shook his black head and scratched his blue crag of a chin in one and the same motion.

"The girl was not bluffing," he asserted, and his voice sounded strangely after the boom of the other. "She meant what she said. She has some queer wild spirit in her that will let her stop at nothing . . . and she hates deer-stalkers!"

Peter Chisholm eyed his friend significantly. "And you said she was bonny?"

"I did not!" That was definite. "Bonny is the last word for her. Beautiful she might be, as the green cloak of a bog is beautiful; as the sullen amber pools of yonder river are beautiful, and not good for a man, neither the one nor the other."

"Just so!" said the other, smiling his huge smile. "Poetry, too!"

Jonathan went on. "I've been making one or two judicious inquiries about the girl, off-hand questions here and there, to Betsy Ellen ben the house; to Duncan Henderson her dad down at the croft; and Alec Macvicar the one keeper-stalker-gillie and general dictator of the place. It's a queer story. . . ."

"But they're queer people, the Neills. I've met the Captain!"

"Aye! Well, this girl's his daughter, there's no doubt about that, but she's hardly proud of the fact; proud as Lucifer about the House of Neill—or rather Macarthy, I suppose I should say—and the clan and all that, but not of her father. Scarcely to be wondered at, as you say. But she loves her dad so little as to refuse to live with him. Accordingly she has lived at Buidhe Bheag with a sort of superior crofter and his family for the last four or five years. Never goes near Inverfeith House when her father's there, and won't spend a night under his roof. This man Macarthy, that she stays with, is apparently no tenant of the Captain's, but proprietor of his own farm. She seems to have a passion for the deer, amounting almost to a derangement, and roams the hills in all weathers like a wild thing. In fact, it's my opinion that the good folk hereabouts think that she's just a little bit mad—though, mind you, they didn't say so."

"They might be right, too, from all I've heard about the Neill family." Peter Chisholm filled his pipe leisurely. "So we are to have our stalking spoiled for us, are we?" he questioned the world at large, and amiably.

"By heaven, we are not!" And that was not amiable at all.

The two men sat on canvas chairs on the rough lawn before the house, and looked down over the haugh-lands of the Feith River, and the smoke of their pipes ascended in gentle spirals into the still evening air, rivalling the busy columns of the midges. Across the wide valley the brown rolling hills rose and rose, up out of the crouching shadows into the pale translucent yellow of the evening sky, and in that languid light their immobility was stark and terrible.

To right and left the river wound its way through its ample strath, and here and there along its twisted links the burnished pewter of its sheen coldly reflected the chill of the sky. Yet the night was warm, with a warmth that seemed to come out of the warm heart of the land and never out of the frigid immensity of the heavens.

Peter Chisholm, his great form overflowing and sorely testing his frail chair, watched the pillar of his pipe-smoke and spoke musingly. "Did you ever hear tell of the death of Alastair Neill, the Macarthy's son, and brother to your mad girl?"

Jonathan was interested.

"This is the first I've heard of Captain Neill having a son," he said.

"Oh, yes. Alastair Neill was more than a son to his father, he was something like a reproduction . . . and in more than his looks, from all I've heard. He died in France early in 1918 along with quite a number of his contemporaries, only,

72

as was to be expected from a member of his family, his end was rather more—er—spectacular than some. My brother Bill told me the story—he was with the Artillery people in the same sector as Neill's lot, the Black Watch—and though he wasn't actually an eye-witness of the affair, he heard all about it from a pal who was. It was in the Coulaincourt sector, during a pretty lively spell, that this fellow—Evans, his name was, and in the same battery as Bill—was sent up from Battery to the line as Observation Officer. On his way up he fell in with a crowd of the Black Watch going up to take-over some new positions—new for them, at any rate—from the Seaforths. They were commanded by Alastair Neill. Since they were apparently heading for the section of line which contained his observation post, Evans attached himself to them. It was a dark night, and he did not get any clear idea of Neill—not that he was particularly interested—except that the man did not seem to be very steady on his legs, and it was only when they got to the Seaforths' company headquarters that he discovered that the Black Watch captain was fully half-soused. Evans, judging by the fellow's looks, got the impression that he had probably been in that condition for a considerable time; but he wasn't the first one to go that way—conditions were apt to lead in that direction—and it was none of an Observation Officer's business, anyway.

"There were six of them in the dug-out at the time, Neill and two of his subalterns, the Seaforths' captain, Macrae, and his one remaining junior, and Evans. Macrae, a small dour-like man, looking as though he badly needed a quiet spell behind the lines, produced a small tot of whisky apiece, finishing a half-empty bottle, which was accepted gratefully enough. Neill thereupon fished out a pint flask from his pocket, and was proceeding to dole it out into the cups when the Seaforth stopped him. Neill was insisting, when Macrae told him that he, for one, knew when he'd had enough. He was not very tactful, perhaps, the way he said it, but after a long spell in the line tact was not always noticeable. Neill took it badly. It was an uncomfortable situation for the juniors. Then Macrae, probably with the idea of smoothing things out, made some not very inspired remark about Neill having more need for the liquor than he had, the Black Watch going into the line while he was going out. Alastair Neill, apparently, was at the aggressive stage, or perhaps he was that way by nature. He took it that he had been insulted, that his nerve had been questioned—Dutch courage required, you know, and all that. The whole affair was absurd, of course, everybody saw that except Neill, and Macrae seems to have decided, sensibly enough, that the best thing to do was to get out without any more of it. He slung on his haversack and the rest, stepped over to a corner of the dug-out, and took down something from the wall and handed it to his subaltern—Malcolm was the fellow's name, I think—Neill keeping up a running fire of abuse the while. Anyway, this lad Malcolm, before gathering up his own kit, lays the object from the wall down on the table right under Alastair Neill's nose. It was a margarine-box lid on which had been drawn a pretty good representation of the Seaforths' regimental badge, a stag's head—the Mackenzie crest, you know. Evans said the thing was quite well done—it turned out that Macrae was, in private life, an art master in a Glasgow school. The badge wasn't just drawn-in in the usual way, but outlined and the background blacked-in, which made the stag's head stand out quite effectively, suggesting the silver cap-badge, I suppose—though what on earth they were doing with such a thing up in the line, goodness knows! Perhaps Macrae had done it there, to while away a spot of unpleasant waiting. Anyway, whatever its uses and artistic merits, Neill didn't like it. In fact, it seemed to send him plumb crazy. He let out a yell, grabbed the masterpiece, threw it on the floor and stamped on it, then without warning he rushed at Macrae, cursing him and bawling something to the effect that he

74

needn't think that his damned dirty stag would save anybody who called a Macarthy Neill a coward. Macrae was evidently so surprised that he made no attempt to defend himself, and Neill landed him an almighty wallop that bowled him right over. Unfortunately the poor devil struck his head on falling, on the edge of something hard—extremely hard—enough to break his neck for him. It was a pretty rotten ending for a man who'd come through the Somme and the rest, eh?"

"Damnable!" Jonathan agreed briefly.

"Neill was tight, of course, but that sobered him. Evans said he thought that the man was going to break down altogether, while the others gaped at each other, open-mouthed. However, he seems to have pulled himself together pretty quickly, gave his second-in-command one or two brief instructions and walked out, saying he was going into the front line to have a look around, alone. That was all. He did go, too, and alone. A search-party found his body next day out in no-man's land."

For a minute, perhaps, they smoked in silence. Then Jonathan spoke slowly. "And you—or at least Evans—thought that it was the drawing that did it, that had some strange effect on Alastair Neill's fuddled mind?"

The big man nodded. "What else is there to think? The others thought so too, apparently, though none of them could imagine anything like a reason for it all. Evans said the drawing was really rather good—quite effective. Of course, the man must have gone mad, something must have snapped in his brain—not altogether to be wondered at, the strain those poor devils were living under."

The other stared out over the darkening moors to the black mysteries of the brooding hills. "So that was Barbara Macarthy Neill's brother!" he mused. "And her with a kink on the subject of the deer. I wonder now . . . !"

And after that the silence of the evening claimed its own.

IV

THEY had had their two days at the grouse over dogs—
Alec Macvicar's dogs—and the stiffness of the Law
Courts had lifted off Peter Chisholm's enormous limbs like
dew in the sun of summer. Also they had had a couple of
evenings with the cunning brown trout in the brown pools
of the Feith River . . . and good for their souls that had
been, too! But their hearts were in neither the one nor the
other; they were just playing themselves, with the real business still to come. They were a sore disappointment to Alec
Macvicar, an old man and stiffening, who much preferred
dogging amongst the birds in the heather, and smoking the
contemplative pipe above industrious fishermen on the river-
bank, to clambering about the corries of the high-tops after
the elusive stag. Poor man, he scarcely knew whether to be
relieved or offended when he was informed that his services
would not be required on the hill, save in an advisory
capacity in the matter of geography, traitorous wind-currents
and the like. As he confided to Duncan Henderson down at
the croft, "The chentlemen will be amusing themselfs and
doing neffer a bit o' harm to a'body, but 'twill pe a dommed
meericale if they effer get within shooting distance o' a peast
an' the staag no' deeaf blind an' nebless!"

It was still early when they left the Lodge, and the mist
lay heavy on the hills and clung in twisted strands to every
corrie and crevice of the soaking brae-sides: nevertheless, the
morning held the promise of fine weather, and the boisterous wind of the two previous days had sunk and died and
was no more. Without much difficulty they had enlisted as
their pony-gillie Johnny Henderson, brother to Betsy Ellen,

76

and a silent stalwart of seventeen Highland summers. Nor was silence the only quality he had brought to the task of gillie-ing; optimism he had too, for he arrived with two shaggy neat-footed ponies instead of the one stipulated. Could amateur stalkers have received a prettier compliment?

According to Alec, vaguely disapproving of the whole venture, and openly cynical over Johnny Henderson's twin shelties, with the weather that was in it there *should* be deer amongst the lower corries of Carn Garbh, though they would be apt to lift higher as the day wore on, or again if the promise of the morning held, there might be beasts on the long hog-back of Meallach Mhor, or again there might not! Either way, one was to realise, would make but little difference to the ultimate result, in the opinion of Alec Macvicar.

Their route lay through the dark belt of the pines that held the chill of death in their black solitude, up over the shelving moors behind the Lodge, where the dew lay like spangled lace on every heather-clump and all the world crouched grey and toneless beneath the sullen blanket of the mist. But half-way up the long browning-purple slope, the heavy blanket thinned to a curtain, a curtain that was strangely shaken and agitated and permeated with a weird refulgent glow, and then lifted smoothly, swiftly, soundlessly, as a good curtain should, to reveal the vast stage of the hills bathed in the flooding sunlight, boundless, terrifying, after the pearly constriction of the mist.

The little cavalcade, then, moved upward and onward through the radiance of the morning, the two men in front and a little apart, and the lad with the ponies a few yards behind, with never a word between the lot of them. Nothing else moved in all that wide vacancy of the heather, nor any sign of life manifested itself, save only the black speck that was an eagle, hanging high in the deepening blue of the sky, and even it hung motionless, immutable.

That is the sort of morning it was.

Their deer grazed high on the mighty breast of Carn Garbh, up on the lip of a long corrie that splashed the brown hide of the mountain with a weal of vivid green, a small herd loosely scattered, and all stags. It was too far to pick out heads—the herd was all of two miles off—but the glasses showed that there were one or two heavyish heads amongst them, and the fates might be kind!

Between men and deer yawned a great trough of the hills, the glen of the infant Allt a' Coire Garbh that gushed from the west side of the mountain even as the twin streams that united in Gleann na Mallach spouted from the east. A great mass of a hill was Carn Garbh, and ample mother of more streams than these.

This gulf had to be crossed or skirted, so much was self-evident. The problem was, which course was advisable, or at any rate, least inadvisable? To cross the glen meant that at least one-third of that crossing must be accomplished in full view of the deer. To make a detour to the right, round the head of the valley and so on to a flank of Carn Garbh, was to work right into the beasts' wind, while to skirt over to the left across the wide mouth of the glen and so on to the mountain via the haunch of Meallach Mhor, would entail half a day's journeying.

Peter Chisholm, back against an outcrop, knees up and open and telescope supported on right knee, stared long and intently, and gave his opinion. "It's the head of the glen for us, wind or no wind. There's no choice."

Jonathan Maitland, sitting back, shook his black head. "I'm not so sure. . . . I shouldn't like to risk it," he muttered. "I've a great respect for those brutes' noses. What does Johnny Henderson think?"

Johnny Henderson had no doubts. "What for must you be giving the beasts your wind, sirs? Go you the direct

78

road down into the glen . . . you'll not be frighting the brutes at that distance, if they're not hearing or smelling you. They'll not shift a yard, and you not setting the whole brae moving . . . but you'll have to be watching yon screes like the deevil . . . and once you're in the foot o' the glen, it's easy, and the bit burn to the left taking you right up bang into the middle o' them. Losh! It'll be as easy as shelling peas, yes!" Johnny Henderson, as has been indicated, was an optimist.

Jonathan laughed his quiet laugh. "I doubt it will not be quite as easy as all that, Johnny boy. It's risky, and I'm not over keen on an up-hill stalk. Still, I think we might chance it—it's better than making that enormous circuit to the left, and less hopeless than making the beasts a present of our wind, as Mr. Chisholm suggests."

Peter Chisholm yawned hugely. "Have it your own way," he yielded slightingly. "It was agreed that the first stalk should be yours anyway. Show yourself as much as you like. We'll march down your hill arm in arm singing *Onward, Christian Soldiers*. We might even get Johnny to execute a Highland fling on the ridge here, just to help things along. Nothing like keeping the brutes amused."

Amiably the dark man eyed his friend. "You shut that great cavern of a mouth, Peter Chisholm!" he murmured pleasantly. "We will walk cannily down this brae into the cover of the glen, and we will climb up the burn just as Johnny suggests, and two-thirds of the way up we will leave it and work up behind that jutting shoulder into all those outcrops and peat-hags. Probably I'll leave you there, for after that good stalking will be required. I will then climb up that bit that looks like a dried-up burn-channel but which will doubtless be full of particularly damp water, and thereafter I will shoot my stag just a hand's-breadth behind the fore-leg. And that will be that!"

"Aye!" said Peter Chisholm expressively.

They took from Johnny the rifles in their waterproof cases, and Jonathan gave his instructions. "You will wait here till I fire my shot. If I miss, we will move over the flank of the hill to see what's doing on Meallach Mhor. If I grass my stag we will drag it downhill as far as we can, and you will come for it with those cynical animals of yours. Also you will pray for me . . . or if you cannot do that, you will at least think kindly of me in my extremity!"

The walking down the steep side of that glen was a distressing affair. Even had they been crawling down on the flat of their bellies they would have felt more at ease, but this casual strolling in full view of the deer, distant as they were, was nerve-racking, embarrassing even. Soon it came to be that they dare not lift their eyes up to the deer but had to keep them glued on the ground a yard ahead of their toes, for all the world like a pair of guilty children approaching an irate parent. Throughout, they had to trend steadily to the left to avoid the treacherous aprons of the screes where a quiet man, with the tread of an angel, might make noise enough for an army. But the one remark was passed on that downward journey. "Deer-stalking!" That was Peter Chisholm.

It was with sighs of relief that they reached the bed of the glen where a bend of the hill hid them from the herd, and the youthful Allt a' Coire Garbh welcomed them noisily. They kept its cheerful company over a hundred yards of its boulder-strewn highway, till a satellite burn tumbling in on the right received them into its steeply convenient channel. The long ascent of that watery staircase presented no difficulties to climbers sound in wind and limb and head and who didn't mind a wetting, and steadily the Allt a' Coire Garbh shrank and diminished beneath them. The rifles, certainly, were apt to be a nuisance, but as a discomfort

rather than an impediment, and only a modicum of exe-
cration was expended thereupon. Presently they lifted out
of the gut of the glen and the summit of the opposing
ridge came into view, and with it a handwave from Johnny
Henderson signalising that the deer had made no move. So
far so good, the fine stalkers they were!

They made a striking contrast in the manner of their
ascent, those two, the big fair man and the slight dark one,
good hillmen both. The big man carried his weight easily,
lightly, climbing like a cat, with almost feline niceness, to all
appearances practically effortless. The other resembled a
steel spring rather, flexible, inexhaustible, climbing with an
assiduousness, a resolution, that was indomitable, with
never a jerk nor a falter to mar the rhythm of his motion. It
might be that the one typified power and the other energy.

In due course they reached the loop in the burn's career
where it was forced to encircle a great rocky shoulder of the
hill that jutted forth like the prow of a battleship. Here they
left their burn regretfully, to creep along the base of this
shoulder till it led them into a tossed and tumbled, though
steeply-sloping, wilderness of peat and rock interspersed
with the jagged stumps of ancient trees, relics of a mighty
race that had flourished there, high above the present tree-
line, when Scotland was young. Fine cover, this carried them
well on their way, and the deer now little more than a
quarter of a mile off, though still out of sight.

Jonathan's burn-channel proved to be dried-up indeed and
offered a passable means of approach, though the loose
stones of its bed had to be watched, carefully. Once indeed,
Jonathan, leading and bent double, slipped on a stone that
was less firm than it seemed, and was brought to his knees,
thereby dislodging a fragment of rock which leapt merrily
downward intent on a headlong career, to be checked by
Peter Chisholm's useful bulk thrown desperately across its
path. Unfortunately in this hasty manoeuvre the big man's

81

rifle came into violent contact with the embedded stones of the bank, and its muffled clatter sent two hearts into two mouths. Scarcely daring to breathe they crouched, waiting for the patter of sharp hooves . . . waited, and breathed again.

Soon however, their stony ladder shallowed and unfolded and disgorged them out on to the open heather, and the deer in full view less than three hundred yards away. It had been a comparatively simple stalk, with both men old hands at the game, but the next hundred-and-fifty yards or so would require clever stalking. And there was no hurry at all, so they waited and watched and let the tattoo of their heart-beats sink and diminish to their normal throb.

There were eight or nine stags feeding fitfully on the lip of the great corrie, mainly youngsters with one or two heavier beasts and but the one passable head amongst them, an eight-pointer with a good wide span. He nibbled apathetically on the outskirts of the herd, in quite a good position, and the sun gleamed splendidly on his red flanks.

Behind a heather-ridge Jonathan Maitland held out his rifle at the stretch of his left arm to test his steadiness. There must be no wounding of beasts. After the first waver the weapon remained motionless, firm as a rock, and the young man nodded and loaded-up, spitting on the first shell for luck.

"I will go now," he whispered, "and Heaven preserve me from firing too soon! Coming?"

The big man shook his head. "I'll bide here," he grinned. "I hate watching a man in his disappointment. Go to it . . . and aim low!"

That next hundred yards or so was not easy at all, but the man was a born stalker, with a stalker's intuition and eye for cover. Every heather-clump, every peat-ridge, every outcrop, every hollow and scar in the face of the hill, he utilised and profited by. He took his time—there was never a bit of hurry and the day still young, and surely if slowly the ground was covered, and the herd fed on.

He still would be, perhaps, one-hundred-and-eighty yards from his quarry when it happened; shrill and clear in the thin atmosphere of the hightops, rose the vibrant scream of an eagle, harsh and fierce.

Jonathan started and gazed upward and cursed beneath his breath, but as far as he could see, the sky was empty. The deer also started, nervous. Anxiously the man waited; well he knew how the deer hated the eagles, seldom indeed though it must be that the birds attacked aught but a new calf. This was the devil's own luck!

Minutes passed sluggishly, and one by one the deer resumed their feeding, but warily. Five minutes he gave them before he once again moved forward; thirty or forty yards now, and that stag would be dead meat. He must not shoot too soon, eagles or no eagles!

A quarter of the way was not covered before once again the savage scream rang out, and once again the deer started and bunched together, anxiety in every graceful line of them.

Jonathan gazed over to the right across the width of the corrie. He could swear that the screaming came from there . . . and yet no sign of an eagle! He noticed that the deer were also gazing that way, and he realised with a shock that they were staring downwards rather than skywards. Even as he watched a third scream pierced the silence of the hills, a silence that was further disturbed by the clatter of a couple of score of cloven hooves, as the herd swept off, heads up, antlers back, haunches low, a vision of the poetry of movement . . . for a spectator disinterested!

And across the corrie floated another sound, not the screaming of an eagle, but a light mocking laughter, clear and derisive in the idle air.

V

"ISN'T she the very devil? Didn't somebody once suggest that the Devil was a woman?" Jonathan Maitland was very annoyed. "The girl's just playing with us . . . must have been watching us all the time and lets me get almost within range before she ups and does the dirty . . . doesn't just get up and shout either, as you might expect, but scares the brutes sort of naturally with a mighty fine imitation of an eagle's screaming. She's a proper pest!" He was very annoyed indeed.

"And the pest of a proper stalker, too," the big man put in. "She was pretty near-in to the wind, up there."

"Oh, agreed! She's all that, more's the pity. This is the second exhibition of her ability she's given me . . . she has both of us licked hollow. That's just the devil of it, the besom's going to take some beating."

Peter Chisholm grinned cheerfully. His cheerfulness was practically damp-proof. "Yon lassie needs a man to handle her," he decided. "She needs laying over a good beefy knee, and her behind spanked, long and hard! You couldn't effect an introduction, could you?"

Dryly he got his answer. "It would be necessary to catch her first." Jonathan stared out over the sun-filled valley to the waiting ranks of the hills. "But I'm hanged if she's got us beat! We'll try Meallach Mhor and use what brains we've got between us, heaven help us!"

They stood just over the ridge above the corrie of their humiliation, and looked across to the long curve of Meallach Mhor, a great hog's-back of a hill, lower than the summit of Carn Garbh by some three-hundred feet. Thitherwards the fleeing deer had bolted. Of the woman there was no sign—

84

nor had there been. The land lay spread before them vacant, solitary, beneath the midday quiet.

"I have them," Peter Chisholm was busy with his glass again. "They may not be the same deer, but deer they are. See that beallach, that bite out of the ridge of Meallach Mhor, away at the far end? Well, down from it and half-left, four-hundred, six-hundred yards maybe—half a mile even, it might be. See them?"

"I do not! I see heather and stones, any amount of them, and nothing else. Can't you give me a landmark of sorts?"

The other scratched his head. "Man, it ought to be easier to spot the beasts themselves than to find a landmark on that bald sweep of a hill. Bide a wee! D'you see that burn that the sun's catching? Well, along from it there's a patch of stuff a bit darker than the rest, probably old heather. Got it? Now up, and up some more. There!"

Jonathan's glass moved along and up, and up and down a little, and steadied to the sharp intake of his breath. "Got them!" he breathed. "The same beasts too, by the looks of them." He was silent for a bit, and his telescope roved. "Peter boy, how's this for a ploy? We'll split up . . . it's your stalk anyway . . . and you will do your damnedest with those beasts, while I get me round the back of the hill and up to yonder beallach, where I'll sit tight. Then if that misbegotten wench interferes as she did here, the chances are two to one, or maybe three to two, that the deer will bolt up for the beallach—you know how they nearly always bolt up-hill and will always make for the lowest crossing on a ridge—and I stand a chance of getting a shot of sorts."

The big man considered. "It would largely depend on where the woman was working from, of course, provided she keeps her game up. If she was as close into the wind as she was here, it is conceivable that the beasts might head for the flank of the hill instead of going over the top. Still, it's worth trying. There's always a chance . . . blast her for a lady-dog!"

"Amen to that!" And that was heartfelt.

They slipped back over the ridge and slanted down through the heather and blaeberries of the long slope up which they had so lately toiled. Far down on the opposite side of the glen three slow-moving specks, outlined against the pallor of the screes, proclaimed that Johnny Henderson and his shelties were carrying out instructions received. The sight of them and the direction that they were taking was, somehow, an added humiliation, and drew from Jonathan Maitland, beneath his breath, a vehement "Damn!"

His friend nodded comprehendingly. "Aye!" he said, and they went on in silence.

Down at the water-meeting, where the Allt a' Coire Garbh joined a lusty stream hurrying round from the far flank of Carn Garbh, they came up with Johnny.

"No luck, sir?" Polite he was, and grave as a judge . . . even if the ponies seemed more cynical than ever.

"No luck!" Jonathan agreed shortly.

Peter Chisholm elaborated. "Over many eagles about, I'm afraid!"

"Oh! Eagles wass it?" The politeness fairly stuck out of him.

"Eagles!" the big man nodded.

"Uh-huh!" said Johnny, and the march was resumed.

They were now at the hub of three valleys, the glen they had just descended, the valley that separated Carn Garbh from the crescent of Meallach Mhor, and a narrow ravine which precipitated down from the high plateau of An Moine Liath. Here, amidst a group of gnarled and twisted Scots pines, the party split up, Peter Chisholm to do his damnedest with the deer, Jonathan to his lofty perch in the beallach, and Johnny and company to wait where they were, optimistically or otherwise.

And the quiet of the watching hills was but little quieter

for their parting.

Jonathan's task was simple enough, entailing nothing more subtle than steady climbing with only a weather eye to be cocked lest he alarm any stray deer and thus arouse the countryside. Half an hour saw him in the mouth of the beallach, breathing deeply but unhurriedly after an un- eventful climb over bracken, short heather, and granite- cropped peat-moss. He picked his vantage-point with care. The beallach was a little pass through the ridge of the hill, perhaps a hundred yards long and some thirty or forty yards wide at its base, with a fair amount of loose rock about it. He ensconced himself behind a great lichen-grown boulder a short distance to leeward above the floor of the beallach, where he could command a wide view of the southeast face of the hill, and settled himself to wait.

With loose stones and moss he deftly constructed for himself a back-rest and a rifle-rest, also from a flat slab, a table, shaded, for his chocolate and Abernethy biscuits. Jonathan liked to be comfortable, when possible.

It was some time before he discovered his deer, the lack of recognisable landmarks and the beasts' protective colouring making their location on that smooth curving slope no easy matter. Once he had found them, however, he realised that they had not moved more than a few yards at most. Three or four of them were lying down chewing the cud peaceably, amongst them the eight-pointer of the morning, and with nothing more on their minds than the vague irritation of the flies, necessitating an occasional lazy scratching of rump with white-tipped antler. So far, peace reigned on that sunflooded brae-side.

With a sigh of contentment Jonathan laid aside his glass and settled himself back amongst his stones. Probably he would have a longish wait—if that meddlesome girl would only keep her fingers out of their pie—for Peter Chisholm would have to wait for that stag to rise, to give him a decent shot, and that might be shortly or not so shortly! He could remember many such waits on a sitting stag, the optimistic commencement, the snail-like passage of time, the growing impatience, the consideration of the possibilities of a sitting shot and their wise, if regretful rejection, the gradual cramping of limbs and stiffening of muscles, the ultimate despair and bottled-up fury, and then the sudden rising to its feet and lightning-like flight of the miserable brute pursued by nothing more lethal than a volley of violent half-frozen curses. Might the big man meet a kinder fate!

It was pleasant lying up there in the smile of the sun with half the land spread out below him for his delectation. He could well sit there for a time, a short time or a long time, and let the kindly warmth console him and the kiss of the breeze seduce him and the calm of the spreading hills edify and instruct him, and he would be the better man and the wiser man for his waiting. Even, in course of time he might come to think less hardly of the Neill girl with her queer dark wildly-wistful beauty and her queer wild proud spirit. Up here, halfway to Heaven, in this remote quietude that might be remotely benevolent or remotely indifferent, it was easier to think less hardly of such human failings, or at any rate, to place human interests and activities at their proper level, and be charitable accordingly. "God, what is man . . . ?"

"You look very comfortable, Mr. Maitland. You will be admiring the fine view?"

For all the sweetness of the voice, Jonathan started as though he had been bitten. "Damn!" he exploded, and swung round on the word.

She was standing a few yards behind him, dressed as before in kilt and jumper, and the breeze of the high-tops caressed her lithe girl's figure lovingly.

"I beg your pardon!" she said politely. "I'm afraid I

disturbed you. I said you will be admiring the fine view?"

"It was a good view," the man acceded meaningly. He was silent for a moment, watching her, considering. "You make a very fair imitation of an eagle's scream," he said at last.

She acknowledged that with a small smile. "I can imitate all the sounds of the hills," she said, quite simply.

"You are very fond of the hills and the things of the hills?" he suggested.

"I love them!" Sincerely she said it.

He nodded and looked away over the stones and the heather. "Isn't it a feature of the life of the hills that all things therein mind only their own business?"

"Except to give warning of a killer!" she flashed. She was quick.

The man swallowed hard. "I don't like your choice of epithets, Miss Neill." He spoke levelly.

"No doubt!" she gave back, cool as a cucumber.

Jonathan examined the toe of his boot carefully. "You and I don't appear to hit it off together, do we?" he murmured. "But then, I was never much use at dealing with ladies."

The girl made no answer to that, just watched him, disconcertingly hostile.

Jonathan reflected. The girl was a plague—several varieties of plague—and he did not desire her company one little bit. But if she was up here talking to him, she could not be down the hill spoiling Peter Chisholm's sport. His course, therefore, was obvious. She must remain up here talking or being talked to, whether he liked it or not. Also, she wasn't doing old Peter any good by standing up openly in the mouth of the beallach, even though partly hidden by the rocks . . . deer will seldom look for trouble from above unless the wind warns them, but one never could be perfectly sure. . . .

"Won't you sit down?" he suggested then, brightly. "I can

recommend these stones . . . most comfortable."

Strangely enough she did sit down, as a woman sits, legs half under her and kilt carefully arranged—though, being only a kilt, it could not quite cover those peeping knees. Jonathan sat down beside her and watched her, brows wrinkled. At any rate, she was no gusher . . . she seemed well content to sit tight and let him do the talking. All very well, but.

"Miss Neill, would you mind telling me just what brought you up here?" he asked of her.

"You did!"

"Well?" He waited.

She was quite frank. "I was watching you from the shoulder of Carn Garbh . . . and I was watching those stags also . . . and I knew what you would do—it was the obvious thing to do. When the deer were disturbed they would almost certainly bolt up for this beallach . . . and when I saw you split up I knew that you knew that too. So I followed you. That's all."

"And why didn't you follow my friend, Mr. Chisholm?"

"Because I can do all that is necessary from up here."

"Oh!"

She turned to him, smiling a little. "You will think me a foolish wilful creature?"

"I think you are a damned nuisance!" he said, simply.

She laughed at that, a quiet laugh of sheer amusement. She had a curious faculty, this girl, of becoming transiently detached from the tone or trend of her prevailing attitude to appreciate fully a momentary impression or passing side-play, and to revert thereafter easily, smoothly, to her original viewpoint.

Jonathan went on. "Might I enquire what you intend to do now, Miss Neill?"

"Certainly, Mr. Maitland. I shall wait till your friend crosses that semi-circle of old heather, as cross it he must, then I will get up and scream once or twice. That's all!"

"And supposing—just supposing, I say—that I was to stop you?"

Coldly she answered him. "You would not, Mr. Maitland!"

"I wonder!" He spoke musingly, as if to himself. "I think that I am stronger than you."

She stiffened on the word and the colour flamed in her face. "You wouldn't dare touch me!" she cried. "I. . . ."

"Yes, I know. You are Barbara Macarthy Neill and daughter of a hundred chiefs. Perhaps you're right . . . hullo, what's that?" and he pointed beyond her, over to the left.

She turned to look, and even as she turned Jonathan acted. He leaned over and his left hand grasped her left arm at the elbow, slipped down to the wrist, pulled backward and then upward, and there she was with her arm doubled behind her back, a position not painful as long as she remained still; but sheer agony if she attempted to move. It was a simple enough grip, but very efficacious.

Furiously, she swung on him, to find her face close against his. If that made her hesitate for a moment, who can blame her? Jonathan Maitland's face could be pretty grim. Nevertheless, she was no less fiercely angry. "You beast!" she almost hissed. "Oh, you beast!"

"No need for excitement, Miss Neill," he advised calmly. "No need at all." He was strangely calm himself considering that this was the first time that he had attempted this sort of thing on a lady. "If you keep still, you will be perfectly comfortable, but any movement you make, especially a jerky movement, will be apt to hurt."

Her eyes blazed into his. "Release my hand at once, Mr. Maitland, or. . . ."

"Yes?"

For answer she made as if to leap to her feet, an idea which progressed little beyond its inception, before the agony in her arm forced her down. She sank back with a sob of

91

vexation.

The man, his lips like a band of steel and brows contracted, loathed himself, and spoke very gently. "That was unwise, Miss Neill. Please don't do it again." He looked away from her. "And don't think that I enjoy this any more than you do. But . . . you have spoiled enough sport for one day!"

"I can still scream," she reminded him, and her voice was bitter, bitter.

"Of course, so you can!" With his free hand the man drew out of his breast-pocket a large many-hued silk handkerchief, held one corner between his teeth and twirled it round till it formed a roll of sorts. "This is, shall we say, moderately clean," he informed her brusquely. "Will you be gagged, or will you promise not to scream?"

"I'll promise nothing!" she snapped. Resolute she was, and her eyes stared straight before her.

Jonathan sighed. "A pity!" he murmured. "It's an ill use to put my old wiper to. It has seen some useful service, all the same, this handkerchief. One of its last jobs was to act as a bandage to a dog with a festering paw . . . oh, and I forgot, since then it came in very handy to carry bait in the day we were worm-fishing." He raised the handkerchief to his nose. "I don't think the worms have left any smell, though!"

Still looking straight before her she spoke, firmly but hastily. "I don't think I'll scream. . . . I won't scream!"

Jonathan Maitland nodded solemnly. "Perhaps that is wise," he said.

For a time they sat in silence, and the silence of the hills washed over them and soothed neither the one nor the other. The girl looked calm enough, frozen perhaps, would better describe her, but the man who held her wrist and felt her pulse knew that she was neither calm nor frozen.

As for Jonathan Maitland, there was no calm nerve to his whole body, with it pressed against the girl's. Every movement of her he could feel, every breath she drew, every heartbeat almost, and the warm firm touch of her disturbed him fiercely. As has been said, Jonathan Maitland was an imaginative man.

A score of times he almost dropped that wrist—and did not.

Far below them the deer basked contentedly in the warmth of the afternoon, and nowhere else in all the sweep of the land was manifest any sign of life. Peter Chisholm, like a good stalker, was taking his time.

Jonathan did make the one attempt at conversation. A remark anent the excellence of the September weather and the absence of mist on the hills, was acknowledged only by the turning of a cold profile one degree farther away from the speaker. The well-meant offer of a section of chocolate and an Abernethy biscuit met with no kinder fate; thereafter the man held his tongue if not his peace, dividing his attention between the stags, tranquil in the lap of the brae, and the cloud-shadows drifting on the face of the heather.

It was the ptarmigan that thawed the girl out of her Olympian silence. They came bustling out from amongst the rocks above, a group of perhaps half a dozen, absurdly busy and impertinent, and peep-peeping excitedly as ptarmigan will. Running hither and thither amongst the stones they worked down toward the silent man and the silent woman, and to one at any rate, and perhaps to both, the little busy-bodies' vigorous cheeping was more than welcome.

For a while the girl watched them in silence, while the frown melted from her brow and a dimple came and went near the corner of her mouth. At length a plump fellow, bolder than the rest, advanced to within five or six yards, to peer at them from behind a stone, chest well out, head on one side and bright eyes winking, a picture of rubicund inquisitive importance.

"Good afternoon to you, Mr. Pickwick!" solemnly

Jonathan greeted him, to send the creature scuttling back, fairly bursting with excitement and chirping fit to kill himself.

The girl laughed at that, a low gurgling laugh of sheer amusement. "Isn't he quaint?" she cried. "Just like a lord-provost."

The man chuckled at the implication. "Sir Pthomas Ptarmigan," he nodded, "of Ptarmigan's Ptasty Ptablet and Ptoffee!"

"Ass!" she named him, but the chill had gone out of her voice.

Peep-peeping in perfect imitation, she presently had the whole platoon of seriously curious birds lined up and watching, for all the world like a civic deputation, as roundly important and as fidgety.

She half-turned to her captor, honey in her voice. "Isn't it a pity, Mr. Maitland, that it's your rifle you have there, not your gun? You would probably have got the whole lot with one barrel!"

Warmly, Jonathan protested. "Scarcely fair, I think, Miss Neill!"

Still sweetly, she went on. "Oh, then you do not consider ptarmigan worthy of your prowess? Is it only the deer that you enjoy slaughtering?"

The man sighed resignedly. "You have a bitter tongue in your head, Barbara Macarthy Neill!" he said. "But tell me, why have you such a down on deer-stalking? You, a Highland girl, must know how the deer would over-run the glens in no time if they were not kept down; how already they are becoming over-plentiful in many districts and seriously damaging the crofters' poor bits of crops. You must know all that?"

"I know all that!" she acceded evenly.

"Well then, if you admit that they must be kept down, surely the way we do it, stalking the stag on its own ground, man against beast with the dice loaded in favour of the stag, surely that is the best way?"

She answered question by question. "Tell me, Mr. Maitland, if the deer did not eat the crops, if there was no danger of them multiplying and therefore no need to keep them down, would you forego your stalking?"

"Probably not," he admitted.

"A poor answer!"

He grinned. "Poor enough, but all your hypothetical question deserved." He returned to his point. "But you have not made out your case against deer-stalking. You must hold strong views on the subject to account for your . . . steadfastness?"

"Perhaps I do." Sombrely Barbara Neill stared out over the spread of that tumbled land. "It is not only a question of fondness for the animals," she explained. "Probably you will not understand, but I have a feeling, a presentiment if you like, that no good can come of stalking . . . on these lands."

"So? You will have your reasons?" Jonathan was interested.

"Yes, I have my reasons. . . . My granduncle went out stalking one day thirty years ago and failed to come back at night. He was found next morning in a burn-channel with a broken neck, and that on an open stretch of heather! My uncle also, the Macarthy Neill's brother, was brought home one night by his gillie with half his face torn away and one eye out, turned on and mauled by a wounded stag. There were others too, before them!"

Jonathan looked at her curiously.

"So you think there might be a sort of curse on the place?"

"There might be!"

He was silent. This thing was interesting. Strangely enough he felt no surprise at the suggestion—though it should be surprising enough. Without actually having thought of it, he had been prepared for something of the sort . . . an intuition, perhaps. They were a queer crowd, these Neills . . . and that glen, Gleann na Mallachd—there was something queer about it too! And yet. . . . He frowned at himself. Lucifer! It wouldn't do to let old Peter hear him in that strain . . . the hills getting him again!

"But aren't you an expert stalker yourself?" he argued.

She took some time to answer that. "Yes . . . but I am looking for something."

Jonathan waited.

"Have you the Gaelic, Mr. Maitland?"

"Only an odd phrase here and there. Why?"

"Over on the east side of Carn Garbh there is a corrie called Coire nan Daimh Ban—"

The sharp crack of a rifle cut short her words, a crack that echoed amongst a hundred hills, and over to their left the ptarmigan, still inquisitive, scuttled frantically for the haven of the higher rocks.

Jonathan felt her wrist, her whole body, stiffen to the quick indraw of her breath. "Wait," he whispered, "they will be passing here in a minute."

His rifle lay where he had laid it.

Quiet they waited, watching the mouth of the beallach, with never a word between them. Nor had they long to wait; soft as the whisper of summer rain amongst the birch leaves came the patter of sharp hooves, and eyes wide, ears forward and sterns down, the deer flashed through the little pass, four, six, seven of them . . . and never an eight-pointer amongst the lot.

VI

AT the sound of footsteps Peter Chisholm looked up
from the gory work of the gralloch, his cheerful
countenance wreathed in the largest and most complacent
of smiles, to blink and start and stare. The change from smug
satisfaction to wide-eyed astonishment was comical, almost
ludicrous . . . but then he had hardly expected to see his
friend with a lady—obviously the lady—coming swinging
downhill arm in arm.

"Lord!" he said, and goggled.

Jonathan appeared to be in excellent spirits. "Stout work,
big fellow!" he called. "Congratulations!" He unlinked his
arm from the girl's and released her wrist at last. "Miss
Neill," he intoned impressively, "you have here Mr. Peter
Chisholm, solicitor in the Supreme Courts of Scotland . . .
but not a bad sort for all that. Peter, this is Miss Barbara
Macarthy Neill of Inverfeith."

Peter Chisholm took a deep breath, glanced from the girl
to his friend and back again, held out his hand and then
hastily withdrew it; one can hardly greet a lady with a hand
dripping with blood! "Afternoon!" he said, and stopped.

Barbara Macarthy Neill said nothing at all. With a toss of
her black head and a twitch of her shoulder she turned and
stared away and away.

The big man gazed at her, then at Jonathan, made to
scratch his head, but paused halfway remembering his
bloody hands, and so stood, a picture of dismay. "Lord!" he
muttered again, and fervently.

Jonathan spoke smoothly, easily. "You must excuse Miss
Neill, Peter. She is rather puffed—we came downhill in

record time." He winked solemnly at the girl's back. "A nice stag that, Peter! All of sixteen stone, I should say, for all he's no royal. Tell us how you grassed him, fellow."

Peter eyed the girl's profile uneasily. "It was simple enough," he said. "I got within range without much trouble—plenty of cover in that long tussocky heather and all these stones—and I found this fellow lying down and in a bad position. I had reconciled myself to an afternoon's wait, when something or other over to the right interested one of the young stags—I thought it would be—er—er . . ." He glanced eloquently at the girl, and Jonathan nodded, grinning. "Anyway, one or two of the others got interested too, and presently my old fellow gets up impatiently as though he considered the youngsters a hell of a—sorry—a blasted nuisance. So there he was, and, well, that's all. I got him just nicely behind the shoulder, and he only took one bound."

"Butcher!" The word was flung at him over a half-turned shoulder. Peter looked supremely uncomfortable.

Jonathan came to his rescue. "I think that Miss Neill must have leanings toward vegetarianism," he suggested genially.

The big man nodded and smiled suddenly. "Perhaps the lady didn't quite catch the gist of your introduction," he hinted. "She would seem to have mistaken my profession . . . I am a lawyer, you know!"

The girl whirled round on them, dark eyes ablaze in the pale of her face. "Oh, you are the clever ones, so mighty clever, so witty . . . and that poor slaughtered animal at your feet! I think you are hateful!" And both men stood silent before the torrent of her scorn.

She swung on her heel and made to leave them but turned after a couple of steps. "And don't think that you have finished with me," she warned. "I shall make it my duty to spoil your . . . carnage, wherever and whenever I can."

Jonathan answered her quietly, tonelessly. "Miss Neill, I regret that you should see fit to continue your . . .

interference in what is, after all, no concern of yours. I leased Buidhe from your father, legitimately and in good faith, and if you have any quarrel with that leasing it lies between yourself and your father, not me. Therefore, I shall take such steps as I see fit to prevent any unwarrantable interference with our sport." He smiled then. "I might even go so far as to put into practice a suggestion of Mr. Chisholm's."

"So?" She was very cool.

"Yes, so! Mr. Chisholm suggests that a good way of dealing with an erring and presumptuous female would be to lay her over my knee and spank her good and hard! That was the idea, wasn't it, Peter?"

"In essence, yes. But who stipulated *your* knee?"

But Barbara Neill waited for no more. With a heated objurgation that might have been "Oafs!" or even "Ogres!" she left them, to stride off across the heather, the violent swing of her kilt bearing eloquent testimony as to her humour.

Unsmiling the two men watched her go, and the verve and spirit of her going was not lost upon them. Jonathan, watching, sighed and sighed again. The other nodded. "Isn't she?" he agreed, and sighed also.

And so they awaited Johnny Henderson and the ponies.

"By the way, big fellow, amongst your many accomplishments do you include a smattering of Gaelic?" Jonathan was not optimistic, but one never knew.

"Gaelic is it? Well, now, I know that *Dhu* means red . . . or is it black? And *Mhor* is either great or small or young or old or something, but really, I'm not what you'd call a Gaelic scholar."

"I believe you! I know almost as much as that myself." The dark man gazed up the valley to where Gleann na Mallachd forked into its twin corries. "You shot that stag of yours at a most inauspicious moment, Peter," he complained.

"The girl was just going to tell me something that might have thrown some light on her derangement on the subject of deer." He produced his Ordnance map. "She named one of these corries . . . this is it, Coire nan Daimh Ban. Evidently that name has some bearing on her attitude. Coire nan Daimh Ban! *Ban* means white, that much I know. Corrie of the white something or other. What might *Daimh* mean, Peter Chisholm?"

"Heaven knows! Anything—anything at all. What sort of white objects are connected with this country? White owls, white cockades, white heather . . . or White Horse! Take your choice!"

"Fathead!" Jonathan's brows puckered to a frown. "It may have some connection with the name of this glen . . . Gleann na Mallachd. I mind the girl saying something the other night about it being a beautiful glen despite the name it had. It is a queer glen too."

Peter Chisholm grinned pityingly. "Man, you're developing the devil of an imagination! I should never have allowed you to come up here by yourself . . . you're not safe to be left alone. Morbid!" He looked about him at the green walls of the glen, stained already with the purple shadows of sundown. "What's wrong with the place, anyway? Seems a perfectly good glen to me."

The other was not disposed to argue the point. "No doubt it is," he agreed briefly. He would let the glen do its own arguing.

So they went on together down that birch-lined aisle of the hills, and the burn murmured its story to them and the reeds nodded in hushed unison, and the trees stooped and listened and sighed. They all knew it, they all remembered, though it was such an old story. And presently the dark man, listening with only one ear to the cheerful nonsense that was his friend's conversation, found himself repeating and repeating ". . . because they seeing, see not; and hearing they hear not, neither do they understand." Jonathan Maitland, admittedly, was an imaginative man.

As for Peter Chisholm, he did not admit—nor does he yet admit—that there was anything strange about that glen, or that its atmosphere made any impression, other than that of peace and beauty, on his essentially practical mind. Be that as it may, loquaciously cheerful as he had been during the first half of their progress, by the time that they left the winding path by the burn-side for the firmer road by the Feith River, the big man had been silent for at least a quarter of an hour. And Peter Chisholm was not what one would call a silent man.

Yet it was a very beautiful glen despite the name it had.

Even at that distance, a good quarter of a mile away, there was no mistaking the identity of the man. The figure fairly shouted its elegance, and a man who can look elegant in Harris tweeds at a quarter of a mile is elegant indeed.

"The gallant Captain himself!" Jonathan's voice betrayed no excessive elation. "Aren't we the lucky ones?"

His friend nodded sombrely. "That is so!" he said.

A few more yards, and Jonathan spoke again, musingly, his eyes on the swirling amber of the river. "All things considered, I hardly think it will be necessary to mention Miss Neill's . . . eccentricities to her father!"

The other grinned understandingly. "Right!" he agreed, and grinned again.

"Not that I condone her offence, of course."

"Of course not."

"It is only that I don't see what good it could do."

"Exactly!" He had a terrible grin, that man.

The Macarthy Neill was affability itself. "Well met, gentlemen! A grand evening, is it not?" Cordially he held out a long hand, delicately made and carefully kept. "You are enjoying good sport, I trust, Mr. Maitland? I noticed

101

Duncan Henderson's boy coming down off the moor scarce a mile back, with a couple of shelties, and but the one unburdened."

Jonathan was civil. He even managed a faint glimmer of a smile on that sour hatchet face of his. "That, sir, was Mr. Chisholm's doing. I was less fortunate!"

The big man chuckled.

"You have some devilish annoying birds hereabouts, Captain," he said.

"Indeed?" Edward Neill's fine forehead wrinkled significantly. "Birds?"

Peter Chisholm nodded portentously. "Eagles!" he said. "Scared the wits out of Maitland here just as he was going to shoot . . . scared the deer too! Deuced unsporting!"

The older man was polite but cold. "You don't say so? Most unfortunate!" One could hardly blame him for disbelieving that story.

He was a handsome man, was Edward Neill, with the raven hair of his family showing hardly a thread of silver, for all that he was well past his fifties. His was a long face, keen and finely chiselled, with a noble brow and eyes beneath it that many a woman might envy. The nose was strong and the chin was strong—many would say it was a strong face altogether—and the resemblance between father and daughter was striking. Except for the mouth—and it was the mouth that caught the attention, and held it—the thin scimitar of a mouth, hard and tight and pitiless as curved tempered steel. That mouth, and those woman's eyes! They sent a shiver through Jonathan Maitland . . . who, of course, was an imaginative man. There were one or two stories about Edward Macarthy Neill of Inverfeith, twenty-sixth of his line. . . .

He was speaking now in a cultured, expressive voice that had a strange fascination about it. "I have just been up to the Lodge, Maitland, to beg a favour of you," he said, "a

102

favour which you will refuse at once if you find it inconvenient to grant. I have a guest staying with me just now, a Colonel Tarras, who is most anxious to have a day at the stags. As you will realise, there are no deer on Inverfeith at this season, barring a few roes—much too low-lying—so I promised him to seek your good offices." He smiled, and it was a strange thing to see a smile on that mouth. "I realise, of course, that it is unusual for a proprietor to bother a tenant in this way, but perhaps you will overlook the irregularity this once? Also, there is some rather good duck-shooting on Loch Feith, which I can offer you by way of compensation."

Jonathan said the only thing possible. "We shall be delighted, of course, Captain Neill! Any day convenient to yourself and Colonel Tarras will suit us." The unblushing liar!

"Thank you, Maitland, I appreciate your kindness. I shall come along with the Colonel, of course, but I shall leave him to do the shooting. It is a long time since I did any deer-stalking." He paused for just a moment, and those wide eyes narrowed strangely. "I lost my taste for it." Then he smiled again. "Too energetic a pastime altogether, I'm afraid. I'm not quite so young as I once was." He held out his hand again. "Good night, gentlemen! I will let you have good warning when to expect us. Be sure to inform me, Maitland, if it is not entirely suitable. Goodnight, and many thanks!"

As they watched him go, Jonathan remembered suddenly. "By the way, sir," he called, "could you oblige me with the meaning of *Daimh Ban*?"

Slowly, deliberately, Edward Neill turned and faced them, and they gasped at the change in his expression. From affability it had altered abruptly to a fury and malevolence that was profound as it was inexplicable. "My God!" he almost snarled. "If that is your idea of humour I don't like your taste, Mr. Maitland!" For a second or two he stood glaring, then without another word he swung on his heels and left them, elegant yet.

"Well, I'm . . ." Jonathan floundered. "Well, I'm . . . scuppered!"

Peter Chisholm tapped his great blond head significantly. "Screwy!" he said. "Screwy, the whole blamed family of them!"

And mystified, they went their way.

VII

OF the happenings of the following week there is little to tell. It was a week of mist and rain and low-lying cloud, of fitful winds and rising burns, turning the cordial colours of that quiet country into a grey desolation wherein the noise of water, hissing, falling, leaping, roaring water persisted and endured. Even the small white-washed Lodge turned wan under the glower of the sky, while round it the guardian pines moaned and wept and wore black mourning for the sun.

It was no weather for stalking. Boisterous winds and shrouding mists are the stalker's worst enemies, not so much as productive of discomfort, as for their effect on the deer. A gusty fickle wind will keep the beasts restless and uneasy and for ever on the move, and the ways of swirling perfidious windcurrents in a narrow glen or yawning corrie can drive a good man mad. As for the mist, clammy spectre of the uplands, while assuredly it may hide the stalker from the stag, more assuredly still, it will hide the stag from the stalker. Need more be said?

Once, indeed, in sheer desperation, an attempt was made on the forest, an attempt that was an abject failure as far as sport was concerned, but which did bring forth one result— the discovery of traitors within the camp. This was the way of it.

Sitting on a streaming sodden hillside, just below the sullen pall of the mist, after a fruitless search for deer, the disgruntled sportsmen had noticed a slight movement of stones on the screes of the opposite slope, a movement which, when localised and examined, had revealed the Neill girl watching them from the lee of a great boulder. On the realisation that she was discovered, she had scrambled to her feet and waved derisively, and, following that with another gesture including in its sweep the grey hills, the lowering clouds, and the mist-filled corries, and eloquent as to her conviction of the futility of their efforts, she had turned downhill and left them to the hills and the hills to them.

They had watched her go, grudgingly admiring her easy conquest of the screes and her graceful leaping of the myriad shouting burns of the brae-side: and they had wondered; wondered at her determination, wondered at her hardi-hood—and her cheek, but most of all they had wondered how the devil she had known that they were going to make an attempt on the forest that day. It was not as though she stayed close-by and could keep the Lodge always under observation; the home of her adoption was more than a couple of miles off. Simultaneously the conviction had dawned upon them both—someone was playing the in-former, someone in Buidhe! Who then? There and then they had laid a plot, and this was the hatching of it.

After breakfast the next morning Jonathan had summoned Betsy Ellen, independent maid-of-all-work to that some-what grim household. "Betsy Ellen Henderson," he had said deceitfully, "I want you to run down to the croft and tell that father of yours that we're for another go at those stags today, and could he spare young Johnny and one of his ill-natured ponies?"

Betsy Ellen, with an expressive glance at the streaming windowpanes, had frowned her stern disapproval.

"You'll not be for going today, with the rain that's in it?" she had protested.

Jonathan was firm. "We will so! Go on with you now!"

With a censorious scowl she had gone, and the plotters had betaken themselves upstairs to a certain attic window from which the Hendersons' croft was visible, there to await developments.

Waiting, they had argued it out. If they were being informed upon, how was the information being conveyed? The Neill girl's residence was a good hour's walk from the Lodge, yet her early appearances on the scenes of their efforts argued a swifter method of communication than that carried on two legs. Also, there was no direct road between, so that the use of the Buidhe establishment's one ramshackle bicycle could be ruled out. Again, the two places were not within sight of each other; a great lump of stony hill as well as a long brown slope of moor separated them, so that any form of signalling was out of the question. What then? A solution there must be.

There was, and soon they had it. Betsy Ellen had not been long within the cottage when she had reappeared at the door, and her father and brother with her. Duncan Henderson was stooping down, doing something with a piece of paper; what he was doing they could not see, a stack of peats obstructing the view. Then he had straightened up, and arm outstretched, had pointed away across the hill, and the others had pointed with him. It had been rather reminiscent of one of those early films, where the imperilled heroine and family abruptly become aware of the so opportune approach of the dashing hero, and hasten to point it out dramatically to the breathless audience. The two watchers had gazed nonplussed at this touching scene, until suddenly the answer to the problem had become clearly discernible as it bounded from behind a dry-stone dyke and took the open moorland at a steady lope.

They were hardly to be blamed for failing to suspect Duncan Henderson's mongrel collie sheepdog as express messenger.

Marvelling audibly, profanely, they had descended, lamenting on the perversity and the deceitfulness of human nature.

"They're all in it, every one of them—even the ponies! I

was suspicious of those ponies from the first." That was Jonathan Maitland. "A fine pair of mugs they'll be thinking us!"

"And you told me that the clan spirit was dead!"

A disillusioned pair, they had decided to keep their discovery to themselves—it might come in useful one day. At all events, they did have the satisfaction of watching Betsy Ellen's changes of expression when Jonathan announced that they had decided to change their plans and go to Inverness for the day—and of reflecting on the long uncomfortable walk that Miss Barbara Macarthy Neill would be having that morning, and all for nothing!

At Inverness, grey metropolis of the northern land, their gloom somewhat alleviated by the strangely exciting influence of numerous gunsmiths' windows, they had called upon, and eventually lunched with a legal friend of Peter Chisholm's, one Archibald Fraser, and a man of parts. He had been unaffectedly glad to see them, as much doubtless for their own sweet sakes, as for the opportunity they had presented to escape from his correctly legal and excessively gloomy office in Church Street.

Archie Fraser was an interesting talker and good company, and he told them a lot of things—one or two things too many, according to Peter Chisholm, practical man. As he had announced to Jonathan on the way home that night, "Archie's a stout fellow, and all that, but at times, I doubt, he's apt to let his imagination run away with him."

The smaller man had smiled grimly. "Same as me?"

"Same as you!" he had nodded solemnly. "And a bad thing in any man, but a calamity in a lawyer."

Archie Fraser had been something more than interested when he discovered that they hailed from the Forest of Buidhe. "That district," he said, "is rather interesting . . . to me." He had hesitated for an instant. "You are having good sport?"

"Unbelievable!" That was the big man.

"So-so!" Jonathan had temporised. "But tell me, why did you say that the district was interesting . . . to you?"

Fraser had looked vaguely uncomfortable. "Oh, it's nothing really, just a feeling I had about the place . . . a sort of experience I once had there."

"Ah!" Peter Chisholm had nodded knowingly. "Eagles?" he said.

The other had been puzzled. "Eagles! No, I can't say that I noticed any eagles. It was something about the place itself that affected me."

"Suppose you let us have the whole story?" Jonathan had suggested quietly.

Fraser had glanced from one to the other a trifle anxiously. "You will think that I'm a bit of a fool, I'm afraid, but, well, you've asked for it." He cleared a space among the debris of the luncheon table, and commenced to inscribe circles on the cloth with the pepper-pot. "Let me see," he began, "it would be sometime in the June of two years ago, that at the invitation of the Macarthy Neill—a queer bird that, by the way—I went on a fishing trip to the Feith River. Neill had some people staying with him at Inverfeith, so I had instructions to confine myself to the upper waters. I remember looking forward immensely to that weekend—I am rather keen on the rod, you know—and I had heard that there were some rather good pools in the Feith as well as some excellent trout-streams running into it. I intended to have the two days at it, and I took my old bivvy with me, so that I could doss down or get up just as the spirit moved me.

"Well, that Saturday afternoon and evening, fishing the strung-out pools of the Feith, I drew a complete blank. I never got so much as a rise though I tried everything I knew. The brutes were there right enough, I knew it—I could see them—but I couldn't get even a nip out of them. The water was in good condition too, though the weather was maybe a shade bright—however, that's neither here nor there. It would be about nine o'clock and the hills beginning to creep in on me, the way they do as the dusk comes down, so I gave it up and decided to try an hour or so with the brown trouties in a likely looking stream coming in on the northwest. I thought I'd maybe have better luck with them than with the salmon.

"This burn came out of a bonny bit of glen, and before I started to fish it, I dumped my kit a few hundred yards into the mouth of the glen and got my tent up—it's no joke putting up a tent once it's dark, as maybe you know, with every tent-peg taking legs to itself and vanishing, so I got mine erected while I could see. Anyway, having made everything shipshape, I wandered off up the valley for perhaps three-quarters of a mile and then started to fish my way down again.

"You know, for the next half-hour I could do no wrong! The trout were rising steadily and fair begging for my fly. In that thirty minutes or so I landed seven good fish besides a few small things. It was like black magic . . . but the strange thing was, I never got a kick out of it. I ought to have been wildly excited, especially after a blank day, but somehow or other it left me cold. Though I was taking fish, my mind wasn't on the job—I don't know what I was thinking about, but it wasn't fishing. I remember it suddenly coming over me how lonely it was—which was a strange thought for a man who'd fished some of the quietest stretches of water in this kingdom, and who hadn't seen a soul since morning anyway. It may have been due to my coming into the narrow confines of the glen after fishing all day in the open strath: it may have been the night coming down, or a chill creeping into the air: or it may have been my empty stomach asserting itself: but there it was. I presently discovered that I was forcing myself on from one run to another, making a duty of it, with every inclination urging me to reel-in and call it a day. Well, I wasn't going to be beat by any attack of

110

the nerves, or whatever it was, so I kept at it and at it right down to my camp, but damn it, you'll hardly believe the relief I felt when I saw the white of the tent in front of me.

"I was hungry enough, so I made a fire and cooked myself one or two of my fish and a can of cocoa to wash down some sandwiches. Afterwards, feeling a bit better in my little Mary, I sat over my fire and smoked a contemplative pipe and wondered what the devil had come over me.

"It was a wonderful night, still as the grave beneath one of those washed-out skies with a tinge of yellow in it somewhere, and the steep birchgrown sides of the glen outlined black against it. There was not a sound except the noise of the water, not even a tree rustling or a night-bird crying. Talk about peace . . . it was the savage peace that reigned before there were living things! How long I sat there before I found that I was shivering and my pipe out, I do not know. My mind had sunk away down into some queer depths of the semiconscious, a sort of purgatory of half-born thoughts.

"Cursing myself for a fool, I gathered some bracken for a bed and wrapping myself in my blanket settled down for the night. I decided I'd get up early, soon after sunrise, and have another go at the river before it got too bright. Strangely enough, I must have fallen asleep almost at once, though I'd hardly expected to. I was tired, of course; I had been on my feet all day, and it would be pretty late by then.

"I wakened some time later, Heaven knows when, near gibbering with fright. What woke me I do not know—I never shall—but I do know that I lay there for what may have been minutes or hours, scarcely daring to breathe, with the fear of death on me. I can't tell you exactly what I felt. Really, I think that I felt nothing but a wild unreasoning desire to get up and bolt from that place . . . and a still stronger dread of doing so. I grant you I'm not cut out for a hero, but I'm not particularly nervously inclined, and I went through the war as a machine-gun item and was in one or

111

two sticky places, but I've never felt as I did that night either before or since. It was as silent as ever, but a silence about as peaceable as hell.

"I have no means of judging how long I stuck it there—it never struck me to look at my watch—before I jumped up and out of that tent. It was not very dark, in fact it was lighter than when I'd lain down, a pale moon having risen over the shoulder of Beinn Buidhe. I've no doubt that it was a beautiful scene . . . but I didn't wait to admire the view. I grabbed only my waterproof and my fishing-basket—goodness knows why I should have taken that—and I left everything else and was off at the double down that glen, nor did I slacken up till I felt the good firm metals of the strath road beneath my feet. I walked fast for a bit down that welcome road till the panic died in me, and my pace dropped to an aimless daunder. Eventually, as the dawn was reddening the tops of the hills, I discovered a convenient shooting-butt quite close to the road, wherein I curled myself in my waterproof . . . and slept like an ox.

"I may say I felt about the biggest fool on God's earth as I made my way back up the strath in the sunshine of the morning, but for all that, though I cursed my fears of the night, I could not laugh at them. There was a queer feeling too, round about my stomach, when I turned from the road to follow that burn up its glen again. I found my tent and things just as I had left them, and I took a reasonable, if not a hearty breakfast. For the sake of my own self-respect—much blown-upon already—I made myself get busy with the rod on that stream again, but after about an hour of it, I gave it up. Not only was my heart not in it, but the wretched place was still having an effect on me: not the horror of the night before, but a feeling of sadness, melancholia if you like, that was hard to reconcile with the smile of the sunny glen. Just a reaction, I've no doubt! Anyway, I packed up and took myself off—I didn't even have another try at the salmon—so you can appreciate the state I was in."

He paused, and grinned self-consciously. "A so-and-so yarn, you'll say?"

Jonathan Maitland shook his head soberly. "I will not!" he said. "You don't know just how interested I've been in your story, Fraser. Tell me now, was there a broken-down wall and some grass-grown ruins in that glen of yours?"

The other nodded, surprised. "Yes, there was, now you mention it. It was within the wall that I pitched my tent."

Of course, as Peter Chisholm pointed out, Archie Fraser, like Jonathan Maitland, was an imaginative man.

VIII

COLONEL TARRAS was a spare man, spare in build, spare in hair, spare in speech, and, according to Peter Chisholm, who was in the way of finding out, spare in patience. He had displayed no noticeable enthusiasm over meeting his temporary hosts, nor for that matter over the day's prospects, despite the fact that the day's arrangements had been made for his special benefit. In Tarras you had that ultimate pinnacle and perfection of our national character, an Anglo-Saxon gentleman, who whatever the circumstances allowed no hint of his feelings to become evident.

The Macarthy Neill, however, made up for him. Having decided, apparently, to overlook the obscure if serious affront put upon him at the last meeting, he was as suavely affable as ever. His greeting to Jonathan had been next to effusive, despite the small encouragement he had received from the rest of the company. If he had noticed a slight lack of warmth in his reception, he had not shown it; his geniality had been as thinly easy, his smile as coldly ready, and his laugh as scrupulously unforced as ever, so that Jonathan Maitland, for all that he could not stomach the man, found himself admiring and responding. That was the Macarthy Neill.

It was a morning of clouds and showers and patches of brave sunshine, with just a shade more wind than made for perfect stalking conditions. Still, as Alec Macvicar—very much to the fore today, with the "laird herself" on the ground—put it: "I am thinking on one or two obsteecles worse than a pickle wind to be overcoming this day, an' that's Goad's truth!" He was a sour old cynic, was Alec Macvicar.

114

It was decided to form two parties, for more reasons than that Barbara Neill, smart on the hill though she might be, could not be in more than one place at one time. Peter Chisholm and the Colonel, with Alec Macvicar as guide and philosopher if not friend, not forgetting Duncan Henderson weaned from his croft to act as pony-gillie, were to take the Carn Garbh beat, while Jonathan and the Macarthy Neill arranged to make for the Braes of Druie on the opposite side of the forest altogether, where a wilderness of small hills occasionally produced a passable beast and a possible shot—this according to the Captain himself. They would thus be out of each other's way, and it was to be hoped that if the interfering daughter of the House of Neill must go on inflicting her attentions on anyone, she would concentrate upon the triflers on the Braes of Druie rather than on the business-like main body up on Carn Garbh. For Jonathan was hardly hopeful—nor desperately keen, what with one thing and another—and Edward Neill came along, at his own request, purely as a guide and spectator. However, young Johnny, complete with pony, was pressed into service just for the look of the thing, and the arrangements were complete.

Before parting company Jonathan had a word with Peter Chisholm. "This day hardly looks like being a picnic for either of us," he commiserated. "All the same, I should say you've got the lighter end of the log, dried-up husk of an old sinner though this Tarras would seem to be. How would you like to spend a day alone with Edward Neill?"

The big man was emphatic. "I'd sooner spend it with Lucifer's self!" he said.

Separating, the two parties took their respective ways, the one rounding the Lodge to face the long climb toward the grey spread of An Moine Liath and the leeward slopes of Carn Garbh, and the other down-hill to greet and accompany the shining links of the Feith River till it waned and diminished and lost itself in the brown welter of the Braes of Druie.

The first let us leave in the capable if pessimistic charge of Alec Macvicar—their fate will be manifest soon enough—and let us follow the others down to the waterside and what was to be.

The river welcomed them, subduedly cordial, from between its rock-lined banks, and to that kindly accompaniment they moved on through the tree-scattered haugh-land, while the strath narrowed and shallowed.

Edward Neill did the talking, and he knew how to talk—when he cared. Jonathan listening, felt, as had many another, that this man might have done great things had he—or fate—willed it. There was something extraordinary about the man, some strain akin to magnificence which was basic and yet superficial, some queer element of greatness, of authority, which was apparent and yet elusive, dormant perhaps, perverted anyway, inherited from some obscure ancestor or line of ancestors. Of course, Jonathan reminded himself, this man was the Macarthy Neill, a Highland chieftain, little though he approximated to the popular model, the descendant of a long series of autocrats, despots maybe, whose word or whim had been law to a war-like race. But that he was the degenerate descendant, Jonathan had no doubt. There was a streak of rottenness somewhere, maybe more than a streak—it might be that he was rotten to the core. That mouth, now!

The sight of a white cottage agleam against a black setting of pines far on the long flank of a browning hill drew a question from Edward Neill. "You have met my daughter, Mr. Maitland?" and he smiled his smile as he asked it.

Jonathan nodded. "I have, sir," he said briefly.

"To your sorrow, no doubt?"

The young man said nothing.

"I was afraid of it. That girl is a hell-born bitch . . . as was her mother before her!" Easily the foul word was spoken. The man seemed vaguely amused.

116

Jonathan stiffened. "You have said it, sir. Shall we change the subject?"

"As you please." The other spoke carelessly. "Admittedly family troubles are extremely boring to all save those directly concerned."

"That was hardly my suggestion." Jonathan was very short.

"Of course not! Your manners are above reproach."

A hot spark of anger kindled and flamed within Jonathan Maitland, a flame that took a deal of quenching. This man was the very devil to deal with. He had known that, of course: he had been told it often enough, but that didn't make the dealing any the easier. Small wonder that his daughter couldn't abide in the same house with him. Why on earth had the fellow wanted to join this expedition anyway? It wasn't for the sport—so much he had told them—and it wasn't a fondness for his company, that much was apparent. Tarras could have come alone, or at least could have been brought, introduced and left—there was no call for Neill himself to take part. What then? The man must have some object in view!

The man had. After a short spell in which the clippity-clop of the pony's hooves away to the rear alone competed with the garrulity of the river, Edward Neill spoke again. "I have heard that you have been suffering some . . . interference with your stalking, unwarrantable interference?"

So the blighter had heard that much, had he? Doubtless the whole country had heard, then! Jonathan frowned at the path and made no reply.

The other went on blandly. "Naturally, I was most distressed to hear of it, both in my capacity as proprietor and, shall we say, as head of the House? Anything that I can do to help, I will. Perhaps my presence here today may prove to be of assistance?"

"As a deterrent?"

117

"Hardly that, I'm afraid, deeply though I should like to think so," he sighed with mock humility. "But if I was to get personal confirmation of this interference, I could then take appropriate action to have it stopped."

"Oh?" His tenant was not noticeably enthusiastic.

Neill nodded, and spoke softly in that melodious voice of his. "Yes, I could take action . . . suitable action. Miss Barbara needs a lesson. By God she needs it!" And the black smile was as easy as ever.

The young man made as if to speak, changed his mind, swallowed hard and quickened his step, his hatchet-face set. He might have been happier could he have known that even then Barbara Macarthy Neill was carefully picking her way through the desolation of An Moine Liath, on the flank of the particularly cheerless expedition to Carn Garbh.

The Braes of Druie, a tumbled sea of small heather hills from the brown breasts of which were born the countless amber streams that went to form the headwaters of the Feith River, lay tranquil beneath the hush of midday. The quiet of the place was startling, uncanny, a brooding silence that lay over the country, undisturbed and undisturbable, a sombre calm that made the place its own.

It seemed to be a placid land, a smooth rounded womanly land, and not a landmark to the length and breadth of it. Just a succession of low brown hills gently rolling, and shallow open valleys softly sloping, and quiet unhurried streams smoothly flowing, with never a scar of scree nor a steep braeside nor even a solitary tree to break the mild contours of it all.

Jonathan Maitland, staring down into it from the shoulder of a steep sentinel hill, whistled. "The Land of Nod itself!" he muttered. "And an easy place to get lost in, I should say."

Edward Neill, at his side, assented. "Yes, a stranger would have no difficulty in losing himself in there . . . and I can think of pleasanter fates. Fortunately, I know it well, though it is years since last I came here. There are paths, plenty of them. Once there was a road. There were even a few crofts, a hamlet . . . formerly."

"But they went?"

"Yes . . . they went!"

Jonathan scanned the rolling expanse dubiously, and shook his head. "A strange place to find deer," he considered. "Roes, now! I could imagine roes haunting that quiet domain: but stags . . . ?"

"Admittedly, it is not typical deer-ground. For all that, some of the finest heads taken on this forest have come out of the Braes of Druie. Of course, it may be that we won't so much as see a deer. It's all a question of luck. Some days the beasts seem to like this place, others, they'll shun it like the plague."

The young man rubbed the jut of his chin with the back of his hand. "I think I can understand their feelings, too, the wise brutes," he said.

The other turned his back on the brown waves of that still sea, to scrutinise each ridge and fold, each brae and valley, that flanked the infant Feith. "So far, we would seem to have the ground to ourselves," he concluded, and it may have been only in Jonathan's imagination that the expressive voice expressed regret rather than satisfaction.

Lunch taken, they slipped down from their viewpoint into the strange stillness of that featureless territory. Edward Neill led the way confidently, with Jonathan only a step behind and Johnny Henderson and his sheltie close in the rear.

Soon they were on a fair path following the course of a subdued stream gliding over a level bed, and on many a muddy patch of that path were the sharp graceful imprints of pointed hooves.

"They've been here lately, at any rate," Jonathan found himself whispering lest he disturb the silence of the place.

Long they followed that path, which was joined by others small and not so small, and only once did it fork. Neill took the right fork without hesitation. He appeared to have a definite destination in view, and the young man, following in silence, watched and took such mental notes as he could. He had a good head for direction, and it seemed to him that they were trending steadily to the right—though that might be no more than a trick of the ground formation. Vividly he realised how difficult, how well-nigh impossible, it would be to cross this place in a straight line without the aid of a compass—or with one, for that matter. Down amongst them, the hills seemed larger and the valleys less shallow, successfully contracting every line of vision, and the general sameness was even more accentuated. Not once or twice but many times Jonathan could have sworn that they were moving in circles, and that they were back on ground already covered, only the paths, muddy after much rain, revealed no footprints but the neat tracks of many deer.

He gazed about him doubtfully. Their chances of spying deer here before they themselves were discovered seemed remote indeed. Yet Neill appeared to know what he was doing! He tapped the elegant shoulder in front of him. "The windcurrents in this place must be like the devil's circus," he pointed out. "We've probably presented our scent to every beast in the vicinity . . . if there are any. And even if they haven't all bolted, what chance have we of finding deer before we're bang up against them? This is like stalking blindfolded."

Edward Neill was patience itself. "Your anxiety is natural enough," he conceded. "This is not conventional stalking, but then this is not a conventional deer-forest. If it were, this piece of country would, in all probability, be a sanctuary. If the deer are here there is one place and one place only to look for them—at this time of day at any rate—a kind of natural sanctuary which seems to draw them. Mind you, we may rouse a stray beast or two anywhere, but that is a risk you must take in any part of a forest. The place I have in mind is not far distant now. If my memory doesn't play me false, we ought to be able to view it from just around the flank of that next hill." He gave a wintry smile. "You will have ample opportunities to display your undoubted stalking abilities, Mr. Maitland, if we see what I hope to see. I have no doubt that your patience will endure till then."

Those woman's eyes of his swept the gentle slopes that encompassed them. "No sign of interference as yet?"

"None!" Jonathan spoke dryly. "But then, the lady is far too good a hill-man to let us see her before she is ready for us."

"You would appear to admire the jade's—er—talents, Mr. Maitland?"

"I trust that I can admire talent when I see it without prejudice, sir."

The other raised his eyebrows. "Your magnanimity does you great credit," he mocked, and the advance was resumed.

Half a mile more and Neill deserted the path for the lift of the heather, signing to Johnny to wait behind. The two men climbed in silence and the shoulder of the hillock neared and levelled. Presently Neill bent double and so moved forward, astonishingly lithe for a man of his years. Jonathan followed suit, till near the skyline the older man flung himself flat, and the remaining few yards were covered belly-down.

On the ridge that was no ridge but only a gentle arching of the heather, they "froze," and Jonathan whistled soundlessly. Before them lay a wide grassy hollow, or more accurately, a green amphitheatre of the hills, strikingly green in the surrounding brownness, and as grateful to the eye as it was unexpected. Across it wandered a pleasant stream, which here and there widened out to quite a respectable pool that sparkled blithely in the intermittent sunshine. Beyond, a

121

small wood of stunted birches, all silver and gold, made constant warfare with the heather, adding the joy of its colour to that upland haven. But most noticeable of all was the manner in which those small round hills grouped around and hemmed it in, jealous lords of its green loveliness, their valleys radiating from the grass carpet of the arena like the spokes of a wheel. And the place was empty under the sky, save for the sad group of tumbled masonry in its green heart.

Jonathan turned to his companion, his eyebrows raised enquiringly.

Edward Neill, reaching for his glass, pointed to the far right-hand corner where a valley entered, slightly wider than the others. "Don't you see them? There, up on the sunny slope of that valley . . . dozens, scores of them."

"You mean directly behind that centre pool . . . over to the right a bit? . . . I don't. . . By Glory! you're right . . . a whole regiment of them! Snakes! What a sight!"

Neill watched the younger man's enthusiasm amusedly. "I am glad that your . . . patience has been rewarded," he said smoothly. "I don't think that you've seen the full extent of the herd, either. Probably there are many more out of sight farther up the valley." He got to work with his glass again. "I would suggest that we work round the back of those two hills to the right there, to see if we can't find some coign of vantage where you can single out your victim and consider your approach, and I can sit back in comfort and watch the sport."

Jonathan, sniffing the wind, agreed. "As long as we bear well over to the right, we ought to be safe enough, barring accidents." He paused, and then, "I must say you know your hills . . . and your deer, sir," he jerked in admiration if not in warmth.

The other shrugged those shapely shoulders and twisted that evil mouth into its smile. "I have already remarked on your magnanimity, Mr. Maitland," he said, and he led the way downhill toward Johnny Henderson and the pony.

Another hour, and, breathing heavily, the two men gazed down into the trough of the valley from the shelter of a quartz-grained slab of basalt, upended in lonely majesty on the smooth face of another brown hill. Below them the ground sloped quietly down and down to the burn in the floor of the glen, and, as quietly, it rose again on the other side. Halfway up that far slope and perhaps seven-hundred yards from where they lay, the deer grazed peaceably or lay at ease discussing the placid cud, though one or two of the younger stags chafed about restlessly. It was a great herd and loosely scattered. Fully fifty beasts, Jonathan counted, his heart thumping from more than strenuous climbing, and a goodly number of stags among them. And there were more further along in a dip of the braeside: he could see their heads.

Long he studied them judging and comparing, till Edward Neill snapped shut his glass. "There are half a dozen fair heads to choose from," he said, "though you would have difficulty in getting within sure range of most of them. You'll get at them from above and behind, I presume?"

Jonathan nodded. "The only other alternative would be to get into that burn-channel round this side of the hill and work my way down. Apart from the general discomfort and wetness, I don't like stalking from below if I can help it, especially in a valley where the wind-currents may play Old Harry with your scent. No, it's round the back and over the shoulder for me. There's a big beast that looks like a ten-pointer high up there: he's got some hinds with him, but if they remain more or less as they are just now, I think I'd get him." He stiffened suddenly and his glass quivered. "Ye gods!" He gripped the other by the arm. "D'you see what's coming out of that dip behind the main herd? It's pure white . . . a white stag, by all that's wonderful!"

"What!" Edward Neill's voice rose almost to a shout. He grabbed the glass and held it, shaking, for a moment; then he dropped it as though it had burned him. He turned, and Jonathan gasped in amazement. Never had he seen such a change come over a man. Gone the handsome sardonic features of the Macarthy Neill; instead, the wild terror-stricken face of a madman, great eyes starting out of his head, cheeks trembling, and mouth sagging loosely.

He started to his feet, his hands clawing at his throat. "My God! My God!" he screamed, and gibbering something in Gaelic he swung round and was off, stumbling, tripping, sliding down the hill past the bewildered Johnny, his shouts shattering the quiet of that silent land.

Astounded, Jonathan watched him go, watched him running, leaping, falling and running again; watched him, palsied with astonishment, till the little brown hills swallowed him up and the ghastly crying faded and was not.

"Lord!" The dark man found that he himself was trembling. Then of a sudden, he slapped his knee. "Snakes! So that was it! *Nan Daimh Ban*—the white stag! But what did it all mean, what could it all mean?"

He turned and looked out over the glen, empty now, empty as an empty church. So he stood for a moment, his face sombre, his shoulders slightly hunched, then he too left that place for the shadow of the valley.

IX

IT was long before Jonathan and Johnny Henderson found their way out of that brown wilderness. If they had not had their former footprints and the pony's tracks to guide them, they might be there still. As it was, long shadows from the early streamers of a fiery sunset were staining the heather a deeper purple before the kindly Feith River sang them the news of their release, and the open strath lay before them.

It had been a silent journey, with the one subject that occupied both minds not to be mentioned. Anyway, the Braes of Druie was not a place to encourage talk, but rather a deep ruminative silence, in reflection of its own abiding quiet.

In due course they reached the Lodge, to find the Carn Garbh party already in gloomy occupation. Peter Chisholm, that naturally cheerful soul, wandering on the short rough drive before the house, greeted them sourly. "Hail the hunter home from the hill . . . Hell!" He gestured toward the pony. "What's *your* excuse?" Evidently Peter had had a trying day.

"A better one than yours, anyway," the dark man countered easily. "The big brute I fired at was so thick in the hide that the bullet ricochetted back and hit Johnny here on the backside. So we've come back for a field-gun."

"Aye! And whereabouts did you bury your dead?"

"Eh?"

"Edward Neill! What have you done with the body?"

"He's not here then? Well now!" He turned to the interested Johnny. "Get along with you, youngster! That pony of yours looks as though it needed a real good rest after all it has done—and seen—this day. One thing, it can't talk. You're not a talker either, are you Johnny?"

"Me, sirr? Weel . . . no sirr!"

"Good! Well, here's a ten-bob note. See if it'll help you to keep your mouth shut."

Peter Chisholm shook a reproving head. "Shame on you, making the laddie an accomplice after the fact! How did you do it? With the rifle, or with your own hairy hands? Let's have the whole story."

He got it, and getting it his features provided a kaleidoscope of expression, patience, interest, concern, doubt, incredulity, and then toleration: in that order they succeeded each other, and the last was the logical reaction to the others. After all, the man was a lawyer, little though he looked it.

"Astonishing!" he said, the recital concluded. "Astounding! Man, you ought to have been a novelist."

"Meaning?"

"Just what I said. Your powers of description are . . . phenomenal."

"So you don't believe me?"

"I didn't say that," the big man protested. "Far be it from me to disbelieve you. All I was suggesting was that events which struck that supersensitive imagination of yours as momentous and sensational, might affect less gifted mortals—myself, for instance—as merely commonplace, or at any rate as capable of a perfectly normal explanation."

"So! And what perfectly normal explanation would you advance to account for Edward Neill's sudden departure, which Johnny can vouch for, even supposing I have let my supersensitive imagination run away with me?"

The other scratched his blond head. "Oh, off-hand I can't think up anything entirely appropriate. . . . Say he'd been suffering from toothache all day—like enough too, he looks as though he suffered from something mighty unpleasant, though that might be that daughter of his—and suddenly the pain gets too great, and he ups and hops it, clutching his face and hollering loudly?"

126

"Thereby very effectually scattering the deer that he'd spent over an hour bringing me up to?" Jonathan sighed. "You'll have to think up a better one than that, big fellow." "Maybe I will," Peter admitted. "But give me time, won't you? I'm no imaginer."

"You are not!" the dark man agreed. "And while you're waiting for an inspiration, you can give me an account of your own misfortunes this day. Gey bad they must have been to send you home in such a devilish cantankerous condition."

"Me, cantankerous? Man, if you want to see a picture of cantankerosity, go you up to the gunroom there, and take a look at that cross-grained old devil. Scarcely a civil word have I had out of him this day. He was bad enough on the way out—I don't suppose he spoke more than a score of words all the way, with most of them humphs and grunts. But that was volubility itself compared with what he was like on the way back, after both stalks had been a frost."

"The girl again?"

"Presumably. Mind you, we never saw her, but I'm positive that in neither case were we responsible for those deer taking fright. The first time it was the crying of a cock-grouse that did it—cleared a good corrie in a snap of the fingers. The second time we were sitting quietly in a peat-hole, a good six-hundred yards from a small herd, wondering over the best method of approach, when without warning they were up and off . . . and coming half towards us. I'm willing to swear that it was not us that disturbed those beasts. And Alec Macvicar was suspiciously unsuspicious, and too dam' philosophical altogether. Said it was all part of the game, a thing that might happen anytime to anybody, and so on, the old hypocrite. I said nothing, and I don't think Tarras suspected anything, though as I say, it didn't improve his temper. We didn't get another chance after that, so you can imagine the sort of day I've had."

Jonathan nodded sympathetically. "Pretty heavy going, I'll grant you. So the old beauty's up in the gun-room still?"

"Swilling our good whisky!" Peter Chisholm had no good word for the Colonel.

"Well, the sooner we get him dislodged and despatched back to Inverfeith, the better."

"Amen!"

"I should think Edward Neill may be needing him."

"Say deserving him," the big man amended, grinning. "Toothache and Tarras . . . Oh, Lord!"

The fiery sunset of the evening had kept its promise, and a sullen scowling morning succeeded a wild night of wind and rain. The guardian pines around the Lodge were still moaning the story of their night of anguish, their tears fast falling, when the decent silence of the breakfast table was rudely shattered by a hearty thump from the dark man's closed fist. "Peter, man," he cried, "why didn't I think of that before? There's something fishy about the Neill family."

"No need to smash the crockery then. I could have told you that years ago." The other was hardly receptive, but then, it was breakfast time.

Jonathan went on, unabashed. "You are a great scoffer, big fellow, but even you will hardly scoff at this. You'll mind it was you who told me of how Alastair Neill met his death . . . and what helped him to it? A white stag's head, I think you said?"

"Wheew!" Peter Chisholm's whistle held no trace of scoffing. "That is true. Queer, certainly . . . very queer!" He stared out at the glowering landscape, and his frown mirrored the frown of the hills. "But, hang it all, what could it be—I mean what connection can there be? It's a strange coincidence admittedly, but we've got to look at this thing like reasonable beings. It's our intelligence we need to use, not our—h'm—

128

imagination." He shook his big head. "But it's queer . . . all the same."

"It is all that, and it's more than a coincidence, that I'll be bound. It connects up with the rest: with the girl's preoccupation with the deer, with her suggestion that no good would come of stalking on these lands, with her mention of Corrie nan Daimh Ban, with her father's fury at the naming of those two words, and lastly with his panic at the sight of the white beast." Jonathan ticked off his points on his outstretched fingers. "Imagining apart, even your intelligence must perceive a connection between all these."

"Perhaps!" Peter Chisholm was not committing himself. "But what significance could they all have—unless it is merely a form of madness inherent in the Neill family?"

"It might be that. The Gaels are a queer visionary race . . . imaginative, if you like. Some of their folklore and traditions are mighty strange. Second sight, and all that. I wonder. . . ?"

Deliberations were interrupted by the arrival of Betsy Ellen, dishevelled as befitted the hour, and appalled at the news she brought. "He'ss back again . . . the chentleman iss back again."

"What gentleman?"

"The chentleman that wass here yesterday—him that the laird brought. The Cornel man."

"Colonel Tarras!" The two men exchanged glances. "And at this hour of the morning!" Jonathan turned to the girl. "Take him into the gun-room—we'll see him there."

"Yess, sirr. It wass there I took him." Betsy Ellen frowned confidentially. "He'ss at your whisky now, sirr," she volunteered.

"Is he, then?" The dark man was suitably grave. "This requires looking into. We will go now, before it's all done. Many thanks, Betsy Ellen."

Colonel Tarras, on the gun-room hearth-rug, wasted no

time on preliminaries. "Morning!" he jerked. "Neill . . . is he here?"

Their faces gave him his answer.

"Then where the devil is he? Been no sign of him at Inverfeith. Expected to find him there when I got back last night. You told me he'd felt unwell and decided to return alone?"

Jonathan nodded slowly. "That is so."

"Was he very unwell—fit to be allowed to come back alone?" The Colonel's attitude was distinctly censorious. "Damme, the man may be lying in a bog somewhere!"

The dark man chose his words carefully. "When he left me, he was certainly . . . unwell, but it was a mental rather than a physical disturbance, I should say. Not such as would disable him in any way."

The Colonel's luxuriant eyebrows shot up at the term "mental disturbance," but he let it pass—he knew the Macarthy Neill.

"Well, and what are we going to do about it?" he demanded.

"What is there to do about it?" That was Peter Chisholm, genially practical. "Captain Neill is perfectly able to look after himself. He knows these hills better than most people, I expect. He is rather a peculiar man, as no doubt you well know, Colonel, but because he had a strange mood on him, it does not follow that he was not quite capable of taking care of himself. I don't for a moment suppose that he would thank you for sending out search parties or organising rescue expeditions for him."

Tarras humphed. "Something in that. Strange, though—strange man."

"He may have stopped at some croft or other for the night," Jonathan suggested. "It was a wild night."

"You think so?"

"Well, it's possible, isn't it?"

"Humph!" That might have meant anything—or nothing. Jonathan eyed the meagre forehead, practically hidden by eyebrow, the washed-out eyes, the purple face and the fierce moustache over a sagging mouth, and decided that it probably meant nothing. "Strange man . . . strange man." Colonel Tarras seemed to have got into a groove. "Annoying! Going south tomorrow . . . most inconvenient."

"Indeed?"

"How unfortunate!"

Sympathetically the young men regarded him.

Tarras scrutinised the two faces in front of him doubtfully. "Humph," he said. He was rather good at humphing.

Conversation appeared to have reached a standstill. The Colonel frowned at the inoffensive heads of a number of somewhat dejected stags—he usually frowned at something; he was that sort of man. Peter Chisholm smiled amiably at nothing in particular: he was that sort of a man. But Jonathan Maitland was an imaginative man, and he merely looked uncomfortable.

"Well, well!" he said at last, hopefully.

The big man nodded his entire agreement. "Aye!" he said, and smiled again.

Tarras, of course, contributed a series of humphs.

This state of affairs might have gone on indefinitely. Fortunately, however, within Jonathan's dark head an idea was born. "We were just at our porridge when you arrived," he said. "Perhaps you will have a plate with us, sir?" He was very polite indeed.

"Porridge . . . me? No, sir, no porridge!" The Colonel, looking positively startled, moved toward the door. "Must be getting along now," he muttered. "Leave you to your—humph—porridge." At the door he paused to frown ferociously. "Morning!" he said.

"Good morning, sir!" And that was a chorus.

*   *   *

131

Peter Chisholm regarded his friend pityingly. "You will, of course, do what you want to do, that goes without saying. No advice of mine will even scratch the surface of your adamantine obstinacy. Nevertheless, my obligation as a friend remains. You will go to Buidhe Bheag and see this girl, but you will not go conceiving it to be your bounden duty, nor yet as an act of disinterested benevolence. You will go because you want to, and for no other reason. Heaven pity you!"

Pensively Jonathan contemplated the big man. "You are a great source of trouble to me, Peter Chisholm," he complained. "You are like a maiden aunt and a doting mother and a legal guardian rolled into one, with just a dash of the Salvation Army thrown in—the blazes of a thing to be hanging around!" He raised one eyebrow reflectively while resolutely-depressing the other, a trick his friend knew of old. "The girl ought to know of her father's disappearance," he reasoned. "She may not love him, but after all, he is her father. The least we can do is to acquaint her with the position."

"If that is all that's worrying you, all we need to do is to mention what has happened in Betsy Ellen's hearing, and Miss Neill will hear all about it soon enough. No need to go to all the trouble of walking there. As it is, I expect young Johnny will have spread some pretty substantial rumours about."

"Maybe so," the dark man conceded, "but not the sort they would care to communicate to Barbara Neill. This is an occasion for the personal touch, in my opinion . . . not just the thing to placard it to the whole neighbourhood."

The other shrugged. "The neighbourhood is probably well placarded already. What an almighty fuss to make over the mere fact that Edward Neill didn't come home last night! He's perfectly capable of staying away for a week at a time, visitor or no, from what I've heard of him. The man's more or less mad!" He nodded accusingly. "If it had been a son now, at Buidhe Bheag, instead of a daughter, there would be a different story to tell . . . you poor fish!"

Jonathan sighed resignedly. "Man, if you're so frightened for me, why don't you come along yourself and act as chaperon?"

The big man snorted. "Me? Not likely! One fool and his folly's enough to be going on with. Go you your own way, but don't complain afterwards that I didn't warn you."

"And you go to hell!" shouted the other as he took the road to Buidhe Bheag.

X

CROUCHING low under the long sweep of a long hill, Buidhe Bheag was a farm rather than a croft, and the shaggy black cattle and the shaggier black-faced sheep thereof, grazed precariously on six-hundred acres of its own heather and bracken.

A good mile off, Jonathan leant against the handrail of a venerable wooden bridge, looking . . . and wondering why on earth he had come anyway! Doubtfully he stared into the hurrying swollen waters of the burn at his feet, and he rubbed the jut of his chin with his closed fist. It had been well enough back at the Lodge . . . but now, with his destination in sight, he wasn't so sure. What was he going to say, and how was he going to say it—even if he got the chance of saying any darn' thing at all? He might have been better, much better, to have let things be . . . he was not cut out for this sort of thing, anyway. He never had been good at dealing with women, especially angry women. And that Barbara Neill would be angry he had no sort of a doubt. Hadn't he been manhandling her the last time they had foregathered? Gosh! It made him hot round the collar to think of that half-nelson he'd put on her. . . . Mightn't it be wise to go now while the going was good? Wise, indeed, and more than wise—were it not for Peter Chisholm, the great flat-footed oaf! He couldn't go back now. . . .

He lifted his eyes across the valley floor and the mile-wide lift of moor and rough pasture, to where the neat two-storeyed white-washed house and the tidy disarray of the steading cowered beneath the grey censure of the heaven. No figure moved, no sign of life other than the huddled cattle and the scattered sheep showed on the bare face of that long hill. She might be out—she might be out! Slightly cheered, he resumed his journey.

Head down into the chill wind he strode, keeping to the narrow grass-edge of the red strung-out pools that constituted the road, and his weather-worn raincoat flapped about him. A long straight stretch, a bend and a hill, and he would be there! The long straight stretch negotiated, the bend turned, and he stopped in his tracks.

She was coming down the hill towards him, a slim dark figure, outlined against the red of the road and the washed-out green of the hill, and the wind modelled her in its passing—as well it might. She was wearing a brown jumper today, close-fitting and shapely, and over it a tweed jacket, open, that might have been a man's; but the kilt was the same, and the spirit that swung it, also.

Meanly, the man waited while she came down the hill to him, the while desperately rehearsing his exposition.

"Good morning, Miss Neill!" he growled. It was unfortunate that the man always sounded most lion-like when he desired to appear most lamb-like. "Good morning!" she gave back coolly, and waited.

He glanced about him anxiously. "Can I speak to you for a moment?" It was a request even though it sounded like a demand.

"I see nothing to stop you," she answered him, and her voice was as remote as the spirit of the hills that surrounded them.

"Were you going anywhere? If so, I'll walk with you— that is, if you don't mind!"

"I was going nowhere. I saw you approaching, so I came to meet you."

"Now that was kind of you!" He was surprised.

"I came to meet you in order to spare Mr. and Mrs. Macarthy any unpleasantness. That is all."

135

"Oh!" Heartily Jonathan Maitland wished that he had turned back at the bridge—that he had never started at all. This interview looked like coming up to his expectations. "Do you mind if we walk on, just the same?" he enquired. "I talk better when I'm walking."

"Oh?"

He almost shivered at the frigidity of that "Oh." "Just that!" he nodded gloomily, and they moved down that road side by side, but a good yard apart.

"The deuce of a wind!" he volunteered, after a few moments.

She nodded.

"A wild night, it was."

"Very."

"The burns are high, too."

"I've no doubt." She turned just the fraction of a degree toward him. "Might I ask if you came to Buidhe Bheag to discuss the weather, Mr. Maitland?"

"No . . . not at all!" He looked about him miserably, seeking inspiration. Why was he so completely dumb when it was a woman that was to be dealt with? A weakness in his character somewhere. "There are no ptarmigan here, either," he complained.

She seemed to catch the implication, for her voice softened just a shade. "No, indeed," she said, and then pointedly, "nor, of course, an appreciative audience."

"Nor deer, nor eagles . . . nor collie dogs!" he gave back.

She started at that, and darted a glance at him. Jonathan smiled and felt much better.

"Look now, Miss Neill," he began persuasively, "how about you and me organising a sort of truce for the time being? Licked thumbs and white flags and so on, you know."

"Why?"

The dark man was satirical. "Just listen to the fire-eater! 'Why,' she says, 'Why have a truce? Why not go on

136

squabbling now henceforth and for ever?'—as though fighting was the life's blood of her!" He shook his head at her portentously. "Maybe it is, maybe it is, young woman, but for myself, I prefer to live peaceably with my neighbours, where at all possible." Jonathan was coming on.

She regarded him with a trace of astonishment. "Are you prepared to give up your deer-slaying then, Mr. Maitland?"

He grinned. "For today, at any rate," he agreed.

Treating that with the contempt it deserved, she went on. "I presume that you must have had some reason for coming here today?"

"Just what I was coming to," he assented. He was quite himself again now. "We were out on the hills again yesterday, as, of course, you know, and while you were . . . entertaining the Carn Garbh party I was at the Braes of Druie with your father. It is about your father that I have come to see you."

"Indeed?" She stared straight before her. "I'm afraid that I don't feel disposed to discuss Captain Neill with you, Mr. Maitland."

"Maybe not . . . but I'm not discussing, I'm just telling you." The big he-man. "Your father behaved very queerly yesterday. He got a fright—more than a fright—and made off in a hurry . . . and he has not been seen since."

He had her attention now. "What do you mean—a fright?"

Jonathan spoke slowly, deliberately. He did not want to provoke hysteria in another member of a strangely excitable family. "He saw something which affected him queerly. It was a stag—a white stag."

The sharp intake of her breath alone signified that she had heard him.

In the silence that followed, the man watched her out of the corner of his eye. Her face was set and pale—but it was always pale—and he got the impression that it was drawn about the mouth and chin. He could not see her eyes, but he

137

had an odd feeling that they would be like shuttered windows, looking inward only. At any rate, there was no sign of hysteria, for which he thanked all the hosts of heaven.

At last she spoke, her voice coming from far away. "So it is true—the *Laoigh Feigh Ban!*" She only breathed the words. "It is true . . . I knew it, I knew it always."

Jonathan Maitland held his peace.

"And after all this time!" She turned to the man. "Did you see it—this white stag?"

He nodded. "I saw it first. It seemed to be an old beast, a light coat gone white with age, probably—I've seen hinds gone grey before, of course."

Barbara Neill shook her head. "No, it was born white, that one, though old it certainly is."

Jonathan looked up in surprise. "You know it, then?"

"Yes, I know it—though I have never seen it. But I have known it always. It is strange that you should have been the first to see it. And Captain Neill—my father?" In her agitation she laid her hand on his arm.

It was the man's turn to stare straight before him. "When I pointed out the beast to him, he got very . . . excited, grabbed my glass to see for himself, then jumped up, shouting something in Gaelic, and ran off downhill."

"And you let him go?"

"I could do nothing else—I was astounded. . . ."

"Of course, of course! My poor . . . father." She seemed to have difficulty in framing the word. "That it should have come to him too. . . ." With an obvious effort she pulled herself together. "I don't suppose that you are a believer in the supernatural, Mr. Maitland? Probably you will put it all down to a streak of madness in our family—and you might be right, too. But it is a strange story."

They had halted in the lee of a larch plantation. Barbara Neill gestured towards a fallen tree just within the borders of that green wilderness. "Shall we sit while I tell you the

138

story?" she asked quietly. Strange that it should be the girl who suggested their sitting down together.

For a few moments she sat in silence, drawing lines and circles amongst the larch-needles with the toe of her shoe. At her side, Jonathan Maitland watched her busy foot, and waited.

"Over a hundred years ago, that stag was a little white calf," she began, "the pet of an old woman living in the sheiling of Gleann na Mallachd—it was called Gleann Raineach then, the Glen of the Fern. She was very old and reputed to have the 'sight'—some said that the deer-calf was her 'familiar.' Then, on the order of the Macarthy Neill, the glen—like the other glens—was cleared. You have read of the Clearances? Sheep were to make fortunes for the Highland landlords—though the land was not the chief's, it was the clan's. Elspeth Macarthy objected to being evicted, objected violently but unprofitably. The eviction went on, with the young chief, the Edward Neill of that day, looking on. Her roof was fired, and she, either by accident or design, was within when it fell. They say her screaming was heard at Inverfeith!" Barbara Neill, looking away into the feathery confusion of the larch-wood, shivered. "They thought that she was dead when they lifted her out, but she had a spark of life left, enough to curse Edward Neill and his House and his glen all the days of the *Laoigh Feigh Ban*, the white deer-calf. The young chief was the first to go—his pistol burst and killed him as he fired at the calf, thinking to end the curse there and then. There have been others, so many others, down to my grandfather, my uncle . . . and now my father. . . ."

Jonathan interrupted. "Your father is probably perfectly well—why shouldn't he be? He got a shock, that's all."

She went on, heedless. "I have never heard of anyone who had seen the white stag—it may be that those who saw it, saw it too late to tell of it—but always I have believed in it.

139

That is why I taught myself to stalk—I tried to make this place a sort of sanctuary. That is partly why I was so angry at Captain . . . at my father's letting it to you. One day, I felt, the stag would come back, and then . . . and then I would kill it, kill it. It has lived long enough, that stag!"

Long they sat in the shelter of the green wood, busy with their own thoughts, while the slender larches nodded and whispered the story to themselves.

Presently the girl turned to her silent companion. "You have said nothing, made no comment on what I've told you, Mr. Maitland. Do I take it that you do not believe it all?"

Thoughtfully, Jonathan answered her. "There is no question either of belief or unbelief. I accept what you have told me—it is fact. These things happened . . . and I have seen the white stag and its effects myself. And whether these . . . misfortunes, and the stag are connected by aught else than, shall we say, tradition, the result is the same." He smiled whimsically. "Though you might not think it, I'm just a bit religiously inclined—an inherited weakness. I hold no brief for witchcraft and magic, black or white, but I would never deny the existence of evil spirits and the like. It is a strange story that you've told me, certainly, but I'd half expected something of the sort. Anyway," he concluded grimly, "it's high time that stag was shot!"

Barbara Neill produced the ghost of a smile. "We are agreed on that, at any rate," she said. She stood up, her shoulders thrown backward, with the air of one who, delaying no longer, must assume the burden that was laid up for her. "Thank you, Mr. Maitland," she said, "for coming all this way to bring me this . . . information. I am afraid that I hardly deserved so much consideration from you. I must ask you to excuse me now—I mustn't waste more time. Just where was it in the Braes of Druie that you saw the stag?"

"You will know the centre amphitheatre, the hub of the

whole place? Well, it would be in the glen—let me see, now—
the glen coming in on the extreme north-west, one of the
biggest and widest of those small glens, I should say."

Nodding, Barbara Neill held out her hand. "I think that
I know the place," she said. "Thank you again for your
kindness and your . . . understanding. Goodbye!"

"Wait a bit, wait a bit! Might I ask what you're going to
do?"

"I am going to look for my father." Simply she said it.

Jonathan nodded. "I thought so. And wasn't I at the
losing of him? And don't I know the way he seemed to
be taking? And aren't four eyes better than two? Well,
then!"

"But . . ." she began.

"No buts, please!" He was very firm. "I am in this thing
for better or for worse. It is my business too, in a sort of
way—aren't I the tenant of this place?"

Her small laugh had the suspicion of a tremor behind it.
"Are you not a little bit rash, Mr. Maitland? We Neills are
rather an unpleasant family to get mixed up with."

The dark man looked into those eyes, dark and deep as
any tarn of her own hills. "I will take my chance," he
observed enigmatically.

Finlay Macarthy had welcomed the stranger with the grave
dignity of his kind. A tall thoughtful man lean and greying,
he represented what was best in a type that was dying out.
Possessor of his own land, and descendant probably of some
petty chieftain, he would have been a man of some consequence in the old days. Now he fell, as it were, between two
stools; as distinct from the crofter on his rented holding, as
he was from the landlord from the South.

He had displayed no surprise at the advent of another
diner to share the midday meal. "Come you in, sir," he had
said. "If it is a friend of Miss Barbara's you are, you can be

141

sure of a welcome at Buidhe Bheag." A decent greeting for any man.

His wife, a still-saucy ample body from Caithness, had produced as if from a hat a royal repast of broth and cold grouse and pancakes, the while Finlay Junior was dispatched post-haste to Inverfeith to enquire as to whether the laird had returned or no.

Jonathan Maitland had done most of the talking at that meal, listened to by his gravely attentive host and smiling hostess and the great-eyed thoughtful girl. On occasion, given the necessity, the dark man could wax quite eloquent. It was a relief in itself to discover those dark eyes fixed upon him, the slender eyebrows neither fiercely depressed nor frigidly elevated.

After the early brief and unemotional explanation given by the girl, the subject of the Macarthy Neill was not mentioned. Jonathan gathered that the name would be but seldom spoken in that household.

The meal over, Barbara Neill disappeared on some business of her own, and the men took themselves out and sat upon the weathered wooden bench amongst the scarlet tropæolum at the porch. Hidden from the searching wind by all the bulk of the house, they sat and smoked in silence. And if once or twice the girl appeared at the door and stared down the road, there was not anything to be done about it. There was no sense in making a move till young Finlay returned with his news.

"That boy of yours has a longish road to cover," Jonathan said at last. "It will be all of six miles to Inverfeith?"

"It will, indeed, by the road," the other nodded. "But there is a short-cuttie the lad will be taking, a bit path that follows the base of Carn na Braithrean, yon green hill, and saving near on to a mile. It is a good path, too, if the Allt na Braithrean has not flooded it, good enough for the bicycle."

"The burns are high," the dark man mentioned. He gazed

down the shallow valley to where the squat bulk of the green hill lifted out of the reeds and the bog-cotton. "Carn na Braithrean . . . a strange name," he said idly.

"That it is, and a strange story it has to it, also." Finlay Macarthy re-lit his pipe. "As you will be knowing, it means the Hill of the Brothers, in the English."

"Yes?"

"Many years ago, before the glens were cleared, this valley was held by two brothers, Cailean and Seumas, of the Macarthys. They did not love each other, and the land was divided atween the two o' them with the march running down the slope of yonder green hill, following a bit burn that rose from a spring, the only spring there was to all that hill, for all its greenness.

"Seumas was a hard man and ill to be getting on with. On a hot day of a hot summer, with the burns and the bog dried up in the glen, and only the spring still flowing, the two brothers, each at the taking-in o' their oats, left off to climb to the spring to be quenching the fire of the thirst that was on them. Seumas it was that was first at the water, and hasting to drink, he gathered up a handful of earth, and just as his brother was coming up, flung it into the water. 'Now,' says he, as he turned away, 'you can be drinking your fill, brother.'

"Scarce would the ill words be out of his black mouth, and the offended spring was boiling in its fury at the insult that was put upon it, to bubble and sink and disappear, and leave that place dry as the rest o' the brae. And the bit grasses and cresses that were lining the sides of it were withering in the sun.

"On the way back it was, to his bit house on the far side o' the hill—you can be making out the traces o't yet—that Cailean found the stream, sprung out from under a great rock, where no stream had been before. As I was saying, there was no spring but the one to all the hill. So Cailean

143

had the water, and Seumas had to be going to him cap-in-hand whenever there was a drought.

"And to this day Seumas' spring runs only in the moist weather when there is no needing it. And the day that spring dries up, Cailean's starts its running. And that is God's truth!"

After a little, Jonathan spoke. "That is a strange story," he acceded, ". . . perhaps it is a strange country?"

"It is a strange country indeed," the older man agreed. "I know that, who all my days have lived in it. Some queer-like stories there are, told about these hills . . . and myself, I would not like to be denying every one o' them."

Jonathan nodded. "I think that the same thing applies to most hill-countries," he said. "Whether that is due to the hills themselves or to the people that dwell among them, or to some strange atmosphere that pervades both hills and people, I cannot say."

"More like it will be the land than the men, I am thinking." Finlay Macarthy stared over to where Beinn Buidhe thrust its imperious head into the hastening clouds. "I could be telling you a thing that happened to myself, if I will not be deaving you . . . I would not like to be tiring you, whatever."

"You will not, either," the other said.

"Go on, Fionnla Sean." Jonathan turned to find the girl at his side. Gravely he moved along to make room on that bench. She sat down beside him, and he felt the smooth warmth of her where leg touched leg.

"Near on thirty years ago, it will be, and me no more than a laddie of maybe two-and-twenty. On the way home it was from the sale at Inverness, where I had been at the selling of two-three stirks, and the evening coming down on the hills. I had in me just the whisky that had been necessary to the occasion, but I was in no ways drunk, and what with that and what with the good money I had gotten for the stirks, I was no' ill-pleased wi' myself and in the great hurry to be home with my siller and my story.

"The train had carried me as far as Kinauld, and I had eight mile of road atween me and Buidhe Bheag. Soon I tired of yon, and the road weary before me, and I made to cut across the hills, darkening as they were. There was no danger in it, for I knew the country like the palm o' my hand. For all that, a wiser man or me with a dram less inside of me, might have held to the road.

"It was one of those soft grey evenings, soft and grey as a cushat and it calling, and the month only mid-March. Good time I made of it too, till I was looking down and seeing the lamps of Buidhe Mor new lit, against the black of the hill. I made my way down into the valley and I took the bit path by the burn-side and followed it bravely. It was a longish glen, as these small glens go, and easy walking, and the head of it no more than the two mile from home. Dark it was, down in the valley, and stiller than still, and there were black shadows in it, for all there was no light to cast them. And I walked on through that glen, and I walked on and on, and in time my pace quickened and then I was trotting, and after a bit I was running and running hard—nor knowing why I was running either. And in time that was not to be told or reckoned in hours or minutes, I stopped, staring about me, and a doubt growing on me. As I was saying, it was a longish glen, two mile maybe from end to end, but it was near the middle o't that I had entered, and still it lay before me, for all my walking and my running—which was a strange thing. Mind you, I knew all that country and that glen, and there was no branch to it or side glen that a man might be taking and the dark confusing him.

"My watch out, and twisted and turned this way and that, and me with my nose touching it, made it just after eight, and more than two hours since I'd left the road. I took a grip on myself then, and set off again up yon burn-side. Doggedly I walked now, and I mind the reeds were rustling

145

and rustling at my side. There was no pleasure in that walking, and no content within myself either, and me wishing I'd brought some o' that whisky along wi' me, and in a bit I was catching myself looking behind me— nor knowing what I was looking for. And as I went I was aye peering to the one side or the other, trying to be recognising a landmark or two. But in yon shadows the glen was changed, different, and I knew none of it.

"I will not be deaving you with all the walking I did that night nor the running either—and I ran near as much as I walked. I will just say that it was a quarter after nine when I looked at my watch again, and me still in that glen, and sweat running off me from more than hard walking, and the burn still running at my side and the brae-sides rising steep on either hand.

"And some time after that a panic took hold o' me, and I turned and ran back down yon glen as though every fiend o' hell was at the heels o' me, till the necessity for getting out o' the place drove out every other thought, and I turned and rushed and clambered up the brae, wi' every step a struggle, and it trying to pull me back. Better far the bogs of An Moine than this glen and it bewitched. . . . Near eleven it was before I made Buidhe Bheag that night. The whisky got the blame o't, of course, and me sober as a judge—as many a judge anyway." And he smiled gravely.

"I think I could lead you to that glen myself," Jonathan Maitland said, out of the silence.

"I believe you," Finlay Macarthy agreed. He knocked his dead pipe against the heel of his boot. "But there is my boy, and his news with him."

"And I know his news," said Barbara Neill quietly.

XI

THE moor in all its rolling emptiness lay before them, bounded by all the round contours of the brown braes of Druie, and the wind in its inconstant vehemence was behind them, and they strode out the more valiantly for its urging.

Their path was one of a multitude that scored the heather, as generally unassuming and occasionally ambitious, and as persistently irrelevant as were its brethren, laid down by the quiet things of that quiet land for their own quiet purposes. But the girl held to the path's uncertainty with a certainness at which her companion could only marvel, and the brown hills grew nearer and browner.

The girl was not talkative, and the man respected her silence. Even Edward Neill deserved that much, surely! Not that he anyways agreed with the premature conclusion of her queer fatalistic attitude. To his mind there was no reasonable ground whatever to assume that it was her father's dead body that they were out to find, but that, obviously, was the girl's prepossession, a premonition admittedly not based on reason.

This much he did say. "A shock such as Captain Neill received, might conceivably affect the mind of an excitable man, such as he evidently is, but hardly the body. Loss of memory, or some other sort of nervous collapse, I should say, may be the worst results we have to look for."

"Perhaps you are right," Barbara Neill said politely, and that was all.

Later on, out of some sombre train of thought of her own, she spoke again. "You did not like my father, Mr. Maitland?"

Jonathan hesitated. "I scarcely knew him well enough for either like or dislike," he temporised. "We got on . . . well enough."

"I prefer you when you are honest," she told him, frowning. "You are not a convincing liar."

The man had nothing to say to that, and she went on in a strangely level voice. "You must think that I am a most unfilial daughter, Mr. Maitland; I am too, I suppose. I never had any real love for my father—he had none for me, you see . . . and he showed it. I have never known anyone who had a genuine affection for him—save one . . . and he killed her—killed her as surely as if he had shot her dead—as surely, but oh, so much more cruelly."

Jonathan watched a small fist clench and unclench itself, knuckles gleaming white. He did not interrupt.

"After my mother died, I could not stay with him—it was quite impossible. He was . . . hateful, hateful!" She turned to him suddenly, her attitude a strange mixture of humility and defiance. "But I embarrass you, Mr. Maitland? I am sorry. I am afraid I have let my tongue run away with me. I hope you will forgive me?" and he noticed the quiver of her lower lip as she said it.

Jonathan was very gentle. "I hope you will continue, Miss Neill. What you say explains many things that ought to be explained. You owe it to yourself . . . and perhaps even to me. There are times for silence, but there are also times for speaking. . . . And you are not embarrassing me."

"I am slightly over-wrought, I suppose," she admitted. "Perhaps I am a little mad, like the rest of the family—there was a strain of madness in them all, you know. It may be that my father was not entirely to blame for all his . . . faults. A lot of them were inherited, no doubt—a streak of cruelty has run through our house for generations, centuries—but with him it was developed into a fine art. If I had stayed longer in his house I should have killed him, or he me . . .

148

but he could not have killed me the way he killed my mother—I am of the Macarthy blood too, you see!"

Quietly she said it, and suddenly she was sitting in the heather beside the path, her face in her cupped hands, and sobbing as though her heart would break, great shuddering sobs that shook her whole slender body.

Jonathan stooped, hesitant, and then one arm was about those twitching shoulders. "My dear!" he said, and again, "My dear!" and he could think of nothing else to say.

So he held her while those dry rending sobs tore her, and before him was revealed all the pent-up anguish of a lonely aching heart, and the travail of a proud aching spirit. And if he could think of nothing to say to her, no words of comfort or consolation that would not be a mockery or an impertinence, his arm was strong and steadfast about her, and his grip was sure on her shoulder.

And after a while the sobs became less sore and less frequent, and the shudders lessened to an occasional shiver, and her trembling diminished and ceased, and she looked up from the refuge of her hands.

"I am sorry," she said. "Hysteria, I'm afraid . . . you must forgive me," and Jonathan sensed the struggle to control her voice. "What will you think of me, Mr. Maitland?"

That was feminine enough, anyway, and a healthy sign. The man answered her gravely: "Perhaps I had better not tell you that," he said, and he helped her to her feet and they went down that uncertain path together.

They looked out over all the gentle brown slopes of Druie, and Jonathan Maitland shook his head. "A mildly malevolent place that," he said. "I don't blame any man for losing himself in there, however well he knew it. You might wander in there all day and all the day before and all the day after too, and never win out of it. They are all alike, those small smug hills."

"There is a trick to it," Barbara Neill told him. "If you examine those hills you will find that the outcrops and loose stones, where they occur, are only on the one side—the south side. Why that should be, I cannot tell you. It can't be the wind or weather that has done it, for that would be the most sheltered side. Perhaps it has something to do with glaciation . . . I do not know. But I can find my way through them without difficulty—not that I come here often. My father knew them well, too."

"I noticed that. But don't you think that, suffering from the shock he had received, and in some sort of mental disturbance, he might easily have missed his way and lost himself among them?" And the picture that suggestion conjured up in his mind was far from pleasant—of Edward Neill, as he had last seen him, wild and haggard and shouting his fear, running up and down those teeming brown hills, up and down, up and down, through all the violence of the night, a lost soul in a lost land. An appropriate hell, indeed! An imaginative man, Jonathan Maitland shrugged his shoulders to disguise a shiver. "Don't you think that is the likeliest solution?"

She shook her head. "I do not think so," she said.

Presently she outlined her plan of campaign for his approval. "I think if we were to take a line between these hillocks and follow it up, each of us taking one side and encircling every hill that we pass, but always meeting again in the mid-valley, we should cover a lot of ground fairly economically, as it were, without overlapping. If we were to take that valley there, and work right ahead in, roughly, a westerly direction, it would bring us out at that central open space you mentioned—An Foiche Uaine it is called, the Green Meadow. Then we could work up and down from that centre—axis is the word, I think—and so cover most of this side of the country. I hardly think that we need search the far side surely it is unlikely that he would go in that direction! What do you think?"

"I think that is as good a programme as we could make."
He smiled at her. "You know, you are a remarkably practical
young woman for all your wild theories. I've noticed that
before, of course."

"Assuming that you mean that kindly, I thank you," she
returned. "We must be thankful for small mercies, musln't
we?"

"You said it," he answered her doubtfully, and in that
spirit they went down to their searching.

That was a strange way of spending an afternoon, and the
man did not altogether enjoy it, winding in and out and
round about those countless heather knowes, identical in
their featureless roundness, looking for he knew not what,
and seeing—nothing. No life moved on those slopes, no bird
flew in that sky, no prominence distracted the eye from the
brown sameness: the place was lifeless, inert, and the silence
that hung over it was uncanny and best left unconsidered, a
silence that was only deepened by the fitful sighing of a
forlorn wind among the heather. Yesterday at least, the sun
had shone, and there had been light and shadow to break
that undulating monotony.

Nor did he see much of his companion. It seemed as
though the hills on her side were smaller than those on his,
for each time that he arrived back at the inner limit of his
scallop-like progress it was to discover her disappearing
round the flank of the next hill, and a wave of the hand was
all the communion they had with each other. Once, indeed,
he ran all the way round his semicircle in order to make
sure of arriving first at that central aisle, but at the actual
encounter his eloquence had deserted him. There is, after
all, only a restricted range of subjects suitable for light discussion with a woman who is convinced that she will shortly
discover the remains of her father.

In course of time they reached the pleasant oasis of An

Foiche Uaine, and its fair greenness was a solace to the eye and a relief to the imagination. No deer grazed on any of its flanks today, and the pair of mallards down by the waterside had all the place to themselves.

The man and the girl stood for a while and stared gratefully at its gentle loveliness.

"It is a pleasant place, and unexpected," Jonathan said. "The Green Meadow—it is a good name, too."

"Yes," she nodded, "and in June it is greener than now, and that green turf is carpeted with wild flowers. It is lovely then, a lovely peaceful place."

"Peaceful it is," he agreed. "Strange, is it not, that the silence which hangs over all this brown wilderness should be harsh and inimical, while the same silence here is just a kindly quiet?"

"Yes, it is quiet, but it was not always so . . . and the starting of its silence was far from kindly." She pointed down to where, amongst the long grasses and the alders at the burn-side, moss-grown stones lay scattered. "Once, there was clachan there, a little community that lived its modest life among these quiet hills, and children's voices would bring peace out of your harsh silence. But it had to go . . . of course it had to go."

The man glanced at her, struck by the bitterness of her voice, and the expression in those dark eyes held his tongue for him.

"Yes," she went on sombrely, "well may you look! It was the Neills that did it, Macarthy Neill the father of his sept, he turned them out as he did so many others. He wanted their poor bits of pasture for his precious sheep, you see. So they had to go."

"It was hard," Jonathan assented. "But would they not have gone anyway? Not that generation perhaps, or the next, but before our day at any rate, your clachan would have been deserted, would it not? People would not live in a place

152

like this nowadays, cut off from the world. It is not only the Clearances that have cleared the glens."

"Perhaps you are right. Our people have lost their spirit—their soul maybe—and are more at home in their city streets than amongst their own clean hills, and the Gaelic enthusiasts enthuse from their suburban firesides. And so, call it cause or effect, their fine land is given up to the wealthy—er—sportsman from the South—like yourself, Mr. Maitland."

"That is where you are all off the rails, Miss Barbara Neill. I am not any kind of a wealthy man. My resources underwent a considerable strain to allow of my taking this forest." He shook his head at her, gravely reproachful. "And you doing your hardest to spoil things for me too!"

"That is unfair!" she cried spiritedly, and paused, biting her lip. "No," she resumed then, "it was myself that was unfair . . . you were shabbily treated. I am sorry, but—you know my reasons. And you were very rude to me, that first day."

"Wasn't I just?" he agreed, grinning. "I quite surprised myself." Seriously, he went on, "But I appreciate your reasons—now. You are an idealist, a visionary. . . ."

"Say a reactionary or a crank and be done with it," she interrupted him lightly. "Let us be honest with each other at all costs, Mr. Maitland."

"At all costs," he acceded. "And let us also remember who it was that made that suggestion." There might have been the hint of a threat in that.

And so they resumed the burden they had set themselves.

Sometime, as that grey afternoon was drawing into greyer evening, Jonathan Maitland paused in his deliberate going to and fro amongst those cheerless braes, to start and stare. Away over to his right, through a gap in the brown knowes, something had moved; he had caught the movement out of the corner of his eye. And in that lifeless wilderness anything that moved was sufficient to make a man start and stare.

He did not know what it was: he had not seen it—he had not seen anything corporeal—it was movement that his eye had noted. It was worth investigating anyway. It might be Edward Neill, still caught in the maze of that place. It might be only some forlorn beast on furtive business of its own. It might be the Old Man of the Hills himself. . . .

He slanted down and across the small valley and up the slope beyond. Near the round summit, where the heather was short and wiry, he threw himself flat and wormed his way forward. Before him lay a small valley, identical with that he had just left, as shallow, as featureless—and as empty. He might not have moved from his first position. It was strange, he had seen a movement there—he was certain of it, just as certain as he was that he had seen no other movement all that long afternoon. It was worth going a bit further anyway . . . he'd try the hill in front, and be damned to it!

And he did too, a repetition of procedure that was almost uncanny. From its bald head he turned away frowning, to stump disgustedly down the way he had come. The place was unnatural, bewitched! And then, of a sudden, he froze in mid-stride and sank curtly into deep heather. Blazes! So he'd been right after all . . . the old devil himself!

Down near the valley-floor, not two-hundred yards from where he crouched, a white form stood out amidst the browning heather, stiff, still and suspicious. The man groaned in spirit. Oh for a rifle! Ye Gods!

His back turned to the watcher, the old stag stood, his nose questing the air, his ears perked forward, a picture of aged distrust. And that he was aged was manifest in every rigid line of him. He had been a big beast too, in his day, and the great bones of him stood out through a hide that was worn bare with years and furrowed with a host of scars of ancient fights. And he was desperately thin, so thin that his great head and mane seemed top-heavy, quite over-balancing the gaunt back and bony haunches and the long skinny legs. But that head itself was held high, and there was no dimness in those bold eyes, and his sharp antler-tines gleamed wickedly. So he stood, alone in that disconsolate place, a grey shadow of the past, vigilant, a pallid hostile thing that was somehow indecent in its aged-ness. And the man watching, shook his head and cursed beneath his breath, while his finger itched for the trigger of a rifle. That beast should be dead—it would be much better dead. It might not be as old as the girl's story made out, and he wasn't going to credit it with any supernatural powers, but for all that, the brute was too old by far—there was something corrupt about it. Strange that it should have been given to him twice to see this legendary animal! The pity that Barbara Neill was not there to see it for herself . . . just as well not, perhaps, though she would not have made a scene like her father did, he'd wager on that. Bye the bye, she'd be wondering where he had got to—he shouldn't have run off like that without warning her. He had better be getting back . . . there was nothing to be done here, worse luck. But he would come back again, so he would, and he'd bring a rifle with him!

The man was debating as to whether he should just get up and walk openly on his way—which seemed a blatant sort of thing to do—or else attempt to creep away unobserved, when the aged stag took the matter out of his hands. Some wandering windcurrent must have told him its secret, for of a sudden he threw back his head, stamped fiercely, and turning, swept away into the fastnesses of that heaped-up solitude.

And Jonathan was astonished at the manner of its going. Somehow, he had expected it to shamble off stiffly, awkwardly, almost to hear the rattle of old bones—that would have been natural, suitable. But that smooth effortless gliding was unseemly, like a white wraith drifting over the heather. Assuredly that beast would be better dead. . . .

Hurriedly, Jonathan Maitland retraced his steps, skirting the hillocks this time instead of climbing them. Two of these knowes he had to pass, and he'd be back where he had started. And the sooner he was there the better. Barbara Neill would be imagining that he had lost himself!

This would be the place! He stared up and down those troughs in the waves of the heather. No sign of the girl! Strange! Perhaps she had gone on a bit before she discovered his absence, and was waiting farther on? Should he wait there, or try walking on a little way? How long had he been away? Ten minutes or so, perhaps . . . say quarter of an hour at the outside. She couldn't have gone far. . . . He'd stay where he was for a while anyway—that would be wisest. She might have found something herself. . . .

He sat down on the couch of the heather, and took out his pipe. A queer way of spending an afternoon, this! A wild-goose chase, with the Macarthy Neill as the wild-goose! Old Peter would have called him a fool for coming—he had called him a fool already that day. Maybe he was right, too. . . . All the same, he was glad that he had come—the idea of that girl in her distress wandering alone about this unnatural place on her melancholy quest, was hardly cheering. Not that his presence made it a picnic, but it would always help to dispel the sense of isolation, the feeling that she was entirely alone in her battle with fate—fate in the shape of a family curse. It was the least that he could have done in the circumstances.

It was a strange business to have got mixed up in, the sort of thing that was quite out-of-date and discredited in this practical age. There could be nothing in it, of course, nothing supernatural . . . he supposed. A biologist could explain it all away in a few sentences probably. Biologists and the like were good at explaining things away of course—they had explained away most of the Bible already. They would say that this business was all a matter of complexes and repressions, with maybe a dash of insanity and a slice of coincidence thrown in. Perhaps they would be right too. But strange things had happened in these hills.

Out of a brown study that matched the tone of his surroundings, he sat up. The dam' fool he was! This wasn't the valley at all—he was in the wrong place. He had been round the back of that hill when his eye had been attracted by the movement: it was the next valley that he should have made for—the colossal mutt!

He started to his feet and ran down and across and up, and over the shoulder of that next knowe, to meet a view that was an exact reproduction of that of a few minutes before, and that in respect of its emptiness also. He paused, perplexed. She wasn't there. The miserable place had opened its deceitful maw and engulfed her as it had done her father. He smiled ruefully. No doubt she had been thinking exactly the same about himself, too! The ruddy fool he'd been! What should he do now? He could always try using the brassy lungs with which an inscrutable Providence had endowed him.

He lifted up his voice then, and called loud and long: and that place swallowed his cry as it left his mouth. Thrice he shouted and listened and shook his head as the profound stillness absorbed his calling, and without impression. His voice was puny, insignificant against that dominant silence.

No cry answered his: there was no sound, no movement, no sign nor expression of life. The place was empty, inarticulate, soulless, and he was an intruder and foolhardy.

Presently he started up that valley that was no valley but only a succession of links in that vast network of braes and hollows. There was nothing else to do . . . she must have gone. But he went slowly, doubtfully, and as he went he called out regularly, dutifully, and once or twice he climbed to the top of a knowe, that length of vision might be his: but it profited him nothing—those hills were all unvarying, there was none higher than another, none stood from amongst its fellows as a coign of vantage: all that was to be seen was the hill's immediate neighbours and the hollows between.

After a while he stopped and turned. Surely she could not have gone farther than this! There was no good in going on. He had better get back to where he had last seen her and wait there—perhaps he should have waited there all the time, and let her find him instead of attempting to find her— she at least professed to be able to find her way about this wilderness.

So he retraced his steps—or hoped that he did—for he could not tell just how far he had gone, and so at which spot he should stop. There was no landmark, no prominence to distinguish one place from another—he could not tell if he moved in a straight line through that sea of hillocks, even if he was still in the right series of valleys. He could not tell for sure, but he thought that he was: he had taken all the precautions that he knew. Barbara Neill had said that any outcrops or loose stones would be on the south faces of the knowes. Probably they were too—but that didn't help him much now: he should have thought of that before this. Not that there was anything in the way of outcrops and stones to be seen hereabouts: heather apparently reigned supreme.

And time passed and a chill crept into the air and the light failed steadily, and as steadily grew the man's unease. Things did not look particularly cheerful, with darkness coming down and the girl still lost—or was it himself that was lost? Darned if he knew . . . himself more like. It rather looked as though they might have to spend the night in this mournful place . . . not a happy experience for any girl, and her alone. In fact it was the devil of a hole that he'd got her into—for it was his fault, his and that wretched stag's.

Maybe there was something in the yarn of its malevolent influence after all, the nasty brute! Perhaps she wasn't alone of course: maybe she had found her father. That wasn't a happy thought either—whichever way she had found him! At all events, his course was evident. He must carry on, up and down, shouting now and then in the hope that one or two of his cries would penetrate the barrier of that stillness, and she would hear and come to him and put him out of his misery. It looked like being one of those nights. . . .

Sometime that night Jonathan Maitland arrived at the green sanctuary of An Foiche Uaine, green no longer, but at least a shade less black than the surrounding blackness. And he was glad to arrive there. For an eternity he had been wandering vaguely, doggedly, almost hopelessly in a baleful mesh, a reticulate waste of small hills and small valleys, that had caught him and held him and confounded him in its grim network. He had been lost for a long time. The perfidious half-light had had its way with him, and he had strayed unquietly through an unreal land where hills were no longer everlasting, but transient, ambiguous, and unsure of their foundations, and valleys were strung-out pools of gloom that writhed and eddied in silent mockery. Therefore the firm levelness of An Foiche was as a quiet haven to a storm-tossed ship, and the smooth turf was grateful to stumbling feet.

He made for the tumbled stones by the water's edge—it seemed to be the obvious place to go—and sat himself down in an angle of the fallen masonry. The wind had dropped considerably but it still had a bite to it, and the night was chill. He would be as well in this corner as anywhere, with the wind behind him and the alders of the haugh and the long night in front of him.

The striking of a match for his pipe gave him an idea. There would be plenty of dead wood amongst the alders, and he was not so warm that he mightn't be warmer: a fire also was a cheerful thing—and it would give him something to do, to attend to: it might even act as a beacon to a girl who might stray to the edge of that dismal labyrinth sometime in the night. He hardly dared think of Barbara Neill. He had failed her damnably—but he could do nothing about it, nothing except to give an occasional hail into the blackness of the night—and pray that whatever pallid spirit brooded over that place might not harm her.

And those things he did, as in duty bound.

XII

BESIDE the glowing embers of a dying fire the dark man nodded, and the little puffs of woodash, raised by a wanton breeze, provided all the animation to that scene. So he did not see the slim form that materialised out of the soft blue-blackness that was An Foiche Uaine, to stand over him and his wan fire; nor did he feel the gentle re-adjustment of his old trench-coat that it might the more successfully withstand the challenge of the night air; neither did he notice the quiet replenishing of his fire from the store of the alders. Jonathan Maitland slept soundly.

It was the blaze and crackle of eager flames that wakened him. He stared at the fire owlishly, interestedly, surprisedly, to glance up and beyond. "The devil!" he jerked, and sat up.

"Not quite, surely!" There was protest there.

"Oh, it's you, is it?" He sank back in relief. "I thought for a moment that it was . . . your father. Your features are very similar, and this flickering light. . . ." Then as things came back to their proper perspective, he was on his feet, his hands outstretched to grasp her wrists, her elbows. "By Jove, I'm glad to see you!" he gasped. "What happened? Where have you been? Are you all right? I've been scared stiff about you!"

Barbara Neill smiled faintly. "Yes, I noticed that," she remarked.

He ignored her comment as irrelevant. "You must be tired—worn out—cold? See, sit down here, where I was." He had his coat off and around her shoulders. "It's quite comfortable if you lean back into that corner, and it's out of the wind." He brought some more dead wood from the alders. He was very busy. "Where did you spring from, anyway? I'm darn' sorry I was asleep—I can't have been asleep long—the last thing I remember was howling mournfully into the night for the ninety-ninth time and wondering vaguely whether I was fated to go on doing that henceforth and for ever more."

"Poor Mr. Maitland!"

Jonathan regarded her, the bar of his eyebrows uplifted reflectively. The drawn lines of her face, pale even in the glow of the flames, and the slight droop at the corners of her mouth told their own story. "You have had a bad time, Barbara Neill . . . and I have been no help to you," he said then, slowly. "You will be tired!"

"I am tired," she admitted, "tired . . . and hungry."

"And I have never the thing to offer you!" He shook his head at her. "You'll not be a pipe smoker?"

"I don't make a habit of it."

"I was afraid not . . . a pity!" he sighed. "What can we do about it then?"

"We can just sit here and be thankful that we are not . . . back there," she said, and she shuddered as she said it.

Jonathan nodded gravely. "Amen to that!" he said.

For a while she stared into the heart of the fire, and her eyes, dark pools in the pallor of her face, held nothing of happiness. Then she glanced up and spoke almost sharply, irritably. "But sit down, won't you, Mr. Maitland? You can't stand there all night, staring at me! No—over here, out of the wind. Here's your coat. . . . I have my own waterproof."

Obediently, he sat down beside her. "Keep the coat," he recommended. "You need it . . . you are cold—I saw you shiver."

"I did not shiver—I am not cold—I am all right." She did not look at him. "Leave me alone, will you? I am quite all right."

Jonathan opened his mouth, and shut it again. He had his moments of wisdom.

It was at her third or fourth quiver, that he leant forward and slipped the discarded coat over her shoulders again, and as he touched her she shivered once more, violently. Something about that shiver drew a frown from him. He bent over to look into her face, but her face was instantly, abruptly, averted, and the raised shoulder which she presented to him, eloquent as it was, did not tell him what he wanted to know. But he was not to be baulked. Deliberately he stretched across and took that firm chin in a firm hand. Furiously she resisted, but he was gently insistent, and suddenly she yielded and he looked into the deep wells of her eyes.

"So . . . crying?" he wondered, and some gentle spirit prevented him from adding "again" to his wondering. He slipped an arm round her and moved closer. "I have heard it said that a man's shoulder is a good thing to cry into," he suggested.

And she adopted his suggestion promptly, trustingly, as a child might have done, and over her dark head the man smiled whimsically. He was getting quite expert at this sort of thing. Given time and practice, he might develop into something in the nature of a parlour-sheik!

Swiftly, in a manner that was almost businesslike, she got it over. Jonathan was not sorry, either . . . though there was no need for her to retire to her previous position! He lent her his voluminous handkerchief.

"Is this the famous handkerchief that I was to be gagged with?" she enquired, and her smile, if wan, was a smile nevertheless.

"The self-same one," she was assured, but she accepted it for all that.

"I am ashamed of myself," she told him. "You will be thinking I make a habit of weeping . . . I don't really, you know!" She looked away into the obscurity of the night before she spoke again, and her voice was even and rigorously controlled. "I have seen my father," she said slowly. "I am afraid he is . . . insane."

Barbara Neill's version of the events of that afternoon did not make cheerful telling. In that brown valley amidst that brown uniformity, when Jonathan Maitland failed to appear, she had waited for him, waited patiently till out of the brooding silence a sound made her turn sharply. Behind her, quite close at hand, stood the Macarthy Neill, smiling at her. But what a smile that had been—and what a smiler. It had required only the one glance at that wild dishevelled parody of the elegant Captain Neill to discover the truth. Her father was mad! She did not dwell upon his appearance. Presumably he had been following them. He had not spoken to her; just smiled and smiled, and in a fashion that far eclipsed all his previous smiling; till in her horror and alarm she had screamed a scream that had died in a throat that was suddenly parched. His smile had changed to a laugh at that, a laugh which the girl did not describe but which her hearer could imagine, and so, laughing, he had turned and left her, running, leaping—and laughing. And she had followed him, impelled by some urge that was contrary to her every inclination and desire, in and out amongst those knowes, till eventually she had lost sight of him.

And then, like Jonathan Maitland, she had discovered the difficulty of retracing her steps in a land that is devoid of distinctive features. Not lost, since she could have found her way out of that wilderness or back to An Foiche Uaine, she nevertheless could not find the valley where her companion should be waiting. At least, she may have found it, passed and re-passed it, but no man waited for her there. Once or twice she had thought that she had heard cries, but whether they came from here or there or nowhere she could not tell—nor was she certain whose cries they were. So she had wandered, seeking, and finding nothing, and her perplexity had deepened to anxiety, and anxiety to dread as the conviction grew upon her that she was being followed. She discovered that she had got into the habit of swinging round sharply, and staring behind her. It may have been imagination. It probably was. Certain it was that she saw nothing, no-one; yet the impression had lingered. Once, during that grey evening, she had come out to this place of An Foiche in the hope that her fellow-wanderer might have reached its green haven, and it had required all her fortitude to turn her reluctant steps back into the brown desolation.

At that Jonathan Maitland had sworn ably, emphatically, but beneath his breath.

And after that, in the wicked uncertainty of the gloaming, she had lost herself entirely. She had been tired, and perhaps her spirit had failed her for a space, and she had been very completely wretched. She indicated that there had been an unpleasant interlude. In time, however, she had taken a grip of herself, and decided to attempt to make her way back to An Foiche just as quickly as she was able. And that she did—but not quickly; no word less aptly described her faltering progress through that sullen confusion. Then, sometime, she had heard a call, and then another, and a hasty scrambling to a hilltop had revealed to her a point of light. And that was all. She had been glad to see his firelight, she told him. And he had not been asleep long, after all!

The man regarded her, frowning and tight-lipped. He seemed to be at a loss for words. At length he spoke deliberately. "If you were a man I'd ask if I might shake hands with you, Barbara Macarthy Neill," he said.

Out of a long silence Jonathan Maitland spoke. "This won't do!" he said. "You are uncomfortable and you are cold. We will have to arrange things better than this."

The girl, hunched in her corner of masonry, shook her

165

black head. "I am very comfortable and quite warm, thank you," she asserted.

"The shameless liar!"

"But it's true!"

"It is not! You are stiff and chilled to the bone. It's obvious in every line of you. Something will have to be done about it."

"Oh?"

"Yes!" he nodded firmly. "We have still a large slice of the night ahead of us, and I don't want to have a corpse to take back with me in the morning. You're not anxious to contract pneumonia, are you?"

"No—o—o."

"Well then, I think if I were to take your place in that corner and you were to lean up against me, we could make the best use of the two coats and generate some warmth, with a certain amount of comfort thrown in."

"But I'm very well where I am, thank you."

"You mean you won't budge—you'd rather crouch there and shiver than do as I suggest?"

For answer, she nodded determinedly and stuck out her chin. She looked very much of a child squatting there in the flickering firelight, pale-faced and great-eyed, her arms clasped about her knees.

The man jumped to his feet, and his chin stuck out too, a long way. He could look very fierce when he liked—his face was built that way. "You may be one darned little fool, but I'm damned if I'm going to be another!" he barked. "Will you come out of there?"

She stared straight into the fire, and hunched her shoulders a little more, and clasped her knees a little closer, and compressed her lips a little tighter.

They were not so tight as the man's though, not by a long chalk. His were clamped. One step and he was at her side, to stoop and grip her beneath shoulders and knees; a heave,

166

a grunt, and he had straightened up, and she was in his arms, undignified but secure. He took no notice of her kicking and wriggling, nor of her protests. He kicked aside his trenchcoat, fallen from her shoulders, went down on one knee, and then sank back into the corner, his knees up before him and the girl held tight.

"Let me go!" she yelled in his ear, and her fists beat indiscriminately about his head and shoulders. "Let me go at once—you beast!"

"Shut-up!"

"Take your hands off me! I'll bite you!"

"Bite away!"

She did too, but not very hard, and the efficacy of her biting was interrupted by the flow of her invective. "You are a beast, a brute . . . taking advantage of your strength . . . a mean cad . . . you think that because I'm alone. . . ."

"Be quiet!" he said roughly. "I'm not going to abuse you!"

And that silenced her completely.

He did not relax his grip, and in a little she lay more or less quiescent in his arms. But he was not going to be fooled by any foxing tactics, so he continued to hold her tightly.

"Barbara Neill," he addressed her. "You have shown yourself to be both practical and courageous. Why act like an hysterical schoolgirl? It is imperative, tired and dispirited as you are, that you should get warm and stay warm—sleep if possible. And that goes for me too, if I may say so. I have no desire to make a martyr of myself. And don't think that I'm doing this out of any desire to cuddle you. I'm not!" He was very grim indeed.

He felt her stiffen at that, but she said nothing, and her face turned away from the fire he could see nothing of her expression—which was just as well perhaps.

He grimaced over her head at the unpleasant path of duty. "I wouldn't have thought you were a hidebound conventionalist," he added inconsequently.

167

Still she said nothing, and he looked down at her speculatively. With the toe of his shoe he stirred the sluggish embers of the fire and a flame shot up brightly. He looked again. Her eyes were closed tightly, as were her lips. She resembled a child expectant of a blow.

"Well, now . . ." he muttered doubtfully. If his hand had been free he would have scratched his head. This was hardly what he had anticipated . . . you can never tell with a woman. Perhaps he'd overdone it a bit—over-acted his part? Anyway she was quiet just now . . . better await developments . . . leave well alone!

Jonathan Maitland was not brutal by nature. On an occasion for ruthlessness he could, no doubt, rise to it, but it demanded effort and bred distaste—as now. But a man must do what he must.

Warily he watched the dark outline that was his burden. She had gone through a lot that day. She must be pretty nearly all-in . . . though there was more than a kick left in her yet, it would appear, the stubborn little minx! She was lying very quiet though, not a movement out of her. It was like clutching to your bosom a case of high explosives that was liable to go off at any minute . . . should have gone off before this. What was her game? Lulling him into a sense of false assuredness? He'd see about that! And he clasped her closer than ever.

It was rather a strange sensation, sitting there in the dark hugging this piece of young womanhood—that did not want to be hugged. Darned if it wouldn't be quite enjoyable—most enjoyable—if he wasn't waiting for her to explode the next moment. She just about fitted his arms, not too big and not too small—though she was no featherweight, and getting heavier every minute! It was her increasing weight that eventually made him peer into her face, and listen, head on one side. With his foot he again roused the apathetic fire. Great Scott! If she wasn't asleep? The poor kid.

A sudden revulsion of feeling came over the man and for a moment he hated himself. Then gently, evenly, he adjusted himself so that she lay more comfortably; softly he raised her head so that it was propped in the crutch of his arm, in-turned to his shoulder; quietly he stretched over and retrieved his despised raincoat and disposed it about her to the best advantage, tucking it in around her feet and legs and bringing the other end of it round her head and over his own shoulder. Then he eased himself back so that the stone-work behind him gave him the maximum of support, and was still.

The night was black as the pit around him. No stars looked down at him out of the obscurity of the sky. From over long miles of heather the wind came to him with a sigh that plumbed the depths of loneliness in its resignation. Once a disillusioned bird of the night called mournfully, hopelessly, and left the silence no less lonely for its calling.

Aware, the man sat and listened. The isolation, the apartness, of their position came to him vividly out of the darkness. They were alone, this girl and himself, alone in an uncaring waste, as separate from their fellows as though they occupied another world. And she was in his arms . . . and asleep. She breathed deeply, unhurriedly, and his arm about her rose and fell with her soft movement, and somewhere beneath his hand her heart beat steadily. And neither of these sensations was unpleasing! Her head, too, rose and sank gently with the motion of his own respiration, and a wandering hair tickled his nose and chin, so close was her head to his own. It was so very close, that dark head, and the mild fragrance of her hair affected him so potently, that it was extremely difficult just to sit staring out into the night. After all, when a girl's head—and a good-looking girl's head—occupies for a protracted period a situation just two inches below a man's lips, the obvious thing to do is to kiss it . . . sort of natural process. Not that he had any

169

intention of doing so, of course. Entirely out of the question in the circumstances, the girl depending on his chivalry and all that . . . darned silly word, chivalry—chevalrie—what the deuce had horses to do with it, anyway? Not that he'd be doing her any harm by kissing her hair: quite innocuous . . . and she'd never know anyway! All the same, there were things a man couldn't do . . . a man must have his standards.

She was warmer now, he could feel it . . . he was warmer himself: his warmth flowing through to her and her sending it back to him . . . mutual benefit society . . . pleasant idea too. Noble feeling this sort of thing gave a fellow . . . pillar of strength, and so on. What would old Peter have to say to it now? Jealous as a tom-cat. . . .

All the same, he'd be more comfortable if he was to ease down just a shade . . . that was better. Her head was nearer his mouth than ever now . . . just a fraction more and he'd be fine—no cricks in his neck, nothing digging into the small of his back. Good! Would she mind if he rested his chin on her head . . . probably not. He could scarcely do anything else in the position that he was in. A nice perfume her hair had . . . his lips were right amongst it now. No kissing, of course—standards again . . . nice hair . . . she wouldn't mind . . . she wouldn't mind. . . .

And An Foiche Uaine had the night to itself.

XIII

THREE or four times Jonathan Maitland had wakened throughout the interminate extent of that night, and always the girl was sleeping. It might be, however, that her sleeping was not entirely unbroken, for once he had discovered that his coat was rather more snugly tucked in round his back and neck than he had seemed to have left it, and that her left hand was clutching his right arm. He was not complaining, either!

It may have been at the fifth awakening that he made the discovery that he was alone in the grey world of early morning. He sat up, frowning, his head in a maze. She'd gone . . . done a bunk! But where . . . why? Of all the little fools. . . .

And then he saw her, beyond the burn and across the green-sward of An Foiche, running, and running hard. Astonished, he stared. What on earth was she running for . . . from whom? There was no sign of pursuit . . . where was she going, anyway? Had she gone crazy, like her dad?

The manner of her running was strange, too, leaping and jumping for no apparent reason, no steady trotting. Amazing! And then he smiled, he laughed, relievedly, blithely. Of course, she was running because she felt like running—to warm her up, restore the circulation, and so on. Good idea too—a spot of the same medicine would do him no harm at all.

Stiff and cramped, he rose to his feet, and the cold that had seeped into the very marrow of his bones made those first few steps an agony. But he carried on doggedly, and presently his joints loosened and his blood quickened, and

171

he was running, lumbering it is true, with every clumsy foot-fall beating violent time within his head, but running.

He splashed through the shallows of the burn, to turn back and, bending, plunge his head into the icy water, and the sting of it sent him on his way gasping. And gradually his stride lengthened and his footwork became lighter and the last vestiges of drowsiness cleared from his head, and he let out a great bellow that shattered the hush of that place as a stone shatters glass. The girl turned in her tracks at the shock of it, and looked and waved, derisively, challengingly, and resumed her running. And the man swore vehemently and charged in pursuit.

That was a great race she led him, across the dew-laden carpet of An Foiche, through the solemn reeds that bowed under their burden of moisture, over the indomitable heather that no mist nor dew nor rain could coerce, and up into the twilight of the birchwood, where the mist-wraiths lingered and the spangled spiders' webs made a clammy fairyland.

By Glory! That girl could run! Like a hind of her own hills she went, lightly, easily, without hesitation and with-out ever a stumble. No sluggard himself, the man following had his work cut out to keep his distance, let alone overtake her, and with every bound she went up in his estimation. A woman who could run, really run, not the usual leg-waving, arm-flapping, windmill-like business, was a discovery indeed!

He gained on her amongst the birches—probably she allowed him to—and once out in the open, and her heading downhill again through the dull-gold of the bracken, he was but some thirty yards behind. She had discarded her rain-coat and jacket, also, apparently, her stockings—which was wise, since they could not have remained dry for half a minute in that dew-drenched morning—and she ran untram-melled and free, a vision of grace and vigour. All of which the man saw and appreciated, and redoubled his efforts.

And then—at a place where the brilliant green of the grass and moss told its own story, she slowed up and paused and jumped to one side. And Jonathan Maitland was just in time to catch a glimpse of her smile, her grin of delight, as, like a charge of cavalry he was upon her, past her. Too late he saw his danger, as with heels dug-in to stop his career, he slipped, floundered, and fell with a juicy smack on to that sodden ground, scoring long weals in its bright green mantle in the process. Down he slithered, spread-eagled, till the silvery laughter that accompanied him was broken, drowned in the storm of his indignation. "You wicked little besom . . . you perishing spitfire . . . of all the heartless, unnatural lady-devils. . . ." He scrambled to his feet and strode up to her where she stood laughing, to grasp her by her two elbows and to shake her vigorously. "You ungrateful wretch!" he threatened her. "If I was to do to you what you deserve, you'd be a shamefaced woman this day!"

Between her shaking and her laughing and the breathlessness natural to her exertions, her rejoinder was barely coherent. "You look so . . . very funny . . . so purposeful . . . and so futile!" and she continued her unseemly mirth despite his shaking.

Jonathan eyed her sourly. "You ought to be ashamed of yourself, instead of standing there . . . giggling!" he reproached.

"I'm not giggling—I never giggle!" She was very spirited. "And don't you start heavy-fathering me! You're not up to it—it won't come off . . . especially with your face like a badly-worn nail-brush!"

"You are an offensive, unmannerly, young woman, Barbara Neill!" he told her. Dearly he would have liked to have repaid her in her own coin, to elaborate some defect in her appearance, but never a thing could he find to criticise. From unruly head to neat-shod if soaking feet, in her businesslike garb of jumper and kilt, she matched the freshness of her surroundings, and her eyes glistened as bright as any dew-drop. He acknowledged it ruefully. "The devil of it is, you look so dam' nice!" he complained.

She curtsied at that, finger to chin. "Thank you kindly sir," she said.

The man considered her intently. This was a new Barbara Neill. He had discovered that she could be, besides her apparent norm of reflective gravity, both frigid and fiery, austere and tender. But gaiety he had never associated with her. Perhaps, given happier circumstances, this might represent the real Barbara Neill? Perhaps . . . who can tell what is the real, the basic attribute of any woman . . . if there is such a thing? So he glowered at her out of his perplexity till she dazzled him with her smile and confounded him with the enchanting tumult of her breathing. "Come on with you then, you brazen minx!" he almost shouted, and led the way downhill.

And that was Jonathan Maitland, quiet man.

An Foiche Uaine proved to be an oasis to more than the brown weariness of the Braes of Druie. In the intimacy of its fair harbourage Barbara Neill laid aside for a space the burden of her cares and revealed a glimpse of the girl that might have been.

The place held the essence of an abiding peace, the more so in contrast with that still sterility that surrounded it which was the antithesis of all peace, and the brightening light of morning assured that its peacefulness should be fresh, vivid, as compared with the reposeful calm of the previous evening.

Jonathan Maitland, then, was in no hurry to desert its green hospitality—nor, perhaps was the girl, in her new-found levity of spirit—but peace, vivid or reposeful, is not proof against the pangs of hunger; and hunger, prosaic and compelling, held them both in its iron grip. And An Foiche Uaine, for all its liberality, could provide only spiritual

174

sustenance, so that human nature being notoriously material it was necessary that a move should be made, and quickly. Also there were other considerations.

"There may be some good folk rather anxious about the pair of us," the man pointed out. "My friend Chisholm admits that I can take a certain amount of care of myself—though if he knows that I am with you, he will consider me as good as lost anyway—but Finlay Macarthy will be apt to be worrying about his lodger . . . which is a pity!"

She glanced at him quickly. "I'm glad you like Fionnla," she said. "He has been a good friend to me . . . when I needed a friend. And he liked you too—I saw it in the way he spoke to you."

That was a pretty compliment and surely signified something more than the mere statement of fact. The dark man acknowledged it. "We might even have something in common, the two of us," he commented obscurely.

Carefully Jonathan scattered the remains of their late fire, and even brought up some dripping gravel from the burn-floor to cover the scar of the ashes. "Mustn't forget our manners," he explained. "This place deserves better of us than to leave a mess behind us."

"You might almost have the Highland blood in you, Mr. Maitland," she commended, and he was not displeased at the inference either.

Before they left that place the man turned and earnestly considered the niche of masonry that had been to them for shelter. "You will realise, of course," he said slowly, "that a man may sometimes have to say a thing which he does not like saying, and which he does not mean at all, the circumstances requiring it. Such a thing as might silence a woman when it was her silence that was needed." He frowned darkly at the unoffending stone-work. "A man would be glad if such a thing was not remembered against him!"

Barbara Neill nodded gravely. "I think I understand," she

said. "Perhaps I have a bad memory. The thing is forgotten." And that was all the comment that was passed on the events of that night.

Jonathan Maitland was not long in discovering that they had left more than the Green Meadow behind them. Almost from the moment that they turned their backs on that sanctuary, his companion's mood had changed, and as the brown knowes received them and confined them, the girl became the Barbara Neill of heretofore, serious, constrained, vigilant, behind the armour of her reserve. Nor could the man blame her, remembering his own despondency of the previous evening. Even now, on the top of the morning, it was not without its effect on himself. "There is something unholy about this place," he declared.

The girl at his side shook her head. "Not unholy," she said carefully. "Gleann na Mallachd may be unholy—this place is only unwholesome."

"Maybe you are right," Jonathan acceded, and they left it at that.

Neither of them was sorry when at length the land sank and levelled before them, and all the regiments of the braes stood ranked at their back. For the last half-hour the girl had been constantly turning and twisting and looking around her, scanning all the smooth slopes that had hemmed them in— nor was it difficult to guess the source of her anxiety. In the circumstances there was not much for a man to say, and Jonathan did not say it. Only the one reference did his companion make to her trouble. "I feel eyes watching me all the time," she said sharply. "It is foolish—imagination—I know, but it is not a pleasant feeling when the eyes are those of one's father."

And what was he to answer to that?

Ahead of them the sun was rising when eventually they rounded the last of those grim knowes, and faced the clean expanse of the moor, open-faced to God and man. On all the encircling ramparts of the hills the mist lay thickly, its obscure tyranny prevailing yet before a stripling sun, and only the rosy flush that infused its upper stratum proclaiming that its time was limited. Beinn Buidhe alone thrust its august head through the grey pall and smiled austerely to the eager sun. But all the trough of the moors lay clear and distinct beneath the morning sky, each line clean-cut, each contour sharply defined, in the cold radiance of that early sunshine.

For a moment the man and the woman stood still, speechless before the widespread immensity of that view, after the constriction of the land they had left. It was like entering a new world, fresh, essential and alive. Already the larks were shouting their light-hearted challenge to the heavens, and the tumbling pee-wees cried and cried again—though no bird had raised its voice in all the Braes of Druie. Out on the moor, near a group of stunted birches, three roes grazed and skipped and stared, vigorous grace in every line of them, fresh as the morning itself. Even at their feet life was busy, as the ants hurried to and fro about their urgent affairs. "Lord!" the man muttered, "I don't believe I even saw a blessed ant back yonder!"

They crossed the moor by the twisting deer-paths, and all around them the things of the day were stirring. From behind a tussock a cock-grouse eyed them intently, neck outstretched, head perked to one side, ludicrously solemn, and out of a patch of reedy marshland an echelon of mallards rose with their stirring clamour, and the hares, blue ghosts of the uplands, lolloped erratically, apathetically, as is their casual wont. Once Barbara Neill pointed up to where a dark speck was engraved on the colourless plate of the sky. "A buzzard," she said, and with a grimace, "seeking his breakfast."

"Sensible brute!" Jonathan grunted feelingly. "But how do

177

you know it's a buzzard—the thing's barely visible?"

"Too large for one of the hawks or a kestrel, and too small for an eagle," she explained. She turned to him plaintively, "Oh, but I'm ravenous, Mr. Maitland!" she bewailed.

"I believe you! If you are anything like me, the walls of your stomach will be flapping together to the sound of a hollow booming. But why in the name of all that's wonderful must you keep Mistering me? Surely, after all that has happened, it's darn' silly!"

"Well, there's no need to be rude about it!"

"Rude? Rudeness is only comparative. I should say, now, that it was the height of rudeness for you to go on miscalling me Mr. Maitland, as though I was something you'd picked out of a telephone directory."

She stared up at her buzzard. "I think I have heard it said somewhere that a hungry man is an angry man!"

"Maybe so! In that case, perhaps you'd better walk ahead a bit . . . I'm getting hungrier every minute. I'll be unbearable presently."

"Undoubtedly!" She considered for a little. "So you don't like your name, Mr. Maitland?"

He shrugged his shoulders. "It's as good as the next . . . but I don't like it on the lips of my friends."

Barbara Neill gave him the gleam of a smile at that. "Thank you . . . Jonathan!" she said.

And that was that.

So they crossed the spread of the moor and climbed a long hill that looked down on Buidhe Bheag and its whitewashed house and all its green valley, and the morning was valiant about them. They paused at the wooden bridge over the Allt Buidhe Bheag, and the girl leaned, arms folded, on its weather-worn hand-rail and frowned into the swirl of the waters.

Abruptly, after a moment's silence, she spoke. "My father . . . what am I to do? I don't know what to do!" She turned to him, "A little while ago you called me your friend . . .

what can I do about my father?"

"There is not much that you can do—there is not much that it would be wise to do." He was very gentle. "It is probable that your father's . . . derangement is only temporary. His obviously highly-strung temperament has received a shock that has unbalanced it, but in all likelihood it will return to normal very rapidly . . . in which case it would be a pity to do anything precipitate, don't you think? He would hardly thank you for it, afterwards."

"That is true . . . but the thought of leaving him like that . . . running . . . laughing . . . it's horrible! And he may starve . . ."

"He will not starve—even a deranged man will not allow himself to starve. Perhaps, though, you might warn your father's factor—and lawyer. They ought to know, I suppose."

She nodded. "And his friend down at Inverfeith . . . ?"

"Colonel Tarras? If you like, I will go down and see him myself and explain matters—if he has not already cut his stick. He seemed to be in a hurry to be off, did the Colonel. A useful pal to have!"

"I don't know him—but he sounds typical of my father's friends. You think that I should let matters be, then? Just leave my father to his . . . misery, and that white stag? It will not be easy, I'm afraid. . . ."

"He will not necessarily be miserable—the reverse rather, I should think, from what you've told me. And leave you that white stag to me—that's my pidgin." He grinned suddenly. "Hang it all, I'm surely entitled to some sport out of this forest!"

Anxiously she swung on him, her hand urgent on his arm. "You will be very careful . . . Jonathan? That beast is evil— hateful! It has caused so much sorrow already. Promise me that you will be careful!"

Surprised, he regarded her, and his smile was warm. "For that thought I will be careful—I will be circumspection itself," he pledged. "For all that, your *laoigh feigh ban* is as good as dead already, the brute! Now off with you up to the house and that great whacking breakfast that's due you. No, I'd better get right back to Buidhe—Betsy Ellen will be worrying how much porridge to make. . . . Goodbye then, Barbara Neill of the Macarthys . . . and don't go worrying about anything."

She gave him her hand. "Thank you!" she said simply, and went her way.

Looking after her, he called out, "Remember Buidhe Lodge is not so far away at all!"

"I will remember," she answered, and the man took his own road, and despite the hunger that was upon him he whistled as he went.

XIV

THAT day had been no better than the rest. It had been identical in its even lucklessness. Not so much as a glimpse, a sign, nor a trace, had they been vouchsafed for their encouragement, and the two men strode in silence through the gathering shadows, and around them, An Moine Liath brooded over the approach of night.

Jonathan Maitland, shoulders hunched a little, body forward a little, went half a pace in front, his rifle under his arm, trigger-guard resting on his forearm, stock beneath his armpit. The big man, walking long-strided, carried his rifle over his shoulder, army fashion, and his lips were pursed in a soundless whistle as he went. And on neither of them was there any sign of exuberance.

When he did speak, the dark man's voice held that quality, half-apologetic, half-defiant, such as might be expected from a conjuror who has failed to produce the rabbit from the hat. "We will get the brute yet—if it has not left the district altogether! That's the worst of an unfenced forest, a beast may cover half the country in a day or so. But if it has stuck to this area all these years, there's no reason for it suddenly to have cleared out. We've just been unlucky."

"We have!" the other agreed grimly.

"We may have been searching in the wrong place, of course. The Braes of Druie may not be its headquarters at all—it may have been just a chance that I saw it twice there."

"A chance . . . or a hallucination!"

"Have it your own way—scoffer!"

"I will! Tomorrow I go out after real deer—not phantoms!"

For a time neither spoke. Peter Chisholm had reason for

181

his sourness. Anyone who had spent three days probing the incivility of the Braes of Druie, and found only incivility, was entitled to be sour. They had quartered that strange country and its surroundings, losing themselves frequently in the doing of it, and they had scanned all the face of a covert land and seen nothing; no white stag, no deer at all, not even a crazy chieftain. They had been painstakingly thorough, they had used all the hill-craft that they had between them, they had tramped for leagues till their rifles had assumed the weight of cannon, and still the same rifles went uncocked. And Peter Chisholm was a practical man and a lawyer.

Presently Jonathan pointed over to where a group of Scots pines stood darkly out of the sea of the heather. "If we keep to the right of those, and up over that grassy rise behind, we ought to make Gleann na Mallachd," he considered. "It will be our shortest route."

"More spooks!" the other snorted, and they went on.

From the head of the long rise they looked down into the trough of the glen, a green trough filling with the lilac shadows of night, beyond which towered the dark mass of Carn Garbh, brown shot with green and the stark grey of screes, and all washed over with the blue wash of evening, save only the bare brow of the mountain flushed in the rosy regard of a sun that to the rest of the world was but a memory.

"And what do you think of that, scoffer?" the dark man demanded, and in his voice there was a note that might have been triumph, as though the subdued vividness that spread before them explained many things.

"I think it will be a fine day tomorrow," Peter Chisholm said, and he led the way downwards.

It was a still night and the sounds of the glen were peaceful sounds—the murmur of the burn, the tinkle of water falling over rock, the soft yearning sigh of mountain air, restless even in the stillness.

They did not descend right to the floor of the glen, but moved along parallel to it, perhaps mid-way down the slope, Peter Chisholm leading. "Brighter up here!" he said considerately. "Less likelihood of your getting the willies!"

Jonathan Maitland said nothing.

They followed a twisting deer-path along that braeface, leaping the multitude of its new-born streamlets, encircling the scattered outcrops and negotiating a host of tiny screes, and always the shadows were climbing. And presently the colour had drained from off all the face of the land, and the men walked in the grey uncertainty of the dusk.

Out of the silence Jonathan spoke. "We would be better down on the path by the burn-side," he suggested. "Better going than up here, in this light," and he slanted downwards on the word.

They were crossing a scar on the green side of the glen, a harsh place of bare red earth and bare sweating rocks and the gravel of screes, when it happened. Above, Peter Chisholm, confronted by the black bulk of a great outcrop of basalt, hesitated, thought to go round it, eyed the sodden ground at its foot where a burn-let issued, and decided to climb over it. A couple of steps, a hand put down to steady himself, another step, and there was an ominous creaking, scraping, rending, as with a shuddering crash the water-rotted igneous stone collapsed and disintegrated.

Jonathan Maitland, perhaps twenty yards below, startled by the noise, glanced up, to leap and scramble aside almost in the same movement, and so avoid by inches the cataract of stone that hurtled down. As it was, a lump of rock the size of his head caught him a blow on the thigh that nearly sent him headlong, and a variety of small stones and fragments beat a comprehensive tattoo upon his scurrying anatomy. But the main stream of the landslide passed him by and went roaring down into the shadows.

And Peter Chisholm went with it—for some distance, at any rate—tumbling, rolling, tossing, rebounding, amidst a hail of debris. Fortunately, heavy as he was and fast as he went, his career was not so speedy as that of the great pieces of rock, which rapidly outdistanced him, thereby considerably reducing the probability of his immediate annihilation. Fortunate it was also, that there were other outcrops on the flank of that hill, otherwise nothing could have stopped his headlong descent and his ultimate destruction—for the lower reaches of that slope were thickly scattered with jagged rock, the result and witness of many such avalanches. As it was, by the mercy of God and his own gyrations, he fetched up with a resounding thud against a squat boulder that took the shock and stood firm. And, winded and battered, he lay there gasping.

The dark man, rubbing his bruised thigh, picked his way down to him, his heart in his mouth. The body thrown against the back of that outcrop looked horribly still. Reaching him, he stooped over his friend, and their eyes met. The big man winked, grimaced, opened his great mouth— and said nothing. Jonathan stared. "Lord!" he said, and scratched his head.

The other panted. "Winded . . . bloody fool . . . hell of a . . . procession that . . ." and he contorted his face frightfully.

The flood of Jonathan's relief was not to be stemmed. "You great clumsy big-footed blundering idiot!" he roared. "Of all the careless devils! . . . Man, you might have killed me!" He knelt down and set his arm round the other's shoulders. "Any bones broken, fellow?"

Peter Chisholm groaned. "Every last one of them . . . I'm barely alive!" With the help of that arm he sat up cautiously, and his hand went up to his head "Ye gods!" he said.

Jonathan eyed him doubtfully. "Can you stand . . . or is it

184

to be one of Johnny Henderson's shelties? Here, try this!" and he worked round to the other's back and gave him the support of both arms. Leaning heavily and swearing suitably the big man rose to his feet, to gasp suddenly with a spasm of sheer agony. "Ouch! My ankle! Damned if I haven't made a job of it!"

The other stooped, and ran a careful and sensitive hand over leg and ankle. "Hurts, does it? . . . blast yourself! No bones broken, anyway . . . just a strain probably. It'll swell though—I'll loosen your shoe for you, and we'll put a wet pad on it down at the burn. Can you walk?"

His friend snorted. "With you carrying me as the alternative, I'd walk on my hands."

"You would so!" Jonathan agreed grimly. "Will we make a move, then?"

"Wait a minute—where's my rifle? It isn't here—I must have dropped it as I fell."

"Hang on a bit, then—I'll see if I can find it."

He returned in a few moments with the rifle, and silently handed it to his friend. Peter Chisholm, leaning against the boulder, took it and stared.

It was the other who spoke first, and his voice was harsh. "I'm sorry, fellow . . . rotten bad luck! It was a good rifle."

"It was a very good rifle!" Slowly he said it. "I was fond of that rifle . . . the sighting was well-nigh perfect. You'll mind it was with it that I shot that thirteen-pointer on Ben Dearg . . . and the twenty-three stone switch. The rest doesn't matter . . . but that was a good rifle!" Gently he laid it down in a cavity beneath the outcrop. "We will be going now," he said. "Give me your shoulder."

Warily, painfully, they worked their way down through the welter of the stones and on to the more kindly turf, and often the big man bit his lip and cursed softly. At the burnside he paused and looked backward and upward. "The end

185

of a perfect day!" he growled disgustedly.

Jonathan Maitland grinned maliciously. "Gleann na Mallachd," he reminded, "spooks. . . ."

And they went on through the quiet of the evening.

On the strath road to Buidhe they met Barbara Neill. The glimmer of her bicycle-lamp heralded her approach before the half-light surrendered her. "I was hoping I'd meet you," she told them. "I've been up at the Lodge, and got tired of waiting. You have had a long day, surely. Is anything wrong?"

"Nothing worth the mentioning. Mr. Chisholm here, met with a slight accident, that's all."

"It wasn't. . . ."

"No, it was not! Part of the hill collapsed beneath his weight back in the glen there . . . and can you blame it?"

"Your ankle, is it?" She gave Jonathan her bicycle to hold, and stooped and felt the leg with a light experienced touch. "It is badly swollen . . . it will be very painful? You oughtn't to be walking on it, you know."

The big man was very rude. "Having neither wings nor fins . . ." he began.

She ignored him. "Using it like that, you will have a thoroughly nasty leg by tomorrow. No more deer-slaying for you for a few days!" Maybe there was a hint of triumph in her voice.

Peter Chisholm barked. "Deer-slaying! Listen to her! An apt description, eh?" He addressed the girl impressively: "Miss Neill, we have spent three interminable and quite fruit- less days searching for an evanescent and entirely improbable animal rejoicing in the name of Laoigh Feigh Ban or some equally ridiculous title. We have achieved nothing, we have shot at nothing, we have seen nothing, we have only walked and walked—and you accuse us of deer-slaying!"

She was sympathy itself. "Poor Mr. Chisholm, three whole

days and no blood shed! No wonder you are bad-tempered—
man can be tried too hard!" She turned to Jonathan. "If you
like to wait here with the . . . casualty, I'll ride back to the
Lodge and get Johnny Henderson to come along with a pony.
That ankle ought not to be walked on."

"You will do nothing of the sort!" Peter roared. "D'you
think I'm going triumphantly back to the Lodge straddling
a miserable pony the size of an under-fed mastiff—like
Napoleon crossing the Alps? Not on your life!"

"Bear!"

Jonathan intervened. "Perhaps it would be a better plan
to get the car out? Can you drive, girl?"

"Not very well, I'm afraid."

"Well, I'd better go myself. I think I might manage that
bicycle of yours. Will you wait here with that big fellow,
and whisper sweet nothings into his shell-like ear? Being
lame, he's fairly harmless!"

"He would be harmless anyhow!" she retorted. "That sort
always are—all noise. . . ."

The dark man nodded. "You are a wise woman, Barbara
Neill," he commended. "I will leave you to it then, and may
Heaven be with you both!"

Peter Chisholm glared at him. "Deserter!" he snarled
venomously.

The girl laughed. "Do not be long, Jonathan," she called,
". . . and Mr. Chisholm in his distress."

"I will not, with Providence kind—I haven't been on a
bicycle for ten years," and he zig-zagged off into the night.

They sat down by the roadside, Peter protesting. "This is
silly, you know," he complained. "We might as well be
walking on—I've walked a fair distance already."

"You have walked too far already—I know something
about ankles. And you had a man to lean on then."

He looked her over appraisingly. "You're a fine well-set-up young woman yourself!" he hinted.

She returned his scrutiny evenly. "We will just sit here," she said, and that was decisive.

There was silence for a little. From somewhere down the strath, the mallards quacked sleepily in a water-meadow of the Feith River, and from nearer at hand an owl hooted twice. The man took out his pipe. "You don't mind?"

"Of course not!" She smiled. "Jonathan was trying to make a pipe-smoker of me the other day."

"Was he indeed?" Peter Chisholm stared at his pipe, eyebrows raised. Jonathan it was now, Jonathan this and Jonathan that! They were getting on. He'd have to be watching that black-browed friend of his. He might shortly be requiring a friendly clip on the ear! Our Jonathan's sometimes a darn' fool!" he said shortly.

"What man isn't?" she asked simply.

He laughed his great guffaw. "You have me there! What I mean is, Jonathan is a romantic, sentimentalist—despite his face. He is old-fashioned."

"I can think of worse failings—and what is wrong with his face?"

"Haven't you noticed? And he suffers from an imagination, also."

"He is greatly afflicted, isn't he? And you—you are not a fellow-sufferer, obviously!"

"I am a lawyer!" Peter Chisholm spoke with quiet dignity.

"Of course!" She looked away. "I am to understand then, that you, as a level-headed man of the world—as distinct from a credulous dreamer like your friend—do not believe in any supernatural influences or occurrences in our—the Macarthy's—history?"

He answered her carefully. "My contention is that such occurrences could—must—all bear a perfectly natural explanation. I can put no credence in curses and witchcraft and so on. And tradition is an astonishing factor—from my

188

legal work I know that. You've heard the saying, that a thing has only to be repeated often enough to be believed? That's a true word, too. And the Gaels are a highly imaginative race."

"But you will admit that strange things have happened?"

"Of course I do—and they will go on happening, and human nature being what it is, some poor fish will discern in each the agency of the supernatural. It's my considered opinion that if you take tradition, imagination, exaggeration, and coincidence—with a dash of morbid sensationalism thrown in—you'll find the answer to all your black magic."

"I wonder!" she murmured. That was all, but as she said it Peter Chisholm was struck, somewhere beyond his reason and his intellect, with a strange fleeting uncertainty, just the suggestion of a doubt. He spoke forcefully. "And as for that Gleann na Mallachd business, it's all bunk, rot! How could a perfectly normal piece of country exert a malevolent influence, or whatever it's reputed to do, all because of some old woman who's supposed to have died there a hundred-odd years ago? The thing's absurd!"

"How indeed?" she agreed.

"And to suggest that because I fell and twisted my ankle in that blessed glen, the place is bewitched, is sheer bilge, the evidence of a disordered mind!"

"Undoubtedly!"

To the man at her side, her compliance was only provoking, mortifying, nor was he sure why. "You are hopeless, Miss Neill—quite unreasonable!" he told her unreasonably.

She smiled quietly. "Perhaps I have a woman's distrust of reason—as such?" she suggested.

At that he shrugged his great shoulders despairingly. What use was argument against sheer pigheadedness? "It will be a fine day tomorrow, I think," he said heavily.

When Jonathan's headlights found them they were sitting a

little apart on that road-side bank, and the beauty of the night appeared to be engrossing them both.

The dark man surveyed them grimly. "I hope I am not disturbing anybody?" he said.

"You've been the deuce of a long time," Peter Chisholm complained tactlessly. "I—we were afraid you might have parted company with that bicycle."

"Desperately afraid!" Barbara Neill agreed demurely.

Jonathan looked from one to the other. "Well, well!" he observed and he shook his head.

The girl elected to sit in the front of the big touring-car, and Peter Chisholm, with a sigh of relief, sank gingerly down into the back seat and lifted his leg up on to the cushions. His body was one comprehensive ache and his ankle hurt damnably. "Drive gently," he pleaded. "It comes to me that the springs of this bus of yours were never up to much."

So they went slowly, and the sharp night air only ruffled the black tresses of the girl's hair as she stared out into the fairyland that the powerful headlights conjured up out of the jealous darkness. In that wedge of golden radiance every tree and all the lacework of its foliage, every serrated bracken-frond, every humble blade of grass, stood out sharply, outlined against its own black shadow, colourful, vivid, and now and then, from the edge of the gloom a pair of green eyes would catch the glare of the lamps and reflect them strangely. Once, an awkward hare, all legs and ears, dashed out into the brilliance of their path, faltered, made to turn back, wavered, and set off up the road, zig-zagging wildly.

"Silly brute!" said Jonathan.

"Just like you on a bicycle," said Barbara Neill.

At the Lodge, with Peter Chisholm safely, if querulously, disposed of, Jonathan came back to the girl in the gun-room. "That man is like a bear with a sore head," he announced. "He's up there licking his wounds and snarling. What did you do to him when I left you alone that time?"

Her brows puckered thoughtfully. "Let me see, now. We talked of a number of things. He told me a lot of very interesting things . . . and I told him one or two things too."

The man grinned . "Ah well, doubtless he asked for it, the big stiff!" he said callously.

They were silent for a moment or two, and when Barbara Neill spoke again, the tone of her voice had changed entirely. "I came to see you tonight to tell you the position . . . about my father. I have not seen him—no one has seen him, or I should have heard—but Finlay Macarthy tells me that certain of the crofters have been missing things—one a coat, others foodstuffs and the like—and they are beginning to talk. I do not like it."

"Of course you don't—you poor kid! D'you think it's got round—about your father, I mean?"

"Well, none of them have actually mentioned it to Fionnla, but then, they all know of his connection with me. The people down at Inverfeith are almost bound to be talking." She sat down in a chair suddenly. "It is horrible!" she whispered.

Jonathan stepped over and took her hand in his and patted it. "Keep a stiff upper-lip, Barbara Macarthy of the Neills!" he urged, and he sounded her name like a clarion-call, so that she looked up and even smiled a little. "Things are seldom so bad that they mightn't be worse!" That was masculine comfort, and poor comfort at that. He continued, "Your news at least shows that your father is alive and able to fend for himself. That's always something!"

She was slow in answering. "You will think me harsh, hard-hearted, but I think that I would rather have him dead than mad . . . running wild, stealing things from his own people." She drew herself up a little, with pathetic pride. "After all, he is Macarthy Neill!"

He nodded dumbly, and she went on, almost beseechingly. "You do not think me harsh, Jonathan?" With seeming

191

inconsequence, she added, "Always, he hated me."

The dark man standing at her side had a momentary vision of the strath-road and himself and Edward Neill upon it, and the smile on the other's face when he said, "That girl is a hell-born bitch—as was her mother before her!" and he compressed his lips tightly. His voice, when he answered her, was restrained. "I do not think you are harsh, Barbara Neill," he said.

She seemed relieved. "Thank you!" she said quietly. She stood up. "I am sorry to come bothering you with all this, but I feel so . . . alone. I have nobody. We are the last of the Neills, my father and just as well, perhaps! I had a brother, but he was killed in the War. I have to speak to someone."

The dark man spoke with a great gentleness. "You are not alone—no-one is ever quite alone. I told you I was apt to be religious. And I am your friend—you know that!"

"I know that!" They went out into the cool of the night, "I will be getting back, now," she said. "I'm afraid I just came for a little . . . encouragement. I went to see the factor, and the lawyer in Inverness. They have both agreed to let things stand, for a bit, though the lawyer was difficult to persuade." She gave him her hand. "Well, thank you again, for everything. You are very good." She smiled. "I enjoyed that run in the car, with the light so bright in front and the night so dark all round."

"It was very short. If you liked it, let me run you back to Buidhe Bheag?"

"But the bicycle?"

"We'll dump it in the back. There's room enough."

"And Mr. Chisholm, and the meal that's waiting for you?"

"Let them wait!" he gestured airily.

XV

JONATHAN MAITLAND'S ire was roused. "But I tell you, the brute *was* there, right under my eyes, on the outskirts of a big herd. There was no mistaking it—it stood out like a sheldrake among mallards."

"And you raised your hat to it and wished it Godspeed?" Peter Chisholm nodded. He spoke from the depths of an armchair, one leg outstretched in front of him and his sore ankle very much in evidence. "At any rate, you weren't uncivil to the creature—didn't interfere with it, or anything like that?"

The dark man eyed him witheringly. "You are very funny in your armchair, aren't you? Actually, I thought I had him, but. . . . See, it was like this." He got down on his knees on the floor, illuminating his explanation by demonstrations on the carpet. "I spied the herd from near the head of the glen—Gleann na Mallachd—they were well up on the east side of Carn Garbh, right out on the open hill-face, and plenty of them. They would be a good mile-and-a-half away then. I left Johnny and his pony well out of sight behind a spur of the hill and made my way up out of the glen and over the ridge, to get at them from the flank. The wind being almost due west, it wasn't too bad a proposition.

"When I got to within half a mile of them, I discovered a fault in the side of the hill which I could use, a sort of groove with no burn in it, which might take me to within a couple of hundred yards with any luck. But the fault slanted diagonally downwards, which would mean an up-hill approach thereafter and an up-hill shot. Naturally I wasn't keen on that, but there seemed to be no other alternative—the rest of the hill-side was as bare as a baby's bottom!

"Well, I got to the end of that fault all right, and had my first real squint at the beasts. Man, I could have danced a jig—there was my white devil not two hundred yards off, a bit apart from the main herd, but with a small group of hinds quite close. . . ."

"And did you?"

"Did I what?"

"Dance a jig! That might in some measure account for your non-success."

"A humorous bloke, aren't you?" Jonathan regarded the other dispassionately. "Goes with big feet and a wide-open mouth. . . ." Patiently he went on with his exposition. "Anyway, there seemed to be a fair chance of getting the white brute this time. The trouble was to get within a reasonable range—there wasn't enough cover on that brae for a decent-sized grasshopper, nothing but screes and blaeberries and dwarf-heather. However, after a lot of belly-scraping I did cover about another fifty yards, up to the edge of a widish scree of gravel, beyond which I daren't go. One hundred and fifty yards is a much longer range than I like for accurate shooting, but the circumstances were exceptional, so I decided to try a shot. My stag was standing with its head half-turned away from me, and three hinds were grouped pretty close round him. He wasn't in a good position, so I waited for a bit, hoping he'd move round. You know what it's like, waiting for deer, with your heart in your mouth and your stomach in your boots! I can't say I enjoyed it. I was crouched down flat as a pancake, trying to hide behind a blade of grass. I remember loading-up with the rifle held at arm's length in front of me, so as I would not have to raise my body. . . ."

Peter Chisholm yawned dramatically. "Why not have this printed?" he interrupted. "Call it the Saga of the Glen, or something of the sort!"

"Wait you! This is by way of being a confession. You'll not come between a man and his conscience? Well, then!"

Jonathan ignored the other's weary gesture of acquiescence. "I soon got fed-up with waiting. The brute certainly was moving away from me—and the range was a whole lot too long already. It was a risky shot at the best, and normally I'd never have considered it, but . . . well, I wanted that stag. So I settled myself a bit more comfortably and aimed just behind his skinny shoulder, sighting just a shade high—and pulled the trigger."

"Well?"

"Far from it! It makes me weep to think of it—I've never known the thing happen before. The shot never fired! A confounded bit of heather-stem must have got clipped in by the bolt when I loaded up, and was stretched right across the base of the shell. When I pulled the trigger the striker hit the blessed thing and only tipped the shell. It wasn't much of an obstruction, but it was enough to make the strike ineffective. I kept the empty shell-case afterwards—you'll see there are two marks on it, the dent of the shot I eventually fired, and just a scratch for the first.

"Man, I was wild! In my fury I jerked open the breech to see what the devil was wrong, and the snap of the bolt told those deer all they needed to know. I slammed the bolt back, and looked up just in time to see the brutes wheel round, heads up, the whole herd of them." He grinned deprecatingly. "It was a dam' fool of a thing to do, of course, but . . . anyway, I ups with the rifle and sent a wild despairing shot after that white brute. And I hit . . . something." He stared in front of him with great concentration. "I shot a hind!"

"What!" The big man nearly jumped out of his seat, game leg and all. "You killed a hind?"

"I did so! I told you this was by way of being a confession. Shot through the head. She went down with barely a kick. A young beast, too. . . . It was unfortunate."

The other was grim. "It was all that! We'll have to be

getting you an air-gun—you're a menace with a rifle." He was very solemn and quite unsympathetic in that chair of his. Unlike himself, Jonathan Maitland was not just a consistent good shot, but something of a wizard with a rifle. "You should have been down at the Feith River with me," he said. "You couldn't do so much damage among the fish."

"Like yourself!" The dark man got his own back there, for Peter Chisholm's basket had been empty. He went on. "I was in something of a funk. If Johnny Henderson had seen that piece of work, my name was mud. Even if he'd kept out of sight behind that spur while I was actually stalking, he'd be sure to come out for a look when he heard the shot.

"I charged down the hill, bent nearly double, dragging that hind by the back legs, and praying that young Henderson had lost his glass or gone blind or taken a stroke— anything, so long as he didn't see what I was doing. I got the beast down into the fault I told you about, and I set about burying it." He regarded his friend, one eyebrow raised, "Have you ever tried burying a large untidy object weighing perhaps one-hundred-and-twenty pounds, on a bare stony hill-side, open to heaven and earth, with nothing more than a penknife and your fingernails to help you— and an urgent desire that the whole proceeding should remain invisible to an interested individual only a mile away, equipped with a powerful telescope? Ye gods!

"Well, I got the brute sort of half-buried with a heap of stones and what-not on top of her. It wasn't a good job, what with one thing and another—over many legs and things sticking out—and I doubt the crows'll be at her by the morning. I have been thinking that it might have been wiser just to have left the carcase in the fault, as it was. It might not have been discovered for long enough, and it would be presumed that she'd died a natural death."

"Except for the bullet hole in the skull!"

Jonathan nodded. "It would be necessary to smash the

skull a bit, perhaps. I might have a go at that tomorrow—a pleasant afternoon occupation!" He shook his head sombrely. "I had the deuce of a job explaining things to young Johnny. I said I'd fallen on some screes—I gave him to understand that a cut on my hand accounted for the hind's blood I'd got on me. I said I'd completely missed my stag—which was true enough—and I said a deuce of a lot of other things besides. I have a kind of notion that that young man thinks I'm a pretty comprehensive sort of fool."

Peter Chisholm stared at the ceiling. "Out of the mouths of babes and sucklings . . ." he intoned impressively.

XVI

BETSY ELLEN, obviously intrigued, brought the word. "Finlay Macarthy of Buidhe Bheag iss in the gun-room, sirr," she announced. "He says could you be sparing him a word maybe?"

"I could indeed!" Jonathan jumped up. "What wind blew that wise man here, I wonder?"

Finlay Macarthy, grizzled and tall, greeted him, gravely polite as was his wont. "Good morning to you, Mr. Maitland! I will not be disturbing you?"

Jonathan held out his hand. "Not a bit! Delighted to see you. A fine morning, isn't it?"

"It is that . . . though there is weather to come, I'm thinking. It will be coarse by night, like enough."

The dark man assented, and waited.

Finlay Macarthy came straight to the point. "It is a favour I've come to ask of you, Mr. Maitland. Could I be having your permission to shoot a deer—a stag?"

"But you don't need my permission!"

"On your forest I do. I'm no poacher!"

"You mean you want a day's sport on Buidhe Forest? You are welcome to that surely, Mr. Macarthy."

"That is kindly said, sir," he acknowledged. "But it is not exactly the sport I am after. There is just the one beast that I would like to be putting a bullet into."

"I see! It must have been annoying you, surely?"

"Well . . . yes, that is the way of it. It has been annoying us."

"Indeed?"

"Just that!"

198

The two men eyed each other for a moment, then Jonathan laughed. "So you want to do me out of the pleasure of shooting my white stag, Mr. Macarthy? Considering it's the only one we've got, that's not very sporting of you!"

The older man looked embarrassed. "It is not that, Mr. Maitland. It is . . . well, it is not that at all," he ended lamely.

"You have seen the brute, have you?"

"I have not seen it—though I have heard tell of it. But this morning my son says that he saw a white stag when he was putting out the cattle to the high park."

"And you think that you can find it again?"

"Finlay Og will be keeping his eye on it, the ill brute!"

"So?" The dark man rubbed his chin with the back of his hand. "I wonder you didn't try a shot first and enquire afterwards," he said

The other narrowed his grey eyes to a smile. "Miss Barbara advised the same. But it is your forest . . . and I am no poacher."

"You are very anxious to shoot that beast?"

"I am, then!" He turned away to gaze out of the window. "I have a great liking for Miss Barbara," he said deliberately.

"You have reason," Jonathan acknowledged. He had a suggestion to make. "Look here, Mr. Macarthy, why not join forces, the two of us, and hunt down that brute together?"

The Highlandman hesitated. "It's sorry I am, Mr. Maitland. I am indeed, but . . ."

"Just as you like, of course!"

Finlay Macarthy looked uncomfortable. "You see, Miss Barbara was saying I was on no account to be telling you about that stag. She was not wanting me to be coming here at all."

"Was she not, the besom?" The young man shook his head sadly. "Who would have thought that girl would be a traitor?"

"She could no' be that, surely!" She had a champion there.

"It might be that she has an idea that there could be danger in it," he mentioned.

"Well, now!" Jonathan Maitland considered that—and was not displeased with what he took out of it. "And that is your only objection to my coming along?" he enquired.

"To be sure, it is!"

"Well then, the thing's settled. There's no need for Miss Neill to know about me."

The other had his doubts. "She is sharp, that one. I would not like to be facing her, and her angry with me."

"But need she find out? She's not on the hill herself, is she?"

"She is not. She is gone to Inverness—the lawyerman will be wanting to see her. But she will be apt to be hearing about it afterwards."

"Then you will tell her that the man Maitland refused you permission to stalk on Buidhe Forest unless he came along personally to keep an eye on you—the ill-mannered Southron!"

Finlay Macarthy nodded gravely. "And it would ill become me to be arguing with the tenant," he remarked.

"It would so!" Heartily the dark man agreed. "When do we start?"

"It is yourself that is tenant . . . and may the Good Lord be kind to me at the hinner end!"

They walked in a world that was bright under a fickle sun, and on every hand the hills stood out with a strange clearness, their vivid colouring alien to a land of washen-shades and delicate half-tints. The brilliance of that morning held a feverish quality that produced no elation, and over it all a fitful wind came and went.

"It is not just the best weather for the job on hand," Jonathan observed. "That wind will unsettle the brutes."

Finlay Macarthy, a lean figure in faded tweeds, nodded his agreement. "That is so! The light is ower bright and the wind treacherous. But we can but be taking the chance that is given us."

Slantwise, they climbed the long slope up to the watershed of An Moine Liath, and crossed that damp wilderness at its south-eastern extremity, and all around them the mountains were toppling in on them. Beinn Buidhe, Carn Garbh, Meallach Mhor, Creag na Lochain, they stood overwhelming, menacing, in the stark clarity of that morning, their aloof austerity exchanged for a threatening tyranny.

An Moine crossed, they circled the flank of Carn na Braithrean, the Hill of the Brothers, and descended into the valley of the Allt Buidhe Bheag. At the wooden bridge Jonathan smiled to himself about something, and asked, "She is keeping her chin up—Miss Neill—not letting things get her down?"

"She will not do that—but she is having a bad time. She has the gallant spirit, that young woman."

"I have noticed that. And she needs it all, too. This situation is anything but pleasant for her."

"It is damnable!" His voice shook ever so slightly as he said it. There was no doubting this man's affection for Barbara Neill. "You are her friend, Mr. Maitland—herself, she told me that—you would not be believing the hell that girl has gone through with that man that is her father. All her life he has been the hurt of her—but he has not broken her spirit."

"Any word of him—the Macarthy Neill?"

"No word!" His voice was harsh.

"You do not love Edward Neill?"

Finlay Macarthy spat. "That man is brother to the devil himself," he said briefly.

As they neared the farm a figure came running down the hill toward them.

"Finlay Junior," the dark man noted. "Let us hope he has not lost our stag."

Finlay Og had not. "The beast is up on the far side of Creag na Lochain," he told them. "It is in the bit we call the Corrie nan Bodach, and there will be two-three others with him. It will be an auld brute, yon!"

"May it be as auld this day as God meant it to be!" his father hoped piously. "Give me the glass, and run you up to the house for the rifle, Fionnla Og. We will be following the Allt na Braithrean up as far as it will be taking us."

The massive bulk of Creag na Lochain rose gauntly out of wooded foothills to the grim sterility of its triple summits, cradling between them the dark lochan that gave the mountain its name. It was a stern hill, sterner for the light of that morning, and its aspect was sombre where it was not forbidding. The brown of its face was deep brown, and its abundant naked rock frowned blackly at the raw wounds of the screes. Even the rushing shallow burns which scored its every flank were only leaden, where silver was called for. But up in the skirts of the precipices that guarded its three summits a number of small corries, green sanctuaries, divided by great bastions of rock, reproached with their charity the surrounding harshness.

In the lap of the largest of these corries, high above the hidden lochan, the deer were grouped, five of them, the ancient stag, a youthful staggie and three slim hinds. They took their ease in that secure harbourage, with all the land before their eyes, and the wind their friend.

From down amongst the last outposts of the birches, the men eyed them anxiously, their glasses roving. Farther down, where the trees were thicker, Finlay Og kept company with a sheltie and his own thoughts.

"It is a difficult place to get at," Jonathan grumbled. "From below or above the approach is equally impossible, and to get at them from either side will need the feet of a goat or the wings of an angel."

"Difficult it is," the older man agreed, "but maybe no' impossible." Carefully, yard by yard, he covered the environs of that corrie with his glass. "There are deer-paths among those rocks, paths and cover of a sort. It would be difficult . . . but we could be trying, anyway."

"If you think there's a chance. You know the country better than I do. It would have to be from this side, roughly a south-easterly approach, with the wind in the south-west . . . if only we could be sure of it. All that semi-circle of precipices will play the devil with the wind."

The other grunted. "It is the devil of a wind, surely— and the devil will maybe be looking after his own. He has looked after him well this long while. But the saints may be kind. . . ."

"Amen to that!" said the dark man, for all he was no Catholic.

"Our way then, will be back into the wood and along till the bend o' the hill is atween us and the beasts. Then straight up to yon shoulder below the first peak. That far shouldna' be difficult, but after that we will be having a crossing to make—a traverse will be the word—and a lot o' loose stuff under our feet." He scratched his head, tipping his old tweed hat forward over his brow. "And I would not just like to be saying what will be the way o't after that!"

Creag na Lochain was hardly a pleasant hill to climb, even for a man who enjoyed climbing hills. There was over-much loose stone about and over-many screes to negotiate. More than once, for all their care, the climbers' feet started small landslides which clattered ominously in the brooding quiet. "Have to be careful," Jonathan gasped, after one such slip. "I'll be ending up fishing, like my friend Chisholm, with a game leg!"

Both men were breathing deeply when they reached that shoulder, only some two hundred feet below the southern peak of the mountain. That morning, despite the fitful wind, had an airlessness about it that was of no assistance to climbers. They stood for a space regaining their wind. "Aye, that was steep," Finlay Macarthy panted. "I will be getting auld, I'm afraid."

"If that was the effect of age, I must be getting on myself," Jonathan told him. "You showed me the soles of your boots at every step." He cast his eyes over the spread of half a country that lay at their feet. "That is a view-and-a-half!" he said. "I don't think that I've ever seen it so clear. Those hills look as though they were engraved on steel."

"Ower clear it is, by far." He pointed out over the width of that vista. "See you yon great heap o' a hill, away beyond the low ridges o' the Monadh Ruadhs? Yon's Beinn Crochan, and fifty long miles away."

"Fifty? I wouldn't have said twenty!"

"Aye! It will be taking a storm to account for yon."

They were still out of sight of the deer when they commenced that traverse across a quarter-mile-wide slope of scree and broken stone and bare red earth. It was bad going, deer-path or no, with every step a problem in itself, yet cross it they must. Higher up was the menace of sheer black rock, and lower down they would be in view of the deer. A great ridge of naked rock, flying buttress of one of the precipices, hid them from the corrie and allowed them to walk upright, but one false step, one small stone-slide, and the game was up. Ten long ears would quiver to the sound and ten sharp eyes would focus on the cause and twenty pointed hooves would do the rest.

After a seeming eternity it was crossed, and the great bastion of rock rose in front of them. From its ridge they would see what they would see. They worked their way down till a small gap in the serrated edge above gave them all the assistance that they were likely to get. Finlay Macarthy led the way. "Watch you the nails o' your boots on this stone!" he warned. "If you were to be falling here, you'd not be stopping for a bit. These rifles are a damned nuisance!"

Jonathan nodded. "Lead on, Finlay Macduff!" he said.

Cautiously they climbed, with hands and knees and toes, making use of every crack and hollow and spur of the rock, feeling their way with outspread fingers, testing each foothold, using only the edges of their shoe-soles, and cursing the rifles, beneath their breath. There was but some thirty feet to that ascent, but they could have walked half a mile in the time they took to climb it.

The older man lay flat in the neck of the gap and waited for his companion to come up with him. He jerked his head eloquently and said nothing. They were looking down into a small corrie, green amidst grey, bounded by another buttress smaller than that they were on, beyond which the large corrie opened out. The deer, loosely scattered, were not more than three hundred yards from where they lay, and feeding peacefully. So far the wind had not played them false.

"Yon's a big ill brute!" the Highlandman declared. "No more than a rickle o' bones, whatever."

"He can move, just the same," Jonathan assured. "Barring a dose of lead, he's not done yet, that fellow."

The white stag stood some yards below any of the others, nibbling spasmodically, ever and anon staring warily outward and downward, almost automatically testing the wind with wide nostrils. Occasionally he scraped the ground restlessly with an impatient hoof, and once, as they watched, he scratched his rump with a sharp antler tine. And the dark man's pulse beat just a shade faster at the sight.

"How far will he be from that next ridge of rock?" he whispered. "Eighty yards?"

"A hundred, anyway—maybe more. But that will be as near as we will be getting—and us lucky!"

Jonathan examined the rock-face below them, down which

205

they must clamber, and the near slope of the corrie, all under the eye of a watchful stag. "Dam' lucky!" he amplified.

They were lucky, too. All stalking—successful stalking—must be an admixture of luck and skill, with so many factors outwith the control of the stalker. Of a sudden, restless or no, their stag sat down, his back half-toward them, his nose into the wind, and his haunches protruding gauntly. Perhaps the airlessness of the day affected him, perhaps the weariness of old bones was not unknown to him, perhaps his great head had suddenly grown too heavy for his wasted body. Anyway, why shouldn't he sit down, with all the stretch of the hill in front of him, and the stern black rock behind? The other deer grazed carelessly, all with their heads into the wind.

The men exchanged glances. Now was their chance. With desperate care they worked their way over the rim of the gap, and slowly, inch by inch, eased themselves down and along, their eyes ever on that white sentinel. Once, they froze, clinging to the rock-face like leeches, as the stag half-turned to scratch an itching flank with white-tipped antler. Leisurely he rubbed, nose up, head back, in an ecstasy of lazy gratification, the men hardly daring to breathe. Before he at length concluded his languid performance and resumed an upright position, the two stalkers were well-nigh frantic.

If their progress on the ascent of that buttress had been slow, their descent was funereal. Well it was for them that the west side of that ridge of rock, facing the prevailing wind, was more weather-worn than was the east; otherwise they could not have escaped observation.

It was with sighs of relief that they reached the grass of the corrie, with the deer still undisturbed. Making use of every fragment of fallen rock and every ridge and hollow of the ground, they crawled down that slope, flat on their stomachs. Fifty yards of it perhaps, and the mass of the other buttress would hide them from their quarry. It required careful stalking still, for all that, compared with that descent of the rock-face, it was mere child's play.

At long last, in the well of the corrie, safe under the shadow of the dividing ridge, they stood up and stretched their aching backs. Jonathan grinned at his companion. "Good work!" he whispered.

"No' bad," Finlay Macarthy agreed, "thanks to the brute for sitting down. That was real convenient."

Side by side they crept up to face the ridge, that was only a small obstacle after that they had just surmounted. For all that, the metal-shod stock of the Highlandman's rifle, tipping a point of rock and clinking musically, gave them a couple of anxious moments before they eventually pulled themselves cautiously to the brow, and peered over.

The scene was unchanged save that two more of the deer had sat down, and peace reigned on that mountain-side. The range was something over the hundred yards; long enough, but reasonable, with the marksman taking his time. All was well—except the position of the stag. From this ridge, only his head and shoulders were visible above an intervening fold of the corrie. For long the two men lay and surveyed the situation, before, by mutual consent, they wriggled backward and downward for a whispered conference.

"We'll have to wait for him," Jonathan breathed. "No sitting shots for me!"

The other nodded. "Standing, we'd have him fine from here. We'll no' can do other than just wait."

"He's a restless old brute, fortunately." The dark man was optimistic. "Maybe he'll not sit for long."

"Maybe no'—and then you'll be needing to be quick on the trigger."

"Or you will. . . ."

Finlay Macarthy shook his grey head. "'Tis your forest,

Mr. Maitland."

"But it's your stalk—it's your show altogether!"

"No . . . I will be your stalker, that is all."

Jonathan pointed to the other's rifle. "What for did you bring that along, then?"

The older man shrugged his shoulders. "It might be that it could come in useful."

"When I miss?"

The Highlandman looked his reproach. "You will be the grand shot, no doubt!" he averred politely. He was gravely obdurate.

"The tenant it is that does the shooting," he pointed out.

"To blazes with that!" Jonathan whispered fiercely. "Look here, we'll toss for it. Your cry—heads or tails?"

"Heads, we'll say, and a head we're hunting!"

"Heads it is! Your pidgin, Finlay Macarthy!"

The other rose. "I will be seeing he's still there," he said.

Jonathan followed him up. All was as it had been. He glanced at his watch. Nearly one o'clock—he had not realised that it was as late as that! He nudged the other, and pointed out the time. His companion nodded, and with great caution produced from his pocket some buttered scones, or more correctly, a mass of scone and butter, conglomerate but edible. The dark man contributed a slab of chocolate. They ate as they waited, and around them the silence was complete and unearthly, save when a lost wind moaned abjectly against indifferent rock and found no consolation.

Patience is a notable quality, with various forms of expression: patience in disappointment, in provocation, in tribulation, in perseverance, in inaction, patience that is mere passivity. Surely it is a high order of the virtue that is required by those optimists who stalk the red-deer on its own heather!

With the hands of his watch denoting that noon was past by the space of three-and-a-half hours, Jonathan Maitland

208

lay and stared at that scene with eyes that were half-closed and weary with their staring. To lie and watch a stag that you have hunted for days, for weeks, to watch it blink its eyes and snuff the air and scratch itself, to wait, tense, for its sudden movement, movement which never comes, to be within range with a loaded rifle at your side, and to do nothing; to wait for two-and-a-half hours and still do nothing, imposes a strain that is well-nigh intolerable. With every fold and contour, every hummock and hollow, every stone and tussock of that view indelibly stamped upon his brain, the young man stared, out of a head that ached furiously. He looked up now, at a sky that was filling up ominously with great masses of blue-black cloud, crushing the shrinking land beneath their weight, portents of Finlay Macarthy's coarse weather. He glanced at his companion as he lay motionless at his side, a grey figure that might have been carven out of the grey rock that bore him up. Once or twice he had thought that he slept, so still was he and so hooded were his eyes; only something in the tenseness of his carriage and the line of his chin proclaimed his vigilance.

It is at Jonathan Maitland's door that the blame must lie: he leant over and tapped the older man on the shoulder. "Let's have a swig at that flask of ours," he whispered. "The heck of a riot this, eh?"

The other nodded, and half-turning over, reached for his hip-pocket, Jonathan working his way backwards. Perhaps his whisper was hoarse after long silence, perhaps their motions were jerky in their stiffness, perhaps the devil was looking after his own! In that moment the white stag rose to its feet, in two movements, ungainly but rapid, and turned to stare right at them. Only an instant did he give them, his great eyes black against white, his ears forward, suspicious. Dropping his flask with a clatter Finlay Macarthy grabbed his rifle, threw it to his shoulder and fired, even as the stag swung round and was off. They heard the vicious smack of the bullet

209

against distant rock through all the echoes of the shot.

Before the same echoes had quite died away, another shot rang out, and the stag, loping smoothly, stumbled, fell, rolled over twice, thrice, and lay still.

"Got him, by Jupiter!" Jonathan shouted, the rifle still smoking in his hands.

"A grand shot, whatever!" The dark man felt his hand gripped warmly. "Wasna' mine a grand miss, too . . . ?" Scarcely were the words out of his mouth before the beast was up again to its feet, to stand for a moment as though uncertain, and then to hurry off at a shaky zig-zag limping run. "Mother o' God," he finished, "it's only wounded him you have!"

The other, his lips tight as a sprung trap, nodded, and said nothing at all.

XVII

IN silence the two men watched that stag till its unsteady running took it out of their sight. It had chosen a route for itself, in a long slant down-hill, with the valley between Creag na Lochain and the lift of Beinn Buidhe as its apparent objective. The other deer had bolted along parallel to the precipices till a beallach opened above them between the summits, and allowed their escape. For a moment, their slim grace was silhouetted against the sky-line before the hills engulfed them.

Jonathan Maitland spoke regretfully. "Only once before have I done that—wounded a beast. It is not a nice thing to do. It was a foolish shot, too risky, but . . ." he gestured with his hand, "well, there it is!"

"Good shooting it was, for all that, with no time for the aiming, and the brute running away from you. "He was a generous man was Finlay Macarthy, with his own shot a miss. "You have the good eye, Mr. Maitland. You will be following the beast up?"

He got his answer. "I will follow it to the gates of hell, if need be!"

The Highlandman got to work with his glass. "There will be the two roads it may be taking. See, it's turning into the glen now, atween this hill and Beinn Buidhe. That glen is the little more than a great corrie, rising steadily till it opens on to An Moine Liath. Yon beast, and it wounded, will lie-up in some peat-hag on the watershed, or it will circle round this hill and make for its sanctuary in the Braes o' Druie."

"Depending, probably, on how badly wounded it is?"

"Just that!"

"It would seem as though there was not much wrong with its running powers, anyway." Jonathan was rueful.

"Aye, but it will be losing blood, most like—and it doesna' look as though it had that much to lose! I would be suggesting that the one o' us should be following the beast down into yon glen—maybe it will be lying dead there, and its heart no' taking it up the hill to An Moine—and the other making for the beallach there where the other beasts went through, and down the east side of the hill, to cut-off the stag and him heading for Druie."

"Sounds feasible! Who goes where, then?"

"'Tis your choice, Mr. Maitland. You are. . . ."

"Yes, I know—I am the tenant. You have a confoundedly stiff neck on you, Finlay Macarthy! However, since it was me who wounded the brute, I'll follow it up. If you take the beallach and the far side of the hill, what about Finlay Junior?"

"Fionnla Og has eyes to him," his father said briefly. He glanced up at the sky. "I am not liking the look o' the weather. It is lucky we'll be, the two of us, if we're dry home this night."

"I shouldn't wonder!" Jonathan shrugged. "For myself, I'm not greatly caring, so long as I see that white brute dead first."

"Aye, so!" Finlay Macarthy held out his hand. "Good luck to you, then, Mr. Maitland, and watch yourself with yon stag—he is an ill customer. Myself, if I get him, you'll be getting word at the Lodge by Fionnla Og. And if the weather catches you on An Moine, watch you yon bogs like the devil himself!"

Jonathan gripped his hand. "All that I will do . . . grandfather! And watch your own self that you don't get lost in the Braes of Druie—if you get that far. Good hunting, Highlandman!"

And they went their respective ways, and left Corrie nan Bodach to tell the tale of its ravishing to its green sisters.

212

*　　*　　*

The young man slanted downhill between dark precipices harsh in their lofty domination, and the dark lochan, sullen in its profound introspection. Taking, as near as he was able, the line of the fleeing stag, he walked with his shoulders hunched and his eyes on the ground. It was not long before he found what he was seeking, great spots of blood, on which flies were already settling. The sight of it moved him strangely, and he quickened his pace.

Nearing the mouth of the glen, he went more circumspectly. It might be that the brute had only put the first spur of hill between itself and its assailants before collapsing, or at any rate, resting. From behind a rocky knoll he scanned all the reach of that glen, as far up as a bend in its course would let him, his glass moving methodically. It was dark in that throat of the hills, with the ground rising sharp and stark on either side, up and up to the high shoulders of Creag na Lochain and Beinn Buidhe, and it was bare of cover for aught but a rabbit.

Jonathan snapped his glass shut. There was no stag in that stretch of gloom—he wouldn't bide there himself if he was a stag, with his legs able to take him further!

He moved along that trench between the mountains on a twisting deer-path that accompanied a hurrying, shouting burn. Behind him the strange moaning wind came and went, hot and cold by turns, but more cold than hot. Now and then he passed a splash of dark blood staining the grey of stone or the brown of the path. This loss of blood must surely bring the brute to its knees eventually!

At the bend in the glen he made another reconnaissance. As Finlay Macarthy had said, the glen tailed away into little more than a large corrie that drove a ragged wedge into the plateau of An Moine Liath. It was cheerless, it was grim, and it was empty.

213

The man walked long-strided, anxious to be out of that place, and the wind in its sad caprice urged him on. Near its head, he climbed out of the glen on to a scarp of Beinn Buidhe, and making his way up to the ridge, stared out over all the rolling extent of An Moine.

Vast and desolate, the great moor spread before him, dead and colourless under the threatening sky. And the man, looking and looking, shook his black head as the hopelessness of his case dawned upon him. To expect to pick out a stag— any motionless object—in that sea of heather and moss and peat-hags, that fugitive's paradise, was quite out of the question. The proverbial needle in the haystack wasn't in it! Long he searched, for all that, before he turned his telescope on to the eastern slopes of Creag na Lochain. Of Finlay Macarthy there was no sign; a rampart of the northern peak jutted out into the watershed and hid what was beyond.

It was with a sigh that the man pocketed his glass and rose to his feet. It seemed hard to lose the brute now, with his mark upon it, his bullet in it. With the season nearly finished, and his return South only a few days distant, he might not have another chance—if the beast got over its wound. It might not: it might die in some peat-hole, and no-one would be any the wiser. He would have liked to have presented that white head to Barbara Neill . . . he would so!

And then he stopped in his tracks and sank down into the short heather. Below him, not quarter-of-a mile away, the white stag was moving, running with the strange unnatural gait of a wounded beast, running straight out into the open arms of An Moine Liath. Lying-up somewhere near the head of the glen, it had moved only when the man came into view on the ridge above.

For the next twenty or so minutes Jonathan's eyes never left that deer—once having strayed, he might never pick it up again. Straight as a crow's flight the stag ran, unswerving, undeviating, over broken heather and grass knowes, through peat-flats and moss-hags, across burns and bogs, at a queer shambling run. There was something uncanny about the directness of that flight. The man on the brae-side watched and marvelled.

Then, in time, something struck him about the line that the brute was taking. Right ahead of it, at the far rim of the moor, was a group of dark Scots pines—the only group in all that landscape. Of course—those pines were black sentinels at the head of Gleann na Mallachd. So that was the way of it!

He watched with the aid of his glass till the old stag had passed those stern trees and reached the grass slope beyond. It paused at the foot of that slope, as though harbouring its failing resources, and then slowly, deliberately, it mounted the rise, to stand for a moment outlined against the sky-line. Then it passed down into what lay beyond.

And Jonathan Maitland rose up again and squared his shoulders and slipped down into the emptiness of An Moine Liath.

The man would be, perhaps, two-thirds of the way across that trackless expanse when the out-riders of the long-heralded storm galloped upon him. Steadily the sky had been darkening, as the great inky clouds mustered and concentrated and compacted into one murky shroud which covered the earth as with a pall. Jonathan stumbled and nearly fell as the first blast of the squall struck him, a wild fury of wind which sent him staggering along, buffeted and breathless. Above the riot of its shouting, he heard the distant mutter of thunder. Then, sudden as a meteor, came the hail, a biting blinding onslaught of ice-fragments, so dense that visibility was reduced immediately to a matter of feet. His jacket-collar upturned in feeble protest to that slanting fusillade, Jonathan crouched in the lee of a bank of peat while the black grew white around him. Moving onward, it would have been the simplest matter to have floundered into one of those bottomless peat-pools that pitted the face of An Moine, from whose dark embrace there could be no return.

Abruptly as it had commenced, the hail ceased, and in the quiet that followed the man listened to the beating of his own heart. With the passing of the hail the wind appeared to have dropped entirely, and a tense breathless hush hung over the cowering hills. The stormy blue-blackness faded out of the lowering clouds, to be succeeded by an oppressive brown, sullen and repellent. Jonathan, glancing up, frowned and decided that he preferred what had been to what was.

He wasted no time. The sooner he was off the watershed the better for his further well-being. He was no fool to underestimate the dangerous possibilities of his position. Hurrying, frankly running, making the most of what he knew must only be a brief lull in the violence of the storm, he headed for the group of pines, and solid ground. He ran lightly, loosely, his body slightly bent, his rifle at the trail, his heels seldom touching the ground, and the ominous silence was close around him as he ran. Leaping from tussock to tussock, skimming lightly over the cracked peat-mud, dodging the brilliant green that cloaked treachery, jumping or splashing through a host of burns, utilising the security of the heather wherever possible, he sped, and the black pines neared and enlarged.

With the general tendency of the ground-level already rising, he swung round to an evil sound, the unquiet wailing of a tortured wind that came and went somewhere at his back. Behind him, Creag na Lochain and Beinn Buidhe were completely blotted out under a grey-brown curtain that rushed upon him, inevitable, inexorable. Jonathan redoubled his efforts, his breathing sharp and painful in the overcharged atmosphere, and before him those grim trees stood out sharply and the reaching of them became an obsession.

With only some four hundred yards to go the storm overtook him, and he went reeling and stumbling under the vehemence of the attack of wind and rain. In a moment he was soaked to the skin.

It was with a curious sense of relief that he reached the purely theoretical shelter of the pines, no longer sternly aloof in their isolation, but suppliant, groaning in the extremity of their distress. Clutching a swaying, straining tree-trunk, he stood panting, while the gale howled around him and the rain lashed his back.

It was some time before the man made up his mind to leave those ancient twisted trees to their own sorrow, and face the slow incline that lay ahead. He felt a noticeable lack of enthusiasm for Gleann na Mallachd in this weather, stag or no stag. How on earth was he to find the brute anyway, with visibility at something like fifty yards? For all that, he couldn't stay where he was all night, clinging to his tree like a shipwrecked mariner to his spar. He was weather-wise enough to know that this was no passing squall, but a first-rate dyed-in-the-wool rainstorm, that would see dawn at least before it blew itself out. He might as well go now as wait, and be damned to it!

He went, tripping and slipping, with the wind impatient of slow feet on heavy ground, and that grassy slope unsound with the soddenness of saturation. He had the feeling that the creation was liquefying about him, with him as ill-equipped for the situation as St. Peter.

On the ridge, with the deeper gloom that was the glen in front of him, he made no pause—he had no option—and headed downhill at once. He decided that he would be better on the floor of the glen with a path of a sort to walk on—he wasn't wanting any more rock-falls, and the conditions highly propitious. As for the stag, wounded as it was, it would be more likely to choose the line of least resistance.

He took that slant in a crazy hectic rush, largely involuntary, his progress a series of leaps and slides and lurches and glissades, his falls frequent, his pace unchecked thereby. So wet that it was a sheer impossibility that he should be wetter, he went, careless of all but his ankles and his rifle. He reached the foot amidst a hail of small stones and gravel, constituents of a small scree which he had dislodged, practically in its entirety.

Down in the valley the violence of the storm appeared to be even greater than on the heights. Constricted by the enclosing hill-sides, the wind swept down the glen as down a funnel, and the sound of its going was as the sound of a barrage of artillery, through which the hiss of driving rain prevailed as a sibilant menace. Added to the vicious uproar was the outcry of the burn, already in tumultuous spate, its turgid waters a thick murky brown in place of their usual clear amber.

Jonathan, pounded and out of breath, made the best speed he could down that clamorous glen, on a path that was glutinous where it was not submerged. And he did not enjoy it in the least. He would not be sorry to be out of that place. If it had been eerie before, it had now thrown aside its eeriness and become frankly hostile, inimical.

Presently, through rather than above the roar of the elements, he caught the sound of another roar, scarcely louder, but set at a different pitch. He faltered, till the wind and his will drove him on again. Instinctively he knew what that drawn-out rumble meant, the sound that is heard at a quarry after a blast, the ominous sound of falling rock. What had started that, he wondered? No man, surely, on a night like this . . . a sheep, a deer, his own stag perhaps . . . or just the shock of the gale itself on water-rotted rock? Either way, it did not make pleasant contemplation for a man at the foot, with an imagination. As far as he could remember, the rock-lined section of the glen extended only for little over half a mile on one side and even less on the other. After that, the trees started. All the same. . . .

It was not long before he arrived at a place where jagged rock lay thickly on the valley-floor, scattered over the path and in the burn, telling its own story. A hasty glance was all he gave to that grim debris. If his ancient stag lay mangled amongst that wreckage, it could bide there till he came back for it! He went on, and though, undoubtedly, he did not realise the fact, he trod quietly and he kept his head down.

At last he walked between tree-grown banks, and he straightened up again relievedly, with the risk of a cataract of stone descending upon him no longer to be considered. Almost as he did so, a sharp crack followed by a rending crash, from close-by on his left hand, pierced the general hubbub, as a tall shallow-rooted pine gave up the unequal struggle, and came down amongst its brethren and neighbours in confusion confounded. The man ducked again. ". . . and great was the fall of it!" he muttered absurdly. "Ye gods!"

After that, he kept well clear of the trees and close to the burn-side, but even there he was frequently struck by flying missiles, dead wood and twigs, small and not so small, caught up in the fury of the wind. He went on doggedly, since there was nothing else to do, but every time a tree crashed—and not a few crashed that night—he started. That was the sort of state he was in.

Where the glen bent sharply round a buttress of the hill, two trees had fallen across the path, one apparently having brought down the other, and the disorder of their tangled branches made a detour necessary. Jonathan had to climb some little away up-hill beyond the upturned roots, appealing mutely, wide-armed to a heedless heaven, before he could cross some boggy ground that was the secondary cause of the trees' calamity. Thereafter, he did not return to the path immediately, but continued round the bluff, at the same level, on what doubtless was a deer-path. He had started to descend when he stopped suddenly in his tracks. On the

219

path, not twenty yards below him, the white stag stood, head adroop, legs wideset, a pale shadow of evil. The bend in the glen must have carried his wind beyond it, and the din of the storm and his own detour had done the rest.

Even as he paused, the beast looked up and saw him. He felt, rather than saw the malevolence of those black eyes. Quick as thought he slipped the safety catch of his rifle and flung it to his shoulder. It was unfortunate that he stood on a slope that was little more than an apron of running water, over grass firm as a soaking sponge. He slipped as he pulled the trigger. As he fell, he saw the brute lurch, obviously hit, stagger, recover, and make off down the glen at a shuffling run. The man, with his rifle instinctively held out of harm's way, slid, rolled, and gyrated, and ended-up clutching a boulder, with his legs in the burn. It is unnecessary to repeat his comments thereafter.

As fast as he was able, he followed that stag. Wounded twice, it could not last long, unless the devil himself had granted it immortality. It had had the most amazing luck, certainly— he had told Finlay Macarthy that he would follow it to the gates of hell itself. It looked as though he might have to!

He blamed himself for that last shot. He had acted like a child in his excitement. He should have looked to his foot-work first—another second only, and he could have fired with confidence. Three times now, he had bungled, and he was not a bungler normally, not where shooting was con-cerned, anyway. After this he would have to confine himself to clay-pigeons!

Beaten, lashed, bruised, with the frenzy of the storm, he plodded on. He was tired physically and mentally. His body wanted only to lie down and let that rageful wind tear over him and past him and leave him alone. His head was hazy, in a whirl, desirous only of peace and quiet and the shelter of his own roof, with somewhere a pulse throbbing steadily,

220

insistently. But his spirit, the undefinable, unplaceable flame that was the man himself, burning brightly outwith the reach of wind or rain, urged him on after that stag. And since body and head knew that spirit of old, they needs must resign themselves to the inevitable.

With the glen opening steadily in front of him, he moved further from the trees, keeping close to the water's edge— close but not too close. The sudden collapse of a portion of the bank, undermined by the swollen waters, and practically at his feet, taught him his lesson. That glen would have him if it could, curse or no curse!

He consulted his watch. It was nearly seven o'clock. If he was to find that stag before darkness set in, not the dead lifelessness of the storm but the deep black of the Highland night, he would have to be quick about it. If . . . ! With the rain washing out any tracks or bloodstains that might have guided him, he could only carry on as hopefully as possible. There was this to it, that weak as it must be, the brute would hardly be likely to try and climb out of the glen, with the slopes, even here, fairly steep, nor to bolt back into the teeth of the gale. More probably it would keep straight on till it reached the open strath, where it must turn east or west, with the Feith River in front of it—east, most likely, since to go west would entail crossing the burn in its anger. On the other hand, it might lie low somewhere in the widening mouth of the glen, where it would be mighty easy to pass. And to think that he'd had the beast right under his rifle, back there. . . .

Half-running, half-stumbling, he passed the green mounds that had once been the sheiling of Gleann Raineach, and he saluted them gravely as he passed. Just ahead of him, and nearer the burn, should lie the ruins of Elspeth Macarthy's cottage. He had an idea that he would feel a better man when he was past that cottage. An imagination has its drawbacks. But he stopped before he reached those tumbled stones, stopped and then went forward again, slowly, almost list-lessly, as though he had suddenly lost his purpose, with only the gale urging him on. His rifle remained beneath his arm. Before him, only a few yards from the moss-grown masonry, and with his hind legs trailing in the brown waters of the burn, lay the white stag, the Laoigh Feigh Ban, home at last. It required no examination to establish the fact that it was dead. And the man who had killed it saw it and knew no elation.

Long he stood over that gaunt carcase, frowning, while the wind and the rain made vicious tumult around him, and he could not have explained the substance of his thoughts. At length he stooped, and gripping the spreading antlers he dragged the beast back till its feet were clear of the water and its head lay amongst the stones of the cottage. Then he turned wearily to pick up his rifle and follow the burn down to the Feith River.

XVIII

SOMETIME, out of the travail of that night, a new day was born, and with its coming, peace descended upon a bruised creation. When, in its own time, the sun rose over the eastern mountains, it was to look down upon a calm that was but accentuated by the sound of hurrying waters. All else lay tranquil under the lassitude that succeeds violent emotion. Even the waters had no urgency in their hurrying, with everywhere the apex reached and passed and the levels falling.

On the strath road, above the swirling sullenness that was the Feith River, the two men walked, casually, unhurriedly, and the dark man was not impatient of the other's limping. They went a little apart, their hands deep in their pockets, and behind, the clip-clopping hooves of Johnny Henderson's sheltie repeated and repeated that there was no hurry, no hurry in the world, for this or that or anything else, nor would there be ever again. From every sun-bathed hillside the droning bees sent the same message through the scented air. That was the kind of morning it was.

The big man sucked meditatively at an empty pipe, his eyes fixed on the distant unsubstantial line, hazy and colourless, that blocked the mouth of the strath and was the rampart of the mighty Cairngorms. From his expression it would be hard to guess the drift of his thoughts, if he thought at all, with his frown only his eyes' acknowledgement of the sun's shining. His companion did not frown: perhaps the black band of his eyebrows gave his eyes all the protection they required. His face was expressionless, hard, his lips tight. At a guess, a friend might say that something moved him strongly.

"Do you believe in heaven?" he demanded suddenly, out of his cogitations.

Peter Chisholm took his time to answer that. "I might—or again, I might not," he equivocated. "It depends on what you may mean by heaven. It is highly unlikely, for instance, that your idea of heaven and mine would coincide. You see, I like peace and a quiet life and good feeding. My heaven would be a comfortable place."

"Sounds like the Liberal Club! And mine?"

"I can see you running up and down celestial mountains attended by flocks of dark-haired dark-eyed angels attired in kilts."

"You are a blethering fool, Peter Chisholm!" the other told him with conviction. "I was just thinking that this morning and this place and the smell of it all, would make a very passable heaven—after the nightmare of last night."

"Nightmare . . ." his friend murmured, "you're quite sure that the whole thing wasn't just a nightmare? I was always doubtful about that white stag of yours. You were a bit queer when you came in last night. It'll be the last straw if we've to bring this blessed pony home again with no stag."

"The brute is dead." Jonathan spoke shortly. "I tell you I dragged it up from the burn by its antlers. I know a dead beast when I see one."

"All right! There's a saying that seeing is believing . . ."

At their backs, a bicycle-bell tinkled musically. They swung round, one quickly, the other not so quickly. It was Finlay Macarthy, his long shanks ludicrously widespread to avoid the handlebars, his jacket flapping open, reminiscent of a ship in full sail. He wobbled to an alarming stop and his bicycle collapsed, protesting, from between his outstretched legs. He stepped from amongst it, his dignity unimpaired.

"That was a handsome finish, Mr. Macarthy," Jonathan greeted him. "I doubt if I could have done better myself."

The other nodded solemnly. "I am not just a great

224

bicyclist," he acknowledged. "I'm getting ower auld, maybe. A grand morning it is, gentlemen!"

"It is so—and paid for in advance."

"That is a true word. Your foot will be better, Mr. Chisholm?"

"Practically, thank you!" The big man did not go into details. That ankle was a sore spot in more ways than one.

"My friend is like a bear with a sore head over that foot of his," Jonathan explained obscurely. "I think he has a grudge against that hillside for not being able to bear his weight—the unreasonable bloke!"

"Well might he, indeed," Finlay Macarthy agreed politely. He went on. "Back at the Lodge there, I was hearing that you were for the glen, an' a shelt with you. Is it the good news, Mr. Maitland?"

Jonathan nodded. "The white stag is dead anyway," he said.

"Man, I'm glad!" He held out his hand. "I was doubting you'd never be finding it in yon storm. It was a coarse night."

"Coarse is the word." Jonathan rubbed his chin. It stuck out rather as though it had been made for rubbing. "I killed it, but I have nothing to be proud about in the killing. I wounded it again, before I eventually found it. Doubtless it died from loss of blood. Hardly a triumph for me!"

"I wouldna' just be saying that. The shooting will have been the least o't. Yon was an ill brute: the Devil was in it, surely."

"You ought to be sure of a free pass to heaven now, anyway. It's not everybody gets the chance of a shot at the Devil. Maybe they'll make you an archangel!" That was Peter Chisholm.

Jonathan shrugged. "The man is a lawyer," he told the Highlandman. "And how did you get on yourself, Mr. Macarthy?"

"I got gey wet," he said briefly.

225

"I'll bet you did! You would go straight home when the storm started?"

"Just that! I saw you crossing An Moine, and I was thinking to follow you, but the weather that was in it changed my mind. Yon was an awful storm." He smiled gravely. "But it was nothing to what was waiting for me when I got back home."

"You mean . . . ?"

"Aye, she'd gotten back from Inverness, and Fionnla Og had been talking, and him a fool." He shook his head portentously. "I doubt you will be having a visit from her this day, Mr. Maitland."

"D'you say so?" Jonathan looked suitably perturbed. "I'll get Mr. Chisholm here to speak for me. He knows how to deal with her."

"You will not!" The big man was vehement. "You can speak for yourself—you're not so dumb, either. That girl doesn't like me."

"I wouldna' be saying that, Mr. Chisholm," Finlay Macarthy protested. "Miss Barbara was telling me the other day that you were quite a nice young man . . . but inexperienced."

"The hell she did?"

Jonathan Maitland lifted up his voice and his laughter filled the morning. "Barbara Macarthy Neill," he shouted, "for that word, I love you!"

Crossing the hog-backed bridge where the burn joined the Feith River, they turned into Gleann na Mallachd. Finlay Macarthy, leaving his bicycle against the parapet, paused and nodded at the tell-tale stains on the weather-worn masonry. "High, the water has been," he pointed out. "See the mark o't. Another foot and it would have been above the arch o' the brig there. I've no' seen it as high except at a spring spate an' the snow melting."

226

Within the confines of the glen the traces of the storm were more in evidence. Among the trees, the legion of the fallen appealed silently in their abasement, and the flood-wrack that lined the burn was eloquence itself. Perhaps the yellow birches still suffered from the strain of their ordeal, and their delicate apparel drooped dull in consequence: perhaps the gold of the bracken had proved in its trial to be but base copper, and the nodding reeds were broken indeed. But the reeds would nod again anon, and the bracken would wear fresh green again in spring, and the birches would cast-off their faded cloak, as was their wont, and face the winter naked in their slim hardihood, assured of greater loveliness to come. Even the fallen pines would clothe their shame with creeping moss, and the kindly earth would lend them its green canopy. All would be as it had been. And the sun drew sweet incense from the bog-myrtle, and overhead the larks shouted their pæan of praise.

The three men were noticeably silent as they neared the scattered stones that had been Elspeth Macarthy's croft. From the rear came the dirge of Johnny Henderson's whistle in tune to the rhythm of the pony's hooves. Jonathan Maitland, a pace or two in advance, felt an odd reluctance to go forward, an undefinable sensation that was neither apprehension nor embarrassment nor depression, but a combination of all three, and as absurd as it was unaccountable. He had a strange feeling that their presence there was an intrusion, a violation of he knew not what. He could not recollect having felt that way before. He was cursed with an ultra-receptive mind.

As he turned past the broken-down gable, he stopped. They all stopped.

The dark man spoke at last, and his voice held a defensive note. "I left it lying there," he said. "Its head was leaning against those stones. . . ." He swung on the others. "It is uncanny . . . it must have been the spate . . . the water must have taken it with it—you can see that the water has been right up here."

Finlay Macarthy agreed gravely. "The water it would be," he said. "It is a strange thing, surely."

Jonathan turned to his friend. "Well?" he said, and his smile was bitter.

Peter Chisholm was not looking at him. "A nightmare. . . ." He nodded quietly. "You have not produced your white devil, fellow, but the pony will not go home unburdened for all that. Look over yonder!" He pointed across the flood-scarred greensward to where a group of rocks clutched something that was not pleasant to look upon. "You are to have a devil of sorts, after all," he ended.

Finlay Macarthy crossed himself. "Speak no ill of the dead," he whispered. "The Lord God Almighty have mercy on his soul, and him a sinner!"

They lifted the bruised and battered body of Edward Neill, the face sardonic even in its disfigurement, and wrapped it in the sheltie's blanket. In silence they stared down at that eloquent bundle, their hats in their hands.

Peter Chisholm was the first to speak. "Has he been dead long, d'you think? He looks a bit. . . ."

Finlay Macarthy shook his head slowly. "I should not be thinking so . . . no' that long, anyway. You would be noticing the eyes of him? But I do not know. . . ." He shook his head again. "The burn would be bringing him down."

Jonathan Maitland, his lips tight, took a few steps away and back. "Last night, up the glen there, I heard the noise of falling rock. It might have been . . . I thought at the time that it might have been the stag . . . I passed the fallen rock, too, but I didn't stop to look at it. I was in a hurry." He looked down at the covered figure and the frown was a black bar across his face. "The man's devilishly like his daughter," he said.

228

"The face of him, only," the Highlandman observed quietly.

"I know that, Finlay Macarthy! That girl did not inherit his twisted soul. This news will be a shock to her."

"A shock indeed, but not a blow, I'm thinking. Myself, I'm thanking the Saints of Glory for it. I knew that man."

And they lifted the Macarthy Neill, twenty-sixth of his line, on to the back of Johnny Henderson's sheltie, and returned the way that they had come.

XIX

WITH but the one day left before his return to the South, Jonathan Maitland paid a call at Buidhe Bheag. He had seen nothing of Barbara Neill since the day of the quiet funeral down at the Kirkton, when he had held a cord of the coffin of a man whom he had neither loved nor respected. His fellows had been Peter Chisholm and Finlay Macarthy, the factor, the lawyer and the Inverfeith headkeeper. The thing had been decently done, for the sake of the great-eyed calmly-collected girl. Edward Neill would have laughed his enjoyment of that spectacle. That day, a handshake and a muttered word, and thereafter, a short note containing her gratitude and appreciation, had been his only communication with the young woman who was now chieftain of the Macarthys. He had not cared to intrude on her bereavement. It had not seemed the thing to do—for all that her father's death was doubtless a release and a relief. Neither had she sought him at the Lodge—why should she? All the same, he could hardly go off South with never a word: that was less than manners demanded. So he paid a visit to Buidhe Bheag. He was a dutiful man.

Finlay Macarthy, in the steading, welcomed him cordially. "Good day to you, Mr. Maitland! It's the stranger you are, surely."

"Good afternoon, Finlay Sean! I was sorry you couldn't manage that day at the grouse with us."

"Aye, so was I, but the stooks had been lying out that long already. I would have been liking it fine, though. Did you have a good day?"

"Very decent. The birds were slow at rising. We got a

couple of fairly good stags yesterday—one a ten-pointer."

"Aye, I was hearing you were out."

"Were you then?"

"Miss Barbara was on the hill herself."

"Was she? We saw no signs of her." He smiled. "As I say, we got two stags."

"What would be hindering you, and the grand weather for the job?" His left eye dropped almost imperceptibly. "Herself will be pleased to hear you were more successful than you were apt to be a while back."

The dark man considered that. "Is she not here then?" he wondered.

"She is not. She's not that often here these days, and her no' in her bed."

"Indeed? You wouldn't have any sort of idea as to where she was, I suppose?"

"It would be hard to say, Mr. Maitland."

Jonathan nodded understandingly. "You got into hot water the last time you disobeyed orders, didn't you?"

"Did I no'!" he agreed. "Yon was a bad business." He wagged his head solemnly. They were both dutifully solemn.

"I am going South tomorrow," the younger man mentioned. "I will be sorry to go."

"All of us will be sorry to see you go, Mr. Maitland, all of us in this place."

"Thank you, Highlandman."

"But you will be back?"

"I will be back, surely. It is a good place to come back to. I will pay my respects to Mistress Macarthy and Finlay Junior now, and be getting along."

Finlay Macarthy accompanied him to the foot of the hill. At the larch-wood, they shook hands, with the steady grip of friendship. "You will be welcome back, Mr. Maitland. *Beannachd Leat!*"

231

"Goodbye, Finlay of the Macarthys! You might tell . . . no, you might not . . . Goodbye and good luck!"

And as he turned and swung off down the road, the other called after him. "It might be the good idea to be going back by the Allt na Braithrean and Gleann na Mallachd. Yon's an interesting glen and maybe worth a last visit."

"I might do just that," Jonathan shouted back. "Thank you, Highlandman!" And his grin answered the other's gravity.

He walked unhurriedly through gently smiling hills that lay at ease in the reposeful stillness of an autumn afternoon, and the sunshine washed all things in its quiet benevolence. He took the narrow path by the murmurous Allt na Braithrean, and held intimate communion with the burn while he followed its green valley. It was a pleasant burn and a pleasant afternoon, and in the occasional muddy patches of the path a woman's shoe-prints were conspicuous. The man hummed tunelessly as he walked.

He crossed the corner of An Moine, and found no loneliness in all its far-flung vacancy, even with the whaups calling out of their weariness. Always, they must be seeking, seeking, nor knowing the object of their search. Like himself, perhaps. What was he seeking . . . the unattainable? Peter Chisholm said he was a fool—maybe he had the rights of it too . . . but it didn't make him feel like those weary birds. Perhaps, when he had searched as long as they had. . . .

He passed the dark pines, obdurate in their independence, ancient crooked trees and veterans of a hundred storms. He touched his hat to them as he passed. They had been to him as friends that once. With the sun-filled glen before him, he paused for a moment. A number of times now, he had viewed that valley from that stance, and not once had it aroused in him the same emotion or shade of emotion. Grief, menace, fury, melancholy, and an unquiet vigilance, all these he had sensed rather than seen, he had perceived with some inner consciousness, when his eyes had shown him only beauty and stillness or the tumult of the elements. And now peace enfolded it as with a garment, and its serenity was frank under the autumn sun's scrutiny. There was no shadow to all the fair length of it. But the first time that he had viewed it he had thought it peaceful, a peace not of this world, until. . . . It was a strange glen, assuredly.

Jonathan slanted down to the burn-side, and frowned at the water's welcoming chuckle. He had a grudge against that burn . . . he could not trust it, chuckle as it would. For all that, he accompanied it cheerfully, and in a little he was humming again. And the foolish reeds rustled and nudged each other, and the bog-cotton tried to dance to the tune of it, and the birches stooped, attentive. It was a pity that he was not much of a hummer.

With a bend in the glen, the burn twisted in its stony bed— perhaps the burn it was that bent the glen?—and with the twist of the burn the path bent, and beyond each bend was another bend. That was the glen. And the man on the path contemplated the burn and the brae-sides and the hazy rims of the hills and all the pale infinity of the sky: but which of them it was that brought the half-smile to the strangely stern mouth of him, would be hard to say. Presently, he was whistling.

Busy as were his eyes, they missed something. With two-thirds of the glen behind him, he was halted by a voice, halted abruptly. "Jonathan . . . Mr. Maitland!"

She sat above him, on the hillside amongst a group of young birches that thrust up out of the turning bracken, and her dark beauty was in striking contrast to their yellow love-liness. He climbed up to her, his hat in his hand. "Well met, Barbara chief of all the Neill Macarthys!" he greeted her.

She sat still as he came up to her, her eyes searching his face. She had a curiously direct gaze, that girl, that was apt

233

to be disconcerting. "You are very happy, surely?" she said eventually.

"Am I?" The man looked surprised.

"I have been listening to your whistle these ten minutes. Sound carries a long way in this glen on a still day. You are a good whistler."

"You should hear me singing. . . ."

Still she watched him, her face cupped in her hands. "What were you thinking about to make you whistle like that, I wonder?" she asked. She was a direct young woman.

He had his chance there. A plain question could have borne a plain answer.

"I don't know . . . nothing in particular," he lied. "Perhaps it was the glen?"

She looked away at that, and inclined her head. "Perhaps it was the glen," she repeated slowly. "Certainly the glen is changed. I have been here frequently since . . . that day, and I know that it is changed. It is Gleann Raineach once more. You are to thank for that." She stretched out her hand to him. "I have a lot to thank you for."

The man sat himself down at her feet, his arms clasping his knees. "You have nothing in the world to thank me for," he said.

"That stag. . . ."

"I came here to stalk deer," he interrupted her. He meant well, too.

"Of course!" Something of that old coldness that the man knew so well crept into her voice. "How stupid of me to forget!"

Gloomily Jonathan considered the silver ribbon of the burn. "I am leaving for the South tomorrow," he said.

"Tomorrow!" she echoed, and for half a moment he imagined that he heard a note of distress, of bleakness, in her voice. Then he realised that he had been wrong. "Every holiday must come to an end sometime, I suppose," she went on lightly. "One is quite glad to get back to familiar scenes and friends and the usual round. Wonderful what a change can do, isn't it?"

He shrugged his shoulders. "Maybe . . . but I am sorry to be going."

"But of course! Deer-stalking over for another year . . . such fine weather to be leaving, too."

"True, that is the tragic part of it," he agreed. He was very sarcastic.

For a while there was silence between them, a silence that held nothing of ease nor of understanding. The man made one effort.

"I was just on my way back from Buidhe Bheag," he told her. "I would have called before but, well . . ."

"Oh, there is no need to apologise, Mr. Maitland."

"I was not apologising . . . and you were calling me Jonathan."

"So I was! Just a slip, I assure you." That girl was a besom and needed a shaking. "You would be saying goodbye to Finlay Macarthy?"

"I was . . . but it was you that I came to see."

"Was it?" She glanced into his face again. "A pity that you had such a long walk to find me. And what can I do for you . . . Jonathan?"

He stared down at his feet. "Oh, I just came to say goodbye . . . that's all."

She nodded slowly. "Well, we can say goodbye as well here as at Buidhe Bheag," she said. Her voice was as casual as she could make it.

"I suppose so . . ." he said, and stopped. What more was there to say? This thing had gone far enough, quite far enough. He was still a man, thank God, and no girning child to whine over his medicine. He rose to his feet and held out his hand. "Goodbye, Barbara Macarthy Neill!" he said. "I will not forget our . . . friendship, not ever."

She sat quite still, and her hand was limp in his. "Goodbye, Jonathan!" she whispered. That was all.

And he turned and strode down through the bracken that clutched at his legs and would have held him, and took the beaten path without a backward glance. And the girl sat still amongst her birches.

He walked between the widening walls of that valley, and he did not whistle as he walked. What was there to whistle about, anyway? He did not contemplate the burn or the brae-side or the distant hills or the infinity of the sky, but stared at the path ahead of him, with no half-smile on his hatchet-face—though it was the same burn and the same glen and the same sky. What was there to smile about? For all that, it was a grand afternoon, and the sun was pleasant in the valley that again had been called Gleann Raineach, the Glen of the Fern.

Jonathan Maitland walked with the set stride of a man who knew his road, the inevitability of it and the eternity of it, and did not like it. Strange that he should know his road now, when an hour ago he had not known it . . . perhaps, at the root of him he had known it all along? He had been working up to this—Peter Chisholm had warned him, and he had told that big man to go to hell. It was no use blaming the girl. She might have been a little more patient with him, a little less blunt . . . but she was direct in all she did: it was the first thing he noticed about her—after her legs—that day up on An Moine. That seemed a long time ago—five weeks ago, no more, no less . . . but a man could lose his life in a moment, and his head in less. An instant, an hour, a year, eternity: what was time? Only an idea, an illusion of mortality, a factor of no account in the vital things that concern the soul of a man. . . .

He went on at a pace that was neither fast nor slow, and he did not hear what the burn at his side was trying to tell

236

him. It was an ancient burn, and what it had to say should have been worth the listening-to. But the man in his dejection had no ears for its message. His disappointment was twofold—disappointment at the girl and at himself. Neither of them had come up to expectation . . . and yes, there was no denying it now, he had had his expectations. There should have been plenty to talk about. He had sort of fancied himself recounting the story of the hunting-down of that stag—quite an epic he could have made out of it, once he got started. But he had not got started . . . his own fault that was, too. He was no use at dealing with women, of course: always he had known it, but he had thought that he would get on well enough with this girl . . . after that night! She had not seemed very cheerful, somehow . . . hang it, she ought to have been full of the joys, with the family curse disposed of and all the ghosts laid. She had been starting to thank him, of course, and he had stopped her, choked her off—naturally! That time she held out her hand to him. . . . Maybe he should have let her thank him: maybe she had felt a bit hipped, snubbed, maybe? . . . He was not always very good at expressing himself. It might be that he had offended her, some way or other—women were queer creatures. He would not like to have offended the lassie, not for anything on the earth nor above or below the earth. She had seemed lonely sitting there, and he had come to her and left her the more lonely. He could have sworn, too, that her voice had quivered when she heard that he was leaving tomorrow. Maybe he'd been hasty, maybe he'd been unkind, unjust, maybe he'd been a fool?

His pace dwindled to a slow walk, a saunter. He stopped. "You have been a damned fool, Jonathan Maitland!" he said aloud, and the conviction was strong upon him. On the word he turned, and with an odd whimsical smile he returned by the road he had come. "Maybe now I'm the damneder fool than ever?" he wondered.

Perhaps the burn, in its insistence, had delivered its message after all.

She sat still in the place where he had left her, her back half-towards him. There was something strangely forlorn in her attitude, something to do with the set of her shoulders and the poise of her head. Very small she seemed against the lift of the brae.

She did not hear him till he was almost upon her, then she jerked round, her eyes wide, her lips parted. In that instant the man noticed the pearly white of her teeth. "Jonathan!" she breathed.

He went right up to her, and looked straight into her eyes, and what he saw there made him shake his black head. "Barbara Neill," he said gravely, "tell me why you were crying."

She turned away quickly and looked up the glen, away and away to where it lost itself in the mighty side of Carn Garbh. She said nothing at all, but he could hear her swallowing.

"Tell me, Barbara Neill!" he persisted.

She spoke at last. "I was not crying, Jonathan," she said, and her voice was smaller than small.

The man stooped and took her by the elbows and lifted her to her feet. "You are the deuce of a poor liar, my dear!" he said, and they went downhill to the burn together.